# NOT *That* GIRL

## ALISHA PERKINS

HADLEIGH HOUSE
PUBLISHING

HADLEIGH HOUSE
PUBLISHING

*For every heart that hides wounds that may never bleed.*

# PART 1

# 1

This is the last one. I threw the butt on the ground and stomped it out on the grimy cement with the bottom of my new "running" shoes. I had just assumed athletic sneakers were all-purpose. How wrong I was.

Then the hipster salesman at the running store convinced me that my regular arch meant I could wear just about any running shoe, but my inclination to pronate meant these were the exact ones for me. Initially I had hoped that pronating was something he and I would get around to in the stock room, but I came to find out this would be the first of many disappointing running terms I would have to now know. And, with that, these neon shoes that cost almost as much as my rent were going to be the ticket I needed to become the "runner" he had promised.

"Buy me a drink first," I had quipped as he helped me slide my foot into the soft sneaker, an athletic Cinderella but with big feet.

His eyes glazed over and face remained emotionless. I guess he didn't find this process to be as invasive and humiliating as I did.

The man had literally just watched my ass shake on the treadmill as I tried to huff through what I was sure was not even his warm-up, and all he had noticed was my tendency to roll my feet inward.

Damn. I must really need to work out.

The shoes that were going to change my exercise routine and outlook on life now had black ash crushed into the sole to go along with the scuff mark on the front left toe from where the cab driver had dropped my suitcase in an attempt to be "helpful." I knew I should have Ubered.

I picked up my barely used Frye messenger bag, a gift from my mom upon my graduation. A shockingly soft material that felt more silk than stiff, and since I preferred stiff, it wasn't my favorite item. I used it out of guilt instead of want, something I had spent my lifetime perfecting: acting for others. I'm sure it was her way of saying sorry for not being there all those years, for being so despondent. But who was I kidding? Tree, meet apple.

All that work had gotten me a PhD in creative writing. No thanks to her. But she had wanted to buy me a bag, at least.

So after the ceremony, she had insisted that I needed a briefcase, now that I was going to be a real member of the working class. I had refused to conform to societal norms, and I kind of just wanted to be a dick, so we settled on this bag. Half-bag. Half-backpack. Half-briefcase. Half-passive-aggressive revenge. All another forced moment of a fake relationship with a woman I didn't know and one who barely knew the real me.

I made my way through the doors and past the poor suckers who thought vaping was the new smoking. Here I was, still enjoying the faint smell of nicotine on my breath for what I was sure was my last time, and those dicks were trying to make smoking socially acceptable. Give me a break.

*Stop. You are not that girl anymore,* I had to remind myself. *You might have fooled them all for a while, but that is no longer you now. You dropped her on the street with that cigarette.*

Who was I kidding? I left her behind years ago when I left that godforsaken town. I traded cigarettes for Sauconys and Hadleigh for Boston.

That girl. The one I was leaving behind was chaos at her best and horror at her worst. She was lipstick stains on beds of men whose names she didn't know and was always an arm's distance away from the ones she did. She was a metaphor and a mess.

That's why I left her there. She belonged in that small town among small minds and dirty sheets. And though I didn't belong in that small town anymore, here I was . . . going back there.

I wanted to put her behind me. I wanted to be the new me. The better me. The real me. Fuck . . . I didn't want to be me at all. I wanted to be someone in a Hallmark movie. I may have had a hard-to-crack exterior, but those damn movies did me in every time. Something about the consistency and timing soothed the chaotic inner child in me. But, if I was being really honest with myself (which I was trying to do now), I was a hopeless romantic at heart. A flower hidden in the shadows of a gloomy sky. I had gotten used to the shadows, even enjoyed fading into the background, but something about love and the warmth it ignited always left a longing in my heart that I had yet to fill. A mixture of sadness and hope. A cocktail of passion and bittersweetness. And I loved to drink as much as the next person, but it was a cocktail you only drank at home within the safe walls that were free of judgment and speculation. My love of love was the sex on the beach of cocktails. It is fun on a crazy night in when you don't care what the world thinks, but in the light of day, or out at a bar, you wouldn't be caught dead ordering it.

First class airplane-food scent lingering in the stale air and slightly dirty upholstery mixed with the fluorescent lights did little to calm my nerves as I boarded the plane.

"Welcome aboard flight 458 with service to Birmingham. We invite you to sit back, relax, and enjoy the flight." The chirpy, bleach-blond flight attendant winked at me. I sat one row behind first class. Story of my life. So close.

I tipped my head back onto the seat and let the cool, re-cycled, surely bacteria-ridden air gently blow my home-dyed brown hair to the side.

I closed my eyes and instantly starting twirling my chain, a gift from my college roommate, between my pointer and thumb, a habit I did whenever I was nervous or bored.

I needed a cigarette. Fuck.

"I heard that she died from AIDS, and they are trying to cover it up by saying it was cancer."

"No. I heard Laura poisoned her once she found out that she had been sleeping with Tom on and off for like eight years. I mean, can you imagine finding out that your husband had been sleeping with her for that long and you were none the wiser. I know it was a long long time ago, but still. Yuck."

"Stop it, ladies. We are at her funeral, for goodness' sakes. Show a little respect. I will say this though . . . I heard that Finn's dad might have been Tom. Just a little bird talking."

# 2

It is not that I hate flying. To be honest, I am kind of indifferent about the whole process. I find it oddly relaxing to know that everything is out of my control, and if we are going down, the impact is likely going to be swift and the death painless. I like not feeling things just like I like not camping. I prefer to keep my feelings like my friendships—surface and simple, with the rare exception.

I catch a glimpse of the flight attendant through the mesh curtain they somehow think separates the social classes. She smiles, winks again. I can't tell if she is coming on to me or trying to make me feel less like a cretin for not being able to afford a first-class seat. Likely, she is just reenacting the tips she learned for how to be everyone's everything in a flying metal box. Or I am just being vain. Maybe she is not winking at all. It wouldn't be the first time my imagination got the best of me.

What I find myself hating more than the mixed signals this flight attendant is sending me is the forced shared space a plane creates. The artificial camaraderie. How is it people don't understand that just because you share a row number doesn't mean that you share life stories?

Where is the damn drink cart for the peasants?

"Where are you from?" he asks me, breaking my stream of inner bitching that I was so comfortable loathing in.

Is he serious? Didn't he get the "fuck off" memo written across my forehead? Maybe I should have that be the first thing I ask my Botox doctor. I'll take the "fuck off" package, plane special.

"Boston," I reply in the nicest, most natural, moderately friendly tone I can muster. I am, after all, a different me now. Different. Better. Apparently airplane friendly.

"Oh, I love Boston. One time my buddy and I went out to a Sox game at that there Fenway park and . . ."

I know I should be paying attention. The new me should be a good listener, but all I can focus on is the way the spit is accumulating in white, small frothy balls in the corners where his lips meet his chubby, overly red cheeks. I wonder if he is a usual over-salivater or if this story has him wildly excited at the possibility that he may just wow me enough to convince me to give him a quick rub and tug under one of those all-too-thin airplane blankets.

What he doesn't know is that the old me would have maybe been convinced into that scenario if for no other reason than to get him to shut his drooling mouth. Never mind the fact that he was pushing fifty and chubby pushing overweight. I was pushing late-thirties and liked pushing the limits.

I wonder if his penis is as chubby as his cheeks?

"And we ended the night at that bar right off Boylston. Right near where the marathon bomb went off. Crazy, huh? Are you a runner?"

It must have been the shoes that gave him the impression that he had the right to ask this question. I don't know why these inquisitions into my athletic aptitude made me feel so violated, but somehow I couldn't shake this eerie feeling every time it was asked.

"Thinking about it." I smiled.

He gave me an earnest look as if he wanted more.

*Give him more,* I thought. Not too much, but just enough. God—it would be so much easier to speed this along if I was the old me.

"I just bought these shoes and am hoping they inspire me to hit the road," I said as I pumped my fist through the air like a cheerleader giving the football team their all.

*What am I doing? An encouraging hand motion? Really?*

As he laughed, a little of his spittle fell on his lap, and I looked away, yearning for that damn drink cart.

Luckily, my running-intention story sufficed enough to shut him up, and he began watching some version of *Fast & Furious*. I wasn't sure if he was really enjoying it or just trying to be relevant. His mannerisms told me he wasn't a deep thinker, so I was leaning towards him just wanting to be able to talk about Vin Diesel at the water cooler. Poor guy. I was fairly certain that he and the vapers were trying too hard.

*Maybe I should be the old me,* I thought, *just for him, just for ten minutes.*

"I wonder what will happen with that big house of hers now. It is not like Finn would ever want it. That poor child ran for the hills as fast as she could."

"I wouldn't mind getting my hands on it and fixing it up—just like that gal and her husband do on that home show Fix It. Or is it Fix Up?"

"Geez, Bonnie. It is Fixer Upper, and who doesn't love that Chip? I wish I would have found me a Chip after Charlie died. To be honest, I always kind of admired Grace Harper for her free spirit and her love of life . . . and men. I secretly always wished I would have tried a few more men out before being tied down."

"Good Lord, Jan! Show a little dignity. This is not the time or place to be talking about becoming a slut. But speaking of sluts . . . has anyone seen Finn? I hear she is darn near unrecognizable."

# 3

Automatic doors at the Birmingham Airport rushed in the warm stale southern air, bringing with it the smell of rubbing alcohol, BO, and a hint of bourbon . . . or was it rum? Captain Morgan? The captain always brings me back. Back to the girl with mousy brown hair, slightly sunburned skin, and a love of life that was insatiable. Back to eighth grade. The first kiss. First base. First drink. First love. First cigarette. First time a sad lyric made me feel something.

I should have known. I should have seen it coming. Underneath all those Tommy Hilfiger clothes and that Cool Water cologne was just another boy. I played the part of the naïve girl who looked the other way, thinking this would be different, but I had a gut feeling. The kind that good mothers tell you to never ignore. I didn't have that mother. I ignored it. I spent years ignoring it.

I was never that girl. I can leave. If I fall hard enough, I am out. I can quit him.

I was that girl. He abandoned me. I couldn't quit him.

He was two years older and a lifetime of bad stories apart.

He said. I did.

He led. I followed.

I loved him and hated him.

He was my smoking habit, the reason I drank, and the motivation behind my lower back tattoo of a bird that was once the size of a quarter and was now closer to a dime piece. Damn . . . thirties suck.

But here I was again . . . the smell knocking me back in time. I needed a stabilizer. A chair. A pole. Anything. I turned quickly enough to catch my back on the wall before I was on my bird tattoo. I leaned there a while trying to make it look like I wasn't about to have an episode, more like I was James Dean. No one leans against a wall quite like Dean.

James Dean.

Now I'm thinking about a cigarette again. Damn.

"Do you ever wonder if she was in love? I think it is sad to think that she died and never felt love."

"Of course she loved. She was madly in love with Beau Boyton. Remember? And she loved Finn. I think. Well . . . she loved herself anyhow."

"Speaking of loving yourself—did you see Tom crying in the corner? Is he serious right now? You cheated on your wife for all those years, and you are sad because your whore died? What a joke. Did Laura even come?"

"I saw her walk in with her daughter, that pretty blond one. She's pregnant. All those kids . . . Why can't I think of her name? I think she used to be friends with Finn in high school."

**4**

Jiggling fat swung from my underarm, practically telling the world I am not the runner my shoes indicate, as I flag a taxi.

I haven't been back there since I was eighteen. I needed more. I needed space. I needed substance. I needed clarity. I needed a place where people didn't know your name or your story.

I slide into the worn pleather seat and close my eyes as I take a deep breath and barely audibly whisper the address to the driver, as if I don't say it I won't have to go.

Of course, *she* brought me back here. *She* made me face my past. I should have known that I could run but I couldn't hide. Actually, I couldn't run, but it was on the docket. I would have to be here again. I would have to show my face. The irony is that she was never there for me, but now she is actually gone. I am in this cab directing a man back to my past. Back to the old me just to show off the new me. The me I have never let these people know.

The cab comes to an abrupt stop in the way only a cab driver can, shaking me from my thoughts. I peer right for a brief second and my breath catches in my throat. It is him. The him who broke my heart. The him who stole my innocence.

The light changes and we are off. Zero to sixty, and I realize that he was a mirage. I may have willed him to life. There is no way he is still here. Still in the place we once called home. Still in the place I last abandoned my heart.

This town of fewer than two thousand people had always felt way too small, too much like a prison, even if it was just the one I had created inside my own body. Much like living inside an airplane. We shared the same recycled air and the same stories with all the unease of that forced community. My entire body begins to exhale as we turn left onto the dirt road that leads to the old farmhouse. She never really liked that house, but it had been willed to her from her parents, so the price was right. Rocks and gravel popped and cracked under the tires of the taxi as we slowly came to halt, and the weatherworn white house came into view. Memories came fast and hard. The front porch. The back pond. The yelling. The fear. The truth. I was never fond of anything hard unless it came in the form of a drink or a dick. These memories were knocking me on my ass.

"It'll be $21.31," he turns and says.

In this neck of town, it was offensive to not trust your neighbors, so of course the front door opened just by twisting the worn, brass knob. Keep your secrets under lock and key, but keep your front door open. An odd concept, and one I learned from the best.

Two pretty girls, a pretty house, and a pretty life. We made single-woman status look glamorous (or gluttonous, depending on who you asked) back in the day. My mom didn't need a man, and so she filtered through several. I was a girl who learned from the best and struggled to feel comfortable in my skin. Gorgeously pale that bordered on creamy, but beneath a wreck bordered on lies and sex.

The town talked about us. The duo on the edge of town with the vintage farmhouse and rotating door. The men who came in and the truth that never came out. Only the men who stopped by for evening nightcaps and the garbage man who disposed of the morning bottles knew the amount of alcohol that flowed. I was a mistake and she was a drunk.

Yet here I was, back again to clean up her mess. This time, though, I wouldn't have her over my shoulder, watching me with those sad eyes.

Evening sun on my back felt like a warm, gentle shove as I turned the door handle and walked in. Old vodka mixed with Brut aftershave and a faint potpourri, as if to mask her indiscretions. God, I hated those Winstons, even though right about now I would smoke one just to settle the dust of the last eight hours.

I didn't know what to do next. This house used to be my home, but now it felt like a memory. One of those places you recall but feels foreign. Déjà vu, though you aren't sure you have ever actually experienced what you are feeling. I was a little girl here, and I am not that girl anymore. I have worked too hard and come too far to be sucked back into my old lies and faked norms. I knew coming here was a mistake. I knew I wasn't ready. I knew she would force my hand. I hate her for this. I hate her for dying. I hate that she's gone.

Chipped plates and cups still lie in the sink in the kitchen, and the coffeepot sat half full. In the corner was a Winston butt stubbed out in an ashtray I had made in seventh-grade pottery, probably the only thing of mine she kept. The white tile on the floor was now edged in a smoky gray, and the cabinet hardware was tarnished to an aged bronze. In its prime, this place was a palace. The talk of the town. The house that made the front page of the *Hadleigh Gazette*. The huge farmhouse on the edge of town with two porches and five bathrooms. A house with the looks of something this town had never seen. Looking at it now, you would never know it was a thing of beauty. Time and cigarette smoke had draped it in a haze that simply broke its charm. The walls were like her heart—black and lifeless.

I opened the cabinet below the sink, grabbed the half-empty bottle of Grey Goose, and sat down at the counter on one of the stools my grandfather had made. She may not have been good for much, but at least she had good taste in vodka. The freezer opened effortlessly, which probably spoke to how many times she had needed this same ice cube tray. It was somehow miraculous and yet unsurprising that she had remembered to fill them. I grabbed the unopened tonic out of the fridge, twisted the ice tray just enough to let the ice cubes jump out of their respective spots, and dumped them into an old mason jar. Tonic to fill the bottom fourth and vodka the rest, Mom's specialty.

The setting sun peeked through the living room windows, casting a lazy glow across the worn oak floors, and it dawned on me that I might have a harder time letting go of that girl in this place. I never felt like myself here. I was always just following her footsteps. As I let the first sip of my cocktail fall down my throat, I realized that I was her again. Drinking alone. Maybe it was time for that cigarette after all—just to complete the picture, of course.

"I know I shouldn't be like this. I am so ashamed, but I think I loved her once."

"Don't be so hard on yourself, Tom. I am sure you did love her, but I wouldn't go around saying that with all these women present. Hell, I wouldn't say it to any of the other men either. God knows how many others thought they loved her. I, for one, was pretty fond of her from time to time, as well . . . if you catch my drift."

# 5

Peeking morning sun is sending warm, bright freckles across the floor, and once again that brings me back to life as I blink the sleep out of my eyes and sit up on the couch, realizing I must have passed out. I couldn't bring myself to sleep in my old bed, in the place where I left that girl behind. So I drank myself to sleep on the davenport.

I had hoped that everything would look different in the daylight. This place wouldn't feel so painful and the Winstons wouldn't be so tempting. I know that I have a job to do, but I don't know where to start. Part of me wants to light a match and watch the whole thing burn, but instead I shuffle over to the kitchen, empty out the old coffee, and fill the pot with new water and commit to a new outlook. She may not have been the best mother. Hell, using the word *mother* almost felt sour swishing around in my mouth, leaving a bad aftertaste mixing with my morning breath.

She never attended a sporting event, school play, conference, or bedtime story session. She would make random appearances when she must have been hopped up on something long enough to decide to be present. She was an extreme. She was all in or out, usually the latter. A few times, she let me skip school and stay home with her for the day. We would get our nails painted (a failing attempt to girly me up) and eat lunch down at Tin 'n' Grits. We would spend the rest of the afternoon watching trashy daytime TV together and laughing until she "took a nap." She would call those days a "three T day" (toes, tin, and TV). I used to weirdly love three T days. The Frye bag was her new three-T-day experience.

But she is the only mother I ever knew, and I am going to do my best to make her proud. That's what good kids do, right?

Leaning against the cabinets, I fill my coffee cup. Steam escapes out into the fresh air that only comes with being in a small town, and I try to convince myself into a new outlook. New day. New me in this old place. I can do this. I am going to do this and get the hell out of here. I don't need to see anyone. I don't want to see anyone. I am going to clean up and get out. I need to do this alone. I know it would be easier with help, but that was hard to come by, and honestly I fear getting attached. I am here to hit it and quit it, so to speak, when it comes to this house and this town. There will be no reconciliation—no relationship. This is nothing more than a booty call.

The kitchen seemed like the logical place to start. Not only because of proximity but simply because I am sure there is nothing worth keeping here, and so it should be a seamless process. I open each cabinet and empty the contents into boxes. Sell. Give. Store. Keep. Ninety-nine percent will fall into the first three boxes, but I have the fourth marked as more of a goodwill gesture. The plates, pans, and glasses are easy enough to part with. She lived simply and was never the dinner-party type, so the kitchenware is minimal if not comical. She was an introvert with an intoxicating charm that enticed the men and infuriated the women. She had no boundaries and no cares. She cared about three things . . . booze, cigarettes, and me . . .

usually in that order. She tried at times, but I think I always left her disappointed and slightly unnerved. She could never quite figure me out and seemed upset when I was like her and disappointed when I wasn't. She was an anomaly. She was a peacock among pigeons. She was whiskey in a teacup. *And apparently she only had one,* I thought as I set it in the brown box.

She didn't have any expensive wedding china that I should hold on to and pass down. She didn't have any flutes from which she had toasted her anniversary. She didn't own a bread maker that she had gotten from her bridal shower. All that was in these cupboards were the bare essentials of a woman with no morals who harbored her essentials alongside the disappointments of her parents.

She was their only child. Surely they had big plans and a big wedding budget. Dreams too big in a small town, and far too big for a girl who was so short-sighted. They were old money, farming when farming truly mattered and land buying was lucrative, but her new ways sent them to the grave. She bucked tradition and broke their hearts. I guess that is where I got it. I remember the look on her face when she found out that they had bequeathed her the house. I think she had assumed giving birth to a bastard child had been her ticket right out of the will. She was wrong. They had loved her in spite of herself. She was too ignorant and stubborn to see it. Then they were gone, and they wanted to leave her a house. A house, a Frye bag . . . Fuck . . . this is too deep and I am only in the kitchen. How in the hell am I going to get through this house?

I feel trapped.

I need a cigarette.

No.

I am going to go for a run.

•　•　•　•　•　•　•　•　•　•　•　•　•

How to start? How not to look like an idiot? I dig through my suitcase and find the so-called "running" shirt and shorts that the hipster shoe salesman talked me into. I had held the shorts up to my legs at the store and remarked that they seemed a little short. He told me that's how all the "runners" wear them. Since I wanted to look the part, I bought them.

Now putting them on, I am realizing that clothes do not a runner make. Not to mention, these look more than a little ridiculous. I decide that I need to look past my shorts, even if I can barely see them over my upper thigh, and stop making excuses. I am not a smoker. I am not that girl. I am a runner. I am the new me. The girl I ran away from here in this small town with small minds.

The shoes are brighter than anything I have worn since middle school, and again I am questioning "runner's" choices in fashion. Once laced up and geared out, I put on this watch that is supposed to track something or other. I exit the house in search of fresh air and a reprieve that I am still sure only a cigarette can bring.

I push about eight different buttons on this watch. It beeps and vibrates. I huff and cuss.

Fuck it.

My walk turns into a slow jog. A jog that might even be too slow to be considered a jog. I keep putting one foot in front of the other. The dust from the driveway kicks up behind me and gives the appearance that I may actually be running. If only appearances were what they seemed.

I turn left off the dirt road and head towards the tiny road that weaves through what Hadleigh calls a downtown. A downtown where I used to sneak into the bar nestled between the five and dime and the pharmacy. A place called Tin 'n' Grits. Thomas Halvers's dad, Jim, had inherited the bar and grill from his father, Ryan. Thomas snuck us all in, and we helped empty the beer out. It was the kind of place where the regulars came to bitch and the kids came for a pick-me-up.

I had grown up within walking distance of downtown, which boded well for my mother and me. Walking home in the wee hours was a nightly occurrence in the Harper home. I can remember all those nights the walk seemed so short, almost as if time didn't exist, but here . . . now . . . in the light of day and with these running shoes, the bar that brought me up seemed to be miles away.

I reached the edge of Broadhill Ave., where the dirt turned to tar and our little town fakes an urban edge. The scene hit me like a brick wall. I slowed to a walk. The little street I had covered with vomit more times than I would like to admit was so different, borderline offensive.

I never thought I was a sentimental person, especially about this place, but seeing this street brought into the twenty-first century, damn near raped of its charm and resolve, made me want to throw up on that street all over again.

The pharmacy where my mom would send me to pick up god knows what in her little white paper bags was now a Walgreens with its red sign casting a hellish color onto the concrete sidewalks, newly installed. The five and dime where I used to practice my thieving prowess was now a boutique specializing in handmade items and goats' milk soaps. Who in this town was buying goats' milk soap? On the other side of the boutique was a Color Me Mine place where apparently you painted pottery and did other artsy things I was sure no one here ever does. Beyond that was a small law firm, an auto repair shop, and a bed and breakfast. I am not sure what struck me more—the fact that people here were making pottery or that someone would actually want to stay overnight in this place.

I stood still for a moment and was awestruck with all the changes this place had gone through. Maybe I wasn't the only one going through an overhaul. The only consistent, the one thing that brought me back to my youth, was Tin 'n' Grits. The cursive, neon sign still lit dimly over the front door that enclosed all my past indiscretions and secrets. The large, weathered oak door with the peep flap that Thomas had assured us was from pre-prohibition days still stood closed; behind it were all the people I was sure I wasn't ready to see. The nostalgia turned to fear as the bile in my stomach rose and my feet moved again. I needed to get out of here.

I picked up my pace, and for the first time since I left the house, I may have actually looked like a jogger . . . not yet a runner . . . but at least a virgin jogger. I was quickly past the bar and beginning to feel like I needed to turn around for a drink and a quickie in the back bathroom when I noticed the law firm window.

Samson & Brown, the firm handling my mother's estate. The one that had called me in the first place. The guy who told me I needed to come to town, that I needed to hear my mother's wishes.

Grinding my teeth, coupled with pain where my jaw met my skull, made me acutely aware that I was angry all over again. I wasn't ready to hear her wishes. I didn't want to be here. I was not ready to see them.

I turned around before the B&B and became resolute in going back to the bar. Fuck this running crap. I needed a drink. I needed to forget.

The sweat beaded above my right eyebrow. I reached for the brass door handle as I had a million times before. Sweaty palm barely gripping onto the door as I had many times before, except now I was about to swing open the door to my youth, the only place that maybe ever truly felt like home. I knew inside I would find Ryan tending bar, Julie wiping her hands on her apron before grabbing a sweaty glass to fill up and dump the excess foam off of. In the corner booth would be Sandy and Tammy drinking their vodka cranberries, their low-class version of a cosmopolitan. "Like they drink in the city," they would say when you asked. They would be gossiping and hiccupping until their kids got home from school. Bellied up to the bar would be the likes of Harold, Frank, and Johnnie, the local high-school-dropouts-turned-loveable-townies who spent their days passing the time by talking about the weather, the Chiefs, or the bitches in the back booth with their highfalutin martini glasses. Who did those women think they were anyways? Next to the townies would be whatever recent "voted most popular" in high school, failed college jock who wasn't sure where he was without football and pussy. And on the other side of him would have been my mom, or me.

I wasn't sure if it was the sweat or fear, but my hand slid off the door handle. Standing there, staring blankly at a door as if I was Alice in Wonderland, I finally took a step back, took a deep breath, and turned on the heels of my highfaluting running shoes and ran as fast as I could down the road. I am not that girl anymore.

"Who is that man that Tom is talking to in the corner?"

"Oh that's Emily's new husband, Phil. He is quite the catch, huh? I think he grew up around here and recently moved back."

"Oh, so they know each other from high school then, huh? They certainly seem chummy. What do you think they are talking about?"

"JESUS! What is Tom doing?"

"Oh my GOD! That is going to leave a mark. Is he okay?"

# 6

The road veered to the right, and almost as abruptly as it had become a world I didn't recognize, it went back to the dusty roads and desolate futures that I did. I couldn't have been more than a mile into my "jog" when my feet began to ache. Each step was getting a little harder to take, but I wasn't ready to go back yet, wasn't ready to finish what she had started.

As I huffed and puffed my way towards Perchman's Path, it dawned upon me that I had yet to see an old, familiar face. There had been a few randoms roaming the street back near the B&B, but no one noteworthy. I am sure they are still here hiding behind the closed, but not locked, doors, just waiting to jump out and scare me when I least expected it. Ghost of a tried-but-not-forgotten past.

Perchman's Path was a narrow trail worn down by years of runners trekking their way through town and kids trying to find their way through puberty. Among the trees were cigarette butts, old joints, condoms, and abandoned articles of clothing hidden in the bushes. Rumor had it that deep in the woods was a barbed wire fence where the panties of girls who had used the trees as cover during their sexual escapades were hung. Shockingly, my underwear is not among those multicolor sacrifices to the gods of sexual youth. Sure, I had my fair share of fantasies surrounding a romp among the wildlife, but the bar had been my main stomping ground. I preferred to be taken from behind, hands pressed against the cold tile wall as I bit the collar of my shirt, trying to not moan too loud. I was certain the neon light was casting a shadow that brought out the arch in my back and the curve of my ass. The Bud Light was liquid courage, and it did the trick for me. There were few nights that I went home alone or actually used the bathroom to pee. Tin 'n' Grits was my Hit 'n' Quit.

"Behind you!" he called.

I snapped back to the present.

"On your left!" he barked.

I moved as far to the right on the path as I could as he passed me.

He grazed my left forearm. With my mind back at the bar of my past and the sweat of his arm bringing me present, I felt goosebumps run up my back and leave the hairs on my arms standing up.

"Sorry." He looked over his right shoulder peeking out under a tank top. He was strong, not in a muscle head way, but just in the way you like a man to be. He was toned, right where brawny meets brains. I stared at his shoulder too long to even see his face before he turned his head and was on his way.

He quickly became the rabbit I was trying to chase. The face I wanted to see. The ass that was keeping me running even though my legs felt like lead. I probably lasted about twenty seconds tailing him, watching his ass move seamlessly with his legs and wondering what it would be like to reach out and grab it.

He had said six whole words to me, and I absentmindedly had said nothing in return. I watched him fall farther and farther away from me. This was clearly not the first time he had run. Those shoes were far from new, and that ass was burned into my mind. That moment. That touch. The hidden hopeless romantic in me swooned ever so slightly. Damn . . . maybe I was going to like running after all.

I finally made it out of Perchman's Path and slowed to a walk. Who was I kidding with this? I knew I had about a mile to go before I was home, and this body was done running. I felt weirdly rejuvenated, though. Maybe it was the running. Maybe it was the chance encounter. Either way, I was ready to go back to her house and finish what I had yet to really start. The sooner I did, the faster I could get done and out of this place. But first there would be alcohol . . . lots and lots of alcohol. Vodka may not be the answer, but it was worth a shot.

"Are you fucking serious, man? It was a joke. It's not like she was your wife. Chill out."

"Oh my God! Honey, are you okay? What the hell happened?"

"I am fine. A misunderstanding, that's all. Right, Tom?"

"Did Tom just hit Phil?"

"What in the hell is going on over there? Men . . . can't even control themselves at a funeral, for God's sake."

"Do you think that Phil was sleeping with Grace too? Geez!"

# 7

It was mid-evening and my glass was empty as I entered the office and sat at the large, mahogany desk. I ran my hand over the smooth surface, trying to feel for the slightest flaw, knowing that one didn't exist. My grandfather made this desk by hand and had inspected every nook and cranny for any possibility of an inconsistency. Grandpa Al made few mistakes in life, and so I knew there would be no mistakes in this desk. He was a man of men, a farmer who fed, a wood worker. Good with his hands and bad with his feelings. He had a short temper and an even shorter tolerance for breaking the rules. It always looked to me like he loved my mother, but she broke his heart in immeasurable ways. I was the worst of it until I was the best of it.

My grandfather tried his best with me. He took me fishing, hunting, and helped fight the monsters under my bed. He was the first person I saw in the morning and usually the last one at night. He was my best friend and the only father figure I ever knew. As much as he tried to resent me, he loved me the moment he saw me, and life was never the same. His relationship with my mom was forever changed, however. He loved that she gave him me, even if he wanted to hate her.

Gramps and I used to write notes back and forth and leave them throughout the house for each other to find. He would always sign them ISYILY . . . I see you I love you. It became our magical phrase to each other. He saw me and loved me. If he had lived long enough to see what I became in this town, I am not sure he would have felt the same way. He died my sophomore year in high school. It was tragic, sudden, and painless . . . just like he would have preferred it. He was with my grandma now, and I was in hell.

Tears stung the corners of my eyes. I gently wiped them away and forcefully shoved the feelings down. I am not going to cry. I can do this.

The top drawer opens with a little jiggle, more than it needed when I was a kid. Time and pain had forced the wood to tighten its grip, almost as if it wanted to hold on to whatever was inside forever.

There they were, all of the letters that my gramps and I had written back and forth. He had kept every one of them and stashed them away in a time capsule built by his own two hands. I stared for a moment longer than I intended. Grabbed what remained of my drink and downed it. There was sure as shit no way I was getting through these without some tears and a cigarette.

I pulled out the first piece of yellow legal pad paper that was folded neatly into a small square. I could tell this one was from him to me instantly because mine were always folded into whatever was the coolest technique for folding notes in my class. We ran the gamut of footballs, diamonds, rectangles with a tuck-in flap, and origami shapes. I ran my fingers over the weathered edges. I could tell he had read this more times than he would admit. I flipped it over and began to peel back the folds.

I smoothed the creases and stared at his handwriting. As a kid I had never taken the time to notice his beautiful cursive. The kind of handwriting people would pay for on their wedding invitations. It was so smooth and beautiful. The curves of each letter fell beautifully into the next. The kind of handwriting that seems to be long forgotten in the age of iPhones and emojis.

The ashes from my Winston dusted onto the page, leaving a faint gray mark as I brushed them off. My gramps would have my neck for smoking in the house, but I couldn't help it. I had found one single pack left behind by my mother in the chicken-shaped cookie jar in the kitchen, and I needed it way more than I feared a lecture right now.

"My dearest Finn—" he began. Finn, short for Finley. A name I have grown to love but hated as a child. My mother had told me that I was named after my father. The man I never met, but whom I could thank for my blue eyes and strong jaw. She never told me his name or their story. All I knew was that somewhere in his name or nickname or last name was the word *Finn*. He could have been a fisherman she screwed on his houseboat for all I knew. All he passed on to me was an androgynous name and a daddy complex.

Finley Harper. My mother's last name was a pretty one. One I always thought would suit one of my children well if I was that type of girl—the marrying type, the mother type. I wasn't, and so Harper sits unused behind the name of a man I would never know. Poetic justice, I suppose.

When I was little, I used to pretend that my dad was actually a merman and that's why I could never meet him. Finn could only watch me grow up from a distance in the water. If I were to meet him, then I would have to join him and never walk among humans again. *The Little Mermaid* was my generation's *Frozen*, and so my fantasy was certainly better than the reality. I was half-mermaid, and that's why I never fit in. Made sense to me, but I am sure it just made me seem crazy to everyone else. Not that they expected anything different from Grace's daughter. Crazy doesn't fall far from the tree.

*My dearest Finn—*

You may not believe this, but today you were the first thing I thought of when I woke up. Come to think of it, you are the first thing I think of most mornings. You are an amazing kid. I have such a strong afFINity for you, kiddo.

*ISYILY,*
*Gramps*

And just like that, the tears were coming again. I folded it up and laid it on the desk. I sat back in the chair and took a few, deep, nicotine-filled puffs in as I tried to stop myself from losing all control. One minute turned into two, and two into three. I tried my best to contain it, but it wasn't going to stop. The tears were rolling as quickly as the smoke, and I just let them come. Smoke and tears . . . sounds like an old country song . . . one Gramps would have loved.

I snubbed the cigarette on the chair arm and immediately regretted it. I brushed and blew at the ashes left behind, knowing full well they weren't coming off. Dammit. I wiped the snot from my nose on my arm and reached into the drawer to continue the pain, apparently a glutton for punishment. I pulled out one that was obviously from me to him. The folding job was immaculate, minus the fringe from where it had been ripped from my spiral notebook. By the looks of this fold job,

I would guess I had moved from wide-lined to college-lined paper, meaning this one was going to be good—filled with middle-school angst and hormones.

I damn near ripped it apart trying to unfold the stupid thing. The edges doodled with god knows whatever I was into at the time and the handwriting of a kid on the cusp of trying to figure it all out but also thinking she knew it all. Trying so hard to be something, anything, other than who she was.

*Dear Gramps—*

Today was another dumb day. Peyton isn't talking to Sarah because she tried to kiss Peyton's crush. My math teacher did the whole lesson with toilet paper stuck to his shoe, and for lunch they served a hot Italian sub, so I chose the chef salad.

I know you say it gets better, and I hope you are right. Seventh grade is stupid.

*ISYILY,*
*Finn*

It is funny to think that when other girls were writing notes to boys they liked, I was writing to my grandpa. I didn't even attempt to refold this one—there wasn't a chance in hell. I threw it on the desk next to the other, took a swig of my ice cubes that lingered with a hint of vodka, and thrust my hand back in the drawer. It kind of felt like one of those vending machines with the claw. You try to get what you want, but in the end you just get whatever it grabs. What I wanted was relief; what I got instead was a stronger feeling of being itchy in my own skin.

Out came another letter written on spiral notebook but not folded as nice. I could immediately tell that this one was written later, very early high school, probably when I no longer cared and just wanted to get the hell out of this place. I nearly expected to find a condom wrapper accidently stuck to the back. I opened it and immediately recognized the words and was transported back to the time.

*Dear Gramps—*

Do you ever wonder if there is more to life than the one you are leading? Do you ever feel like you are different than the rest? I truly think there is something off with me. Everyone says it is just my age and I will feel more comfortable in my skin as I get older, but I feel like it is more than that. I feel like you are the only one who understands me, and so I feel like there is something I need to tell you. Something I haven't told anyone. I hope you won't be mad. I am—

DING DONG. The doorbell.

*Are you kidding me?* I thought. Who just shows up unannounced anymore? Isn't that what texting is for? I stayed put, figuring if I ignored it, then whoever was there would just go.

DING DONG.

Really? Twice in thirty seconds? Now I definitely didn't want to know who that was. They were obviously crazy.

DING DONG. DING DONG.

And just like that I was up and out of my chair, empty drink in hand, and with a pissed-off regard that would have made my mother proud. This doorbell nonsense was going to stop here and now.

Just as I was reaching for the handle, the door flung open, practically hitting me in the face, grazing the tip of my nose. Damn trusting folks and their no-lock policy; apparently they have an "enter on your own" policy as well. I yelped and grabbed my nose, making sure it was still in one piece when I looked up.

"You must be Finn," he said. "I have heard so much about you."

He reached out his hand. "I am James Brown. Sorry about your nose. I assumed no one was here when I rang a few times with no answer."

"James Brown?" I asked through my cupped hands covering my nose, rendering the question to an echo.

"Your mother's attorney." A tall, tan man with the eyes of James Marsden and a body that you could make out even under his suit. He obviously worked out, but wasn't "jacked"—he was a perfect mix of lean and built. He cracked a sweet smile as his lower right corner of his mouth turned down ever so slightly. This made him seem more attainable and less godlike, thank goodness.

"I left you several messages regarding her will and that we needed to speak. I never heard from you, so I thought I would stop by and get a few things in order of the event you never showed."

"Well, I am here now," I muttered, rubbing my nose again and removing my hands.

"Great. I would really love to sit down as soon as possible and discuss your mother's wishes. How's your tomorrow?"

"Tomorrow is no good," I lied. "I have plans with friends, and I need to finish going through things around here."

"Okay then." He cocked his head a little to the right as if he wasn't used to not getting his way. With a raise of his eyebrow he said, "Maybe the day after?"

"I don't know yet. Can I call you?"

"Sure," he said begrudgingly, probably knowing the odds of me calling were not in his favor.

"The sooner the better," he chimed as he turned and headed out the door. "Night."

In that moment I had the faintest feeling of déjà vu rush over me. Had I met him before? Did we go to high school together? Did I sleep with him?

Then it hit me—his ass. He was the ass I was following on my so-called "run" this afternoon. He was my rabbit. I felt my face start to flush as I called "night" and slammed the door. Holy shit—were lawyers supposed to be that attractive?

"I heard that Grace and Finn haven't spoken since she went off to college."

"That's not true. I am sure it isn't. I know they didn't see eye to eye, but they have to have talked, at least occasionally, right?"

"That Finn is a writer, you know. I bet she could write some real Fifty Shades–type stuff from what she grew up seeing. Poor child never had a chance after the grandparents died. That grandmother was a nut to begin with. I always thought there was one screw loose there. The way she would make stories up and look at you with those dead eyes. Gives me goose bumps just thinking about her."

**8**

I headed back to the kitchen to fill my glass. Why? I am not sure. I sure as shit am not going back into that office anytime soon. I already knew what that letter said, and I had spent so much time since then trying to rectify it. Trying to fix it. I was sure I was a better person now, and I didn't need to read those words again. So I headed into the spare bedroom, figuring that this had to be another safe place to clean. Not a lot in here that would bring me to tears.

A light blush-pink nightstand sat next to an old, metal-frame full bed. Not a decent guest room nowadays by any standard. I can barely sleep alone in a king, much less share a full with someone. This room was my mom's room when Grandma and Gramps were alive. It still looked the way it did then except for the slew of men that were in and out. My grandma used to turn a blind eye while Gramps would turn a shade of red. I used to hear them at night. Their door closed but their voices raised. They would blame each other for my mother's behavior and would argue about how to deal with her, or not deal with her. They thought no one knew their pain—but I did. I heard it while leaning outside their door with my ear pressed against it.

Above the bed was a picture of flowers in a prairie that Grandma had always told me my great great grandma had painted back in Ireland, but truthfully I never believed it and always thought she bought it from Hank's Antiques the next town over. I would smile and nod and she would bask in her lie. We were happy in those moments together.

Grandma was different than Gramps. *Different* might not be the right word. They were similar in the fronts they put on. Both strong, silent, unassuming, and rarely complimentary. The difference was that every once in a while, especially through writing, Gramps would let down his guard and let me see him.

With Grandma, on the other hand, what you saw was what you got, whether you liked it or not. She was not warm and fuzzy; she didn't have a soft side hidden. She was a badass mother who had no time for bullshit or expensive vodka. The cheap stuff got her drunk quicker and with less money spent. Win-win. I often wondered if she was like this before my mom or just after my mom hit puberty. I never got the answer and she never liked me. The few moments we had were when we would be in this room for whatever reason and she would turn to me and say, "Your great great grandmother painted those flowers and brought them over here from Ireland." I would nod and look at the painting as if I was hearing this for the first time. She, too, would stare at the painting for just a moment too long and go before I had a chance to say anything more. I would return to whatever I was doing, half wondering if she was crazy or just drunk again. She couldn't handle my mother, so she drank. She couldn't stand that I reminded her of my mom, so she ignored me.

I looked at this picture on the wall, and though it should have been just a reminder of my terrible, ignorant, drunk grandmother, instead it made me smile. She wanted me to believe that lie so badly that I couldn't help but keep it going. We may not have had much, but we had that picture. Maybe someday I would tell my kids that their great great great grandma painted that picture. Oh geez . . . now I was talking kids. Look what this place was doing to me.

I placed an orange Post-it on the painting—one that stands for "keep it." I looked around the room. The walls were a bland, buttery yellow that once was probably in style but now just looked like something that had seen better days. The dresser on the opposite wall matched the nightstand, and on it was a picture of my mom back in high school. She was laughing while sitting on the back of a pickup truck with her sun-kissed legs dangling below her cut-off jean shorts. She was thin with blond hair that at the time could have still been natural, and a smile that would raise your spirits. Her hair lay in ringlets around her flawless skin and naturally pink lips. She was the epitome of an all-American, farm-raised beauty. Her looks were part of the problem, of course. With a body like that, it was hard to not stop men in their tracks. I picked the picture up to look at it closer and noticed around her an arm of a man who had been cropped out of the camera's view. His arm was tan and strong, his grip on her shoulder firm. For a split second I wondered if it was my dad. The man I never knew but pictured to have strong, manly arms. The kind of arms that hoist his child in the air and fly her around like a plane. Arms that wrap you in them when the first boy breaks your heart. Arms that I was sure would have delivered me a fair share of spankings in my day, but also my fair share of tickles. Those arms allowed me to dream. I placed another orange Post-it on the frame and set it back on the dresser. The woman I grew to know didn't look much like that happy girl in the picture, but I liked the thought that she was once that joyous.

Despite the huge appearance outside, the inside of the house was rather small. Made up of a lot of walls in places they didn't need to be and filled with shit my mother thought she needed. I passed by the staircase that leads up to the rest of the bedrooms and looked for a second too long at the door, thinking about the attorney with the ass. I caught my foot on the corner of the rug as I headed past the kitchen, office, and bathroom, knocking my right shoulder into the hallway wall that was lined with some type of vinery-themed wallpaper. I hit so hard I almost expected to see the print on my shoulder after. With my left hand now clutching my shoulder, I turned my back to the wall and slowly slunk down until my ass was on the floor and my head in my hands. Again I cried. Whether from the bump or the trip down memory lane, I couldn't tell. Honestly, it didn't really matter—both hurt.

A few minutes passed, and I rubbed the tears from my eyes. I pulled myself off the floor.

Once fully back on my feet, I headed toward the far back of the house to one of my all-time favorite spots—the screened-in back porch. The door swung open, and immediately I was inundated with the familiar smells and sounds. This was the only part of this place I truly missed.

Whenever the doctor has to take my blood pressure, I conjure the serenity of this place. The cuff tightens and I drift back to Hadleigh and this back porch.

"I heard that Elizabeth drank herself to death after she finally caught Al cheating."

"Yeah. You know that Grace learned from her father. Back in the day, he used to get around. I think he thought no one knew."

"Poor Elizabeth. Such a crappy existence, and that hair."

"But she was rich as the dickens. I would trade in my looks for that kind of money."

# 9

The screened-in back porch had barely changed over time. Thin mesh kept the bugs at bay but allowed the warm sun to caress your skin. You could hear the crickets in the back woods at all hours of the day, and at night you could see every star in the sky. The frogs were in full croak tonight, calling to their mates and trying to get a piece—something I had certainly done on this porch.

I walked around, listening to each floorboard make a different creaking noise under my feet. I recalled how impossible it had been to sneak back into the house via the back porch without detection.

Not that anyone had really cared how late I was out or where I was, but I liked to pretend sometimes that someone was waiting up for me, waiting to give me a whooping for breaking curfew. I would come in the back sometimes tiptoeing and pretending, hoping. Opening the door and shutting it ever so slowly behind me so as not to wake anyone. I would sneak up the stairs and into my room before they even knew the hour. In my head I was well cared for and watched over. In reality, I had the life most teenagers would have died for: Total freedom and no rules. You always want what you don't have, I suppose, just like the perm I tried to talk Grandma into letting me get after mom had said no in third grade. Curls were all the rage, and fitting in seemed like the thing to do. So if that meant a perm, then that was my best bet.

Against my better judgment, I waited outside on the porch one morning when I had heard Grandma and Grandpa hollering about his "disgusting behavior." I remember thinking it was odd that she found him to be the gross one when she was the one who barely brushed her hair. Although I guess he did always have a piece of hay in his mouth, which used to make me scrunch my nose up, thinking about the bugs that had crawled on that before he put it in his mouth.

I had been lost in thought about the bugs when the door slammed shut behind me, jarring me back to life, bringing my courage to the surface, arriving along with a ball of fear.

"Grandma, can I get a perm?" I queried, hoping my innocent eyes would woo her.

Bottle in hand, keys in the other, she hollered out to me as she stomped past, "Do whatever you want, child. Seems like that's what everyone else around here does."

But as the dust flew up and her tires sped weavingly away, I knew that no one at Amgine would take me to get a perm. I may have had permission, but I needed a plan, and no one around here wanted much to do with those. That was the first of many moments when I realized I was resolved to forever be on the outside of what was in.

I found a resting spot on the large wooden porch swing, big enough for a few people to sit on, another piece of my gramps left behind. The cushion had worn thin from all the time and weight it had carried. The paisley pattern had faded to a sepia tone, due largely in part to all the cigarette smoke it had absorbed over time. I half expected a cloud of smoke to fly up when I sat down.

My feet were flat on the ground as I started to push back and forth. At five ten, rocking flat-footed was no problem. The sky was ink black, something you rarely saw in Boston, and was glittering with the same stars of my childhood. I sipped the last swig of my vodka and let the lone ice cube swirl a little in my mouth before chewing it to pieces and swallowing. This moment, this place, was almost too perfect to get up from, but I was without a drink. I worried that if I sobered up now, I might never finish this process.

I half-hoped that if I sat there long enough my gramps would come out the door and tell me this was all a dream. A bad dream, but one nonetheless. He would join me on the swing and we would rock back and forth, singing "Copacabana." Gramps, weirdly, was a huge Barry Manilow fan, and though it didn't fit his profile, he didn't care. According to him, he and Barry were tight. Barry could do no wrong. So we would sing about Lola, Tony, and Rico. We would sing every word and then discuss just who shot who. We would laugh at the absurdity of the entire song, and then I would beg to sing it again.

I'm humming the tune under my breath when I hear another song off in the distance. For a moment I am utterly confused. I am back in 1989 singing with my best friend. Where on earth was this other music coming from? It takes longer than it should for me to realize that it is in fact my cell phone ringing back in the kitchen.

With a jolt, I am up and rushing back into the house, tripping again on the rug (mental note to fix that), but catching myself before it ends poorly once more. I make it into the kitchen as the ring is coming to an end. I slide the Answer button across the screen only to have missed the call. Damn.

The screen still has that crack across the top from when I threw it across the room after taking the call about my mother and knowing I'd have to come back here. I wasn't sure if I was more upset about her death or having to clean out her house. Either way, I was pissed and the phone took the brunt of it. Three missed calls and four new text messages, all from Letty. It was a sobering thought to realize that in the midst of this mess I had neglected to call my roommate and touch base. Letty was one of the very first people I had met once I got to Boston. She was a tiny, pretty but not stunning, smart but not irritating, little thing from Iowa. It was in the middle of a gay bar on a Friday night that I bumped into her. Literally bumped while trying to get through the crowd and almost stepped on this wispy woman on my way to get a drink. She was on the prowl and I was out of my comfort zone.

"Let me buy you a drink," she offered.

I politely declined.

She elbowed me. "Oh come on! I promise I won't try to hit on you!"

I found out she was a recent transfer out of Iowa. She felt her small town didn't understand her way of life, and she was tired of being an outcast. She was ready for a big city and big dreams. She wanted to be herself and be accepted. A little girl with big aspirations. The open book I had never become. She was a graphic designer by trade and a vixen by night. She got her fair piece of ass, but she was actually trying to look for the real thing. Certain she was going to find it in Boston, if only she could find a place to live that wouldn't bankrupt her.

Letty was a study in everything I wanted to be, sans hooking up with chicks. Coming from a small town where standing out means no chance of ever fitting in, and where letter jackets are more important than grades or life ambitions, watching her thrive in being other was magical. I have been other as long as I can remember feeling anything at all. I hid it, swallowed it down with the bitter pill of shame it brought along with it, but it was there, always in the back of my mind and the pit of my stomach. Letty made it all look so flawless, leaning in to her originality instead of running from it. She was a little person with a big presence, sparkly and distinct, gay and proud of it. I was someone in the shadows, twisty and complicated, my sexuality one of the most confusing things for me. I longed to be close to her from the start, just to orbit around someone that sunny was something I knew I needed in my life.

I had come to Boston a few days earlier and was still living out of my suitcase at the local Red Roof Inn. Boston by way of Austin. I had tried my hand at the southern lifestyle and found it didn't suit me either, so I was headed east, hoping to find what I was looking for.

Hoping to be accepted and live an honest life.

A writer by trade, I actually had already published one book, but you would never know it. I was still not comfortable writing as myself, so I was doing it under a pseudonym. Finnegan Hadleigh was someone comfortable in their skin, unlike Finn Harper, who couldn't even share secrets. Ironically, the true me was a pseudonym.

Finnegan Hadleigh was doing okay when arriving in Boston. No *New York Times* best seller yet, but enough sales to get a few paychecks. Boston was a whole new ballgame, though, and in order to try to make this place home, I needed a roommate and a new book idea.

The bar was bustling with people trying to get laid, and here I was potentially snagging someone to go home with . . . not to sleep with, just to share the rent. A few vodka tonics for me (guess I did get something from my mother) and more than enough cosmos for her, and it was a deal. We were going to move in together. We sealed the deal with a hug at Woody's Bar among drag queens and people trying to look up from their humpr apps. It was an alcohol-fueled decision, and while most would advise against those, I was a firm believer in them. Most of my books had been written while consuming several ounces of booze. Hemingway said, "Write drunk, edit sober." It was the one thing in life I truly believed in.

The next morning while still half-asleep on my rock-hard bed at the Red Roof, I dug through my scratchy sheets as my phone began to buzz.

"Hello, roomie!" she chimed.

"Good lord. What time is it?" I asked.

"Eight a.m. Up and at 'em, Finny. Time to get us some digs!"

I groaned and rolled over. "If you are a morning person, I am not sure this is going to work," I informed her.

"You'll get used to me. I am an acquired taste. But something from last night tells me you might be, as well." She chuckled.

"You might be right," I admitted.

"I'll pick you up in twenty. How do you like your coffee?"

"After ten a.m.," I said with a moan.

"You better stop messing with me or I am going to bring you some fancy pumpkin spice thingy, and my guess is that is not your jam."

"Black. I like it black. Thank you. See you in twenty."

That was years ago. I had hopped into her cute little Prius that fit her personality, and we had found a two-bedroom industrial loft where the air ducting is part of the aesthetic and the floors are all concrete. The location was perfect and the price was doable. We moved in the next week.

After all this time, we had become like siblings. We loved

each other like them and fought like them. We had our moments, for sure, but nothing was ever bad enough to break us. We had never found a reason to leave, and so we stayed. She was still on the hunt for Mrs. Right, and I was still on the hunt for my true self, the one behind the pseudonym.

This was probably the longest we had ever gone without talking, and I was sure that poor Letty was probably convinced this place had chewed me up and swallowed me whole. She was one, if not the only, person who knew just how I felt about Hadleigh. She knew to the extent that I would tell her, and that was enough for her to know this place was going to do some damage.

The phone rang maybe once before she answered.

"Finny! Are you alive? Since when don't you return texts? How awkward that I had to call. I think I even left you a voicemail." She gasped.

"Hey, Letty. So sorry. This place has me all in a jumble. I am not even sure how many days I have been here."

"Tell me all about it, babe. How is it? How's the house? Have you seen anyone?"

She called everyone "babe," as if Iowa was far enough south for her to pull off the southern vernacular. I was never sure if it was an intentional gypsy thing, or if she really thought she was below the Mason-Dixon line. Either way, it was part of her, a part of her I adored.

"The house is fine. Full of memories and pain but still standing. Still reeking with old farmhouse charm that I am sure Chip & Joanna Gaines would love."

She giggled at this; she had been making me watch HGTV's *Fixer Upper*, and I had fallen in love with shiplap just like the rest of the country, though I would never admit it to the world outside Letty.

"Other than that, it has been a lot of drinking and trying to avoid smoking. I did venture out on my first run though."

"You what?" she sputtered. "Like to the liquor store?"

"No, jerk. Like a real jog."

"You went for a jog? How totally quaint and random."

"Yeah, I know. I bought those shoes before I left and intended on this big lifestyle change and felt like running was part of it. Seemed like a good alternative to smoking. Not sure if it is up to the hype, but I'm going to give it a fighting chance, I think. Plus there is not much to do here anyhow. They had cut the internet and cable after she died. So it is just this house, the memories, the booze, and me. Sometimes I need a little fresh air."

"Sounds like a shit ton of fun," she joked. "How long will you be there? Have you seen any ghosts of Finny past?

"No ghosts yet. Hopefully they stay behind closed doors. The only person I have come into contact with is my mother's lawyer. He stopped by to remind me that I needed to come down and hear her last wishes. He was kind of a welcome surprise."

I decided to forgo mentioning his ass and the arm graze out on the run for now. Letty would make something out of nothing, and I was already doing a fine job of that on my own.

"A welcome surprise, huh? Did you let him have his way with you in your childhood bedroom?" She snickered.

"Wow. Straight out with it, huh? I am not sure you are ever going to snag Mrs. Right with a mouth like that," I rebuffed.

"The right one will love all of me. Ass, sass, and crass," she said. I could practically hear her smiling on the other end.

Amidst this mess, she was my bright spot. She was my godsend, as she had been time and time again.

I reached for the vodka and filled my cup while balancing

the phone on my shoulder. Letty went on about her recent adventures while I was gone. I grabbed my glass and headed back out to the porch.

"Letty," I finally interrupted, "I'm exhausted. Can I call you tomorrow?"

"No worries, babe. Just wanted to make sure you were still alive. FaceTime me tomorrow. I want to see this place for myself. Night, babe."

And then there I was, alone again. I lay down on the swing and pulled a hand-knit quilt over me. It was one of the other items in the house my grandmother told me was a hand-me-down from an Irish relative. The quilt smelled of stale cigarettes and Love's Baby Soft perfume, just the way my mother always had.

I took a big gulp of my drink, set it on the floor, closed my eyes, and instinctively started humming, "His name was Rico / He wore a diamond . . ."

"There was no way I was letting Finny do this alone. The poor babe. I know this place is the pits, and I couldn't not be here. I flew through the night to make the funeral. Ugh! I can't imagine going through this. Anyway, how did you say you knew her again?"

"I'm James, Grace's lawyer."

"Wait . . . what? James, I think my Finny mentioned you."

"You're Finny?"

# 10

My breath caught in my lungs, suffocating me and throwing my eyes open at the same time. I wasn't sure if it was the humidity or the stark realization that someone was staring at me.

"Oh my God! I am so sorry!" a woman shrieked.

Jesus, why did people just keep showing up here all the time?

I kept my right eye closed, and through my squinting left eye, I could make out the outline of a woman. I raised my hand to use as a shield over my eyebrows as she came into vision.

She was about my age, straight, blond, recently-colored hair, huge designer sunglasses covering her eyes. Her arms were wrapped around her hugely pregnant stomach. She looked familiar, but the sun still prevented me from seeing her perfectly.

She took a step closer.

"I am so very sorry. I didn't mean to disturb you. I tried the front door, and when no one answered, I came around to check the back. I used to be friends with the girl who grew up here . . . Finn. Have you seen her?" she asked.

I stared at her until it finally dawned on me. Peyton. Peyton, the girl from my note to Gramps in eighth grade.

The girl who was voted most popular in high school despite her outcast of a sidekick. That sidekick, of course, had been me. She was head cheerleader and the top bitch (though she would never use that word). She ran that school like a tight ship. You didn't want to be on her bad side, but you wanted even worse to be on the inside. She always had my back, even though it never made any sense. I made it through high school without the typical slut-shaming thanks largely to Peyton. She knew people wanted to talk about me, but she wouldn't have it.

"Peyton?" I asked.

She looked a little caught off guard until she lifted her sunglasses and met my eyes.

Back then, she had been as good of a friend as a girl could ask for in Hadleigh. But as senior year came to an end, she followed her high school quarterback boyfriend off to Clemson, and I followed a desire to get the hell out of dodge to the University of Texas, Austin. That was it for us. We had run our course. We were too different outside of Hadleigh. We were footprints in the sand at a time when we needed each other most. In my heart it hurt a little, but the writer in me was okay with the poetic end to it all. It seemed so adult and so Austen. But now here she was, on my back porch where we used to have sleepovers, asking if I knew where Finn was.

"Finn?" she questioned.

"Hi. Long time," I said sheepishly. I wasn't sure I was ready to do this without coffee, or alcohol for that matter.

"Wow. I heard you were different now, but I almost didn't recognize you. You look great. Austin is agreeing with you," she stammered.

"Actually it is Boston now," I replied.

"Even better," she said. "Less heat." With that she cracked a smile.

Peyton had a way of making everyone around her feel comfortable. The type of individual that people are drawn to. She could also bring you down just as quick, but that side rarely showed.

"You look great, too," I remarked. "How far along are you?"

"Eight months yesterday." She smiled and rubbed her belly. "Boy number four. Just the way Will wanted it. Me and a bunch of little penises." She laughed.

There she was. The Peyton I knew, polite and endearing with a crass side among true friends.

"Right. How is Will? What is he doing now?"

Will, the quarterback she had followed off to Clemson and married her senior year of college. He had proposed after she cheered his team on to a national championship against LSU. In the parking lot after the big win, he got down on his knee in front of everyone and professed his love to her and sealed it with a giant diamond (with his parents money). She couldn't have cooked it up any better, and she had been posting pictures of their "perfect" life all over Instagram since.

"Oh, William. He is still a lawyer at a firm he started with a friend in downtown. He is great." She cracked a smile that I couldn't tell was real or forced.

"And the kids?" I asked.

That night back at Clemson in the back of his pickup truck, she let the celebration continue and allowed him and his national championship penis to go without a condom as long as he agreed to pull out. He wanted to really feel every moment of that special night, and that meant not having any part of him feeling restricted. Nine months later, William Champ Samson was born. Champ was the apple of his dad's eye since he was a constant reminder of his glory days, or day.

"They're great," she said.

"That's great," I murmured. Then it dawned on me what an ass I was being in not inviting her in.

"Please. Have a seat." I got up and pulled a chair over. "Can I get you anything?"

"You are so kind. Water would be great," she said, looking down and rubbing her belly again as if to signify why water was her only option.

I walked back inside the house and could feel her eyes on me. Why was she here? What did she want?

In the kitchen I started the coffeepot and poured two glasses of water. I had forgotten to refill the ice tray, and so lukewarm water it was. What a space cadet.

While the pot brewed, I filled the trays and set them back in the freezer next to the bottle of vodka.

I poured myself a cup of coffee from the one mug I had left in the cabinet and carried the coffee and her water out to the back porch, leaving my water on the counter once it dawned on me that I only had two hands. Wow. I was certainly winning today.

The door squeaked a little as I pushed it open with my back. I turned around and handed her the water. "So sorry. We are out of ice."

"No worries. I like my water not too cold anyway," she politely responded, smiling into the cup.

I sat back down on top of the quilt in the spot that had doubled as my bed last night and took a sip of coffee, trying to steady myself for whatever this was.

"You look so different. I can't get over it. I mean, I had heard that you changed, but this is not what I expected," she said. "I don't mean that in a bad way. I am sorry—this is coming out wrong. Please don't hate me." She looked down into her cup again.

There it was, front and center. The reason I didn't want to come back. My insecurities laid out on the table, and it made me feel like that little girl again, hiding in her closet and crying. I felt comfortable in Boston. I felt like me. Here I felt like a freak show.

"I was nervous to come," she went on. "I heard you were back in town for the funeral and to clean out this house and I wanted to reconnect." She looked up and we locked eyes. "I have weirdly missed you."

The silence was making me uncomfortable enough that I had to say something. I honestly hadn't thought about her at all since high school and missing her had never crossed my mind. This made things even more awkward.

"Wow." Was all I could get out at first. I took a deep breath and another swig of coffee as she reached out and put her hand on my knee.

"I know this is a lot, and it probably doesn't make any sense, but I think you may have been the truest friend I ever had. I don't know what has become of me. I thought this was everything I wanted. The ring. The husband. The kids. The PTA and the book club that was really a wine club that was really just a gossip session." At this she kind of trailed off and looked off in the distance as though searching for something. With a little shake of her head, she turned back and continued, "But I am now wondering if I did it all wrong. Maybe I should have followed you instead of him. Maybe I should have been more independent and accomplished something with my life like you did. I read your books, you know."

This confession startled me. I have never written a book under my real name. Under Finley Harper I only write puff pieces for the *Boston Herald*. Finnegan Hadleigh was the one who wrote the books. She must be mistaken. She couldn't have read my books.

I took another drink, trying to figure out my words carefully.

"Sounds like you have everything you ever wanted. Everything you ever said you needed when we were in high school. I am not sure you would want my life anyhow. The grass isn't always greener, Peyton," I said, trying to ignore the book reference all together.

"I know that, Finn. I am not saying I want to be you, just that I wish I would have had a little of your reckless abandon. Your guts. Your ability to not give a fuck. For God's sake, the most daring thing I ever did was to have sex without a condom with a man I was going to marry." She looked depleted as she said it.

"Well, that sounds pretty damn reckless," I said. "That's the kind of shit that makes you a mom, which you and I both know I never wanted."

"You know what I mean, Finn." She smirked.

I took another drink before I looked at her. "I don't mean to be rude, Pey, but what is it that you want from me?" I asked.

"Truthfully, I don't know." She looked down at her Tory Burch ballet flats and shifted slightly in her seat. "Maybe just a second chance? I know that sounds so childish and naïve, but I think it is a good place to start."

"Pey—I really appreciate the offer, but I am sure I can handle this on my own. Lord knows I am used to riding solo," I replied.

"Let me help you with this. I knew your mother just as well as you, and I know that this mess has to be driving you mad. She always drove you mad. Let me help. Let me be the friend I haven't been in a long time."

I stared at her. She was just as beautiful as she had been in high school. She was obviously getting Botox on the regular because her skin was free of wrinkles, free of stress. I was sure that a mother of boys was not stress free, and so she must have a good doctor. The only thing that looked different (other than her protruding belly) was the look in her eyes. She looked empty. She was trying to fake it, I could tell. And for most people she was probably pulling it off, but I knew better. I knew her. And it was then I realized that she needed me just as much as I needed her.

"Deal," I muttered.

"Oh, Finn! This is going to be good. You will see! I will make you not want to leave this place!" She smiled.

"There are a couple days until the funeral, and I need to figure out what to say and clean this house out before then, and Pey . . ."

"Yes?"

"There is no way in hell I will stay."

"Yes. Well . . . no . . . I mean not my Finny. My roomie Finny. Did I strike a nerve? Are you and Finny a thing?"

"I don't know. I think there is a lot going on right now, but what I do know is that the other night was pretty amazing."

"The other night? Do tell, babe . . ."

## 11

Pey ran into town to get some lunch from some new café called the Blue Moon that she swore had bread that rivaled the French. Looking at her made me wonder if she had actually consumed a carb in years. She was probably one of those "gluten free" gals who did it for vanity and not allergy.

I got up and brushed my teeth. The mixture of last night's cocktail and this morning's toothpaste/coffee combo made me a little queasy. Spit, rinse, and wipe. The person looking back at me in the mirror was starting to look like a mess.

Peyton was so put together and made everything seem simple. She looked identical to the girl I left years ago, and then there was me. This person staring back in the mirror looked, dare I say it, like my mother? My eyes reeked of misery and strain. I wasn't her, but I sure as hell didn't feel like me here either.

This town was bringing out the worst in me. I was sure it wasn't the booze. It was the environment. I needed a shower. I needed a cigarette. Nope . . . correction . . . the new me needed a run. My second attempt at a new habit, one that wasn't going to be bad for me. I had too many vices already; this was going to be good.

I put on my tiny, little shorts and laced up those fluorescent shoes. I left the watch on the counter this time, damn thing is broken for sure, and wrote Pey a note on a napkin I left on the kitchen counter.

"Went for a run. Yes, seriously. If not back by two, please call the cops. Or just let me go."

I probably should have put a smiling emoji at the end, but I couldn't bring myself to do it. Writing a note had felt so ancient in the first place that I almost felt my hand cramping. What kind of a writer can't write? Good God.

The dust kicked up behind me again as I disturbed the gravel. I was going to take the same route as before. I needed to see the changes this place had gone through again. I almost didn't believe it.

It still didn't feel easy or fun yet. Runners are nuts. If I was going to seriously start doing this, then I should probably invest in Spotify or at least start putting music on my phone to listen to. I wouldn't even know what kind of music people run to. Prince. Maybe he would work. In the wake of his death, there had to be plenty of Prince songs and playlists for free download to pass the time as I did this whole "running/bettering myself" thing. I needed something to help pass the monotony.

It hit me all over again, as if I had happened upon the Vegas strip. The new Hadleigh downtown. The pottery place still made me laugh (not much did these days), and there were more people milling around. God . . . what day was it anyway? Sunday? Was it really Sunday already?

People were walking around still in their church best. I had never owned church clothing. I was always glad about this. I was never a girl for dresses and tights, so if not going to church meant no dresses, then I was all in. It wasn't until I was in college when I first learned about religion. Sure my mother used to say his name in vain all the time, but that was all I ever knew about the man. He was an adjective for profanity.

That's what made this whole funeral thing seem so funny to me. She never believed in a god, but yet here I was holding a funeral in a church as per her wishes. Maybe she had hoped it would wipe all her indiscretions away, one last "Hail Mary."

I noticed the Blue Moon Diner for the first time and hoped Peyton had already left and wouldn't see me huffing along. She was a track star back in the day and probably ran a million marathons a year when she wasn't pregnant. My jogging motion would probably make her laugh. I sped up a little as I passed the diner and the bar. I knew at some point I would have to go in there. I had to make peace. Make nice. But not now. Not today. Today I was out for a run. Oh so healthy of me.

I veered onto Perchman's Path and again thought of the sexual escapades that happened in these woods. The virginity it took and the hymens that were popped. I was thankful my first experience wasn't among leaves and dirt. I may have spent my fair share of time getting dirty, but my first time was not that. My first time was like many firsts. It was innocent, naïve, quick, and in a safe place. It sure as shit was not out here, and it was not meaningless. It might have been one of the only times sex ever mattered to me.

I was fifteen and in love. He was seventeen and horny. We had been together, "going out," for six months. He made me feel safe and I made him lust. It was time. We had talked about it long enough, and I was so sure that I wasn't being my mother that I was okay with it. It had been six months, which was five months and twenty-nine days longer than she had ever made a man wait. So it was time.

My mom was off God knows where and Gramps was tilling the field for the evening when I let Nick Weston till my field. We were under a blanket on our back porch swing, watching the chickens peck the ground, when his hand slipped under the blanket and he whispered in my ear, "Are you sure?"

I nodded and took his hand, leading it under my leggings that I had worn so everything would be as easy as possible. It might have been foreshadowing. I kept my hand on his as he slid his finger inside of me. I moaned quietly and tilted my head back. We had gone this far before, but this time felt different. I thought for a second about my dead grandma watching from the afterlife, shaking her head at me, thinking I was becoming my mother. I wanted to yell, "I am not her. I love him." But instead, I moaned. His face lit up, and he turned and kissed me on the neck. I arched my back and grabbed his hand again. This time I tried to lead his pinky farther south.

I had read once in a magazine about this technique and it intrigued me. I hate to say that I was an ass girl, but I did have a slight infatuation with the butt. I liked men's butts and I liked the feeling of having his finger in mine.

He looked a little caught off guard by this young girl helping him do things he had only seen in pornos, but he willingly participated nonetheless. I moaned as I felt him thrust his fingers in and out and his penis grow harder against my leg. He was into this as much as I was. It was time. I was ready. This was it. I was in love and was going to have him enter me.

I had been taking the pill for three months now in anticipation of this moment. I wanted to feel everything. I didn't want to be hindered by a "do you have a condom moment," so I had gone to Planned Parenthood the next town over and gotten the pill. I had diligently taken it every day, and now it was going to pay off. I wasn't going to have an accidental Finn.

I whispered in his ear, "I want to do this," and just like that, his fingers were out and he was unzipping his jeans. The jeans that seemed to be made for him. The jeans that had gotten us into this situation in the first place. I reached down to feel him, to know he wanted me as much as I wanted him. He did.

He slid on top of me under the blanket on the porch swing. I helped guide him inside. For a minute or two, I wondered if it would even work, but it quickly became apparent that it would. The swing seemed to move in rhythm with his hips and he went in and out, trying hard to make it last as long as he could. He must have thought that I was going to get off, but I was far from enjoying the moment. I was just trying to get through it. Nerves were firing in all directions, sending mixed signals to my brain . . . it hurts . . . it doesn't . . . it feels good . . . I need more. In the end he climaxed and then fell on top of me, breathing as though he had just run a marathon.

I lay there trying to catch my breath and wondering if this was all sex had to offer. Why was my mother so into it if it left you feeling like this? Sore and unsatisfied. There had to be more.

"Hold up. You mean to tell me that Finn flew back here for this? She actually came to speak? Last I heard, she was living in Austin and barely resembled the girl we used to know."

"Yeah. Pey has been spending a bunch of time with her, helping her clean out that old farmhouse. I think Pey secretly wants her to stay, but I am hoping that this goodwill gesture on Pey's part will help us land that house. I would love for the boys to grow up on all that acreage."

"Pey and Finn . . . just like in high school, huh? The odd couple. You think they ever hooked up? Like a drunken night . . . just tried it out? Or is your wife too square for that?"

"Damn! I would pay a premium to see that, but I don't think it ever happened. At least not that Pey ever mentioned, but I guess why would you tell your husband that? I guess it's not beyond the realm of possibilities."

# 12

My sexual escapades were again at the front of my mind when I heard him there in Perchman's Path, just like before.

"Behind you!" he called.

I turned and saw it was the hot lawyer again, the one I had yet to call. Damn. I couldn't have him see me. I turned forward quickly and moved to the right side of the path and turned my head as if I was looking off at something in the woods as he passed me.

I felt his arm brush mine again, almost as if it had been intentional, and then he was gone. I could hear the music in his headphones trailing off and the faint smell of sweet sweat as he ran away. His touch left me in a tizzy again. What was it about this guy? I wanted to find out, but I wasn't going to call him. Not yet. I wasn't going to be that easy. I was afraid of what I would do if I came face-to-face with him again . . . and I wasn't that girl anymore.

I quickened my steps and prayed he wouldn't look back. I wanted to follow him but not too closely. I wanted to see how he did it. How he made running seem so natural, so primal. He looked as though he was floating on the ground. He had music, which I had already made a mental note that I needed, and he had that damn watch thing that I was supposed to be wearing. Guess I need to give that another go. He also miraculously made sweating look amazingly attractive. I was sure that the amount of perspiration coming out of my pores was anything but cute. I studied him for a minute and wondered about his story.

Why was he here? What would bring someone that attractive to this shit hole? Was he single? Married? Straight? Gay?

I squinted my eyes shut, almost as if to stop these thoughts. Maybe if I cared so much, I should call the guy back instead of stalking him out in the woods.

And then he turned his head around and looked at me, as if he could hear my thoughts. I wanted to run and hide, or at least look away, but it was too late. His beautiful eyes had locked on mine and I was awestruck. Lost in the sea of blue, I missed the ground below my feet change and stutter-stepped as I was trying not to fall. I was praying this wouldn't be the moment that my lack of athleticism would show. I needed to look like I was a veteran, like I run on the reg. I caught my balance just in time to prevent an all-out epic fail. I looked back up; he smirked, winked, and ran off. He was there and then gone, like a damn fox.

I stopped for a second now that I was done trying to impress and caught my breath and bearings. Why did this guy shake me like this? I haven't had such a visceral reaction to a man since Nick, and even that was more puppy love than passion. I knew nothing about this guy, and yet I had a deep yearning for him. He could be a serial killer who was stalking me in the woods with plans to eventually do away with me and take my mom's money. While that was a little farfetched, his eyes didn't say serial killer, but truthfully, my body didn't care. I shrugged my shoulders back and tried to focus my adrenaline on finishing the run instead of on his body pressed against mine.

Deep breath.

The second half of the run seemed to go faster than the first. I am not sure if it was because my body was warmed up (in all kinds of places) or that my mind was racing with thoughts of James, the lawyer. Either way, the run had seemed a little more effortless, which was encouraging and made me smile as I walked onto the front porch.

I put my hand on the screen door jamb and used the front of the shoe with the scuffmark to push the other shoe off my heel, and then I used my freed toes to do the same to the other foot. There was something so liberating about taking off your shoes after a run—maybe that is the feeling that everyone looks forward to. Perhaps that is why they like it so much.

I bent over and picked up my neon shoes and walked through the front door. I gently set them on the side of the rug, perfectly, symmetrically, and freeing. I cocked my head to the side to stare at them and smile. Why did I suddenly feel this connection to them? Was it because every time I wore them I saw him? Was it the amount of shit I could leave behind while wearing them? They were just shoes, after all, but they were no longer sneakers. They were my escape from the past and means to the future.

"Hey—you are back! And alive!" she said, breaking into my train of thought.

"What the fu—" I yelled as I spun around, completely forgetting that I had let someone into the house, into my personal space.

She looked at me with her beautiful "deer in headlights" eyes. "Oh my goodness—I am so sorry I startled you. I got back from the diner before you and let myself in and got to work. I am so sorry, Finn."

"Good Lord. I totally forgot. No, I am sorry. My bad. I didn't mean to freak out."

I wiped the sweat from my forehead as she handed me a bottle of lemonade.

"I got you the best lemonade you will ever have. I swear they must mix crack in it. Oh, and your sandwich is on the counter. I didn't know what you liked, so I just went with their special—the chicken salad on whole wheat. I hope that's okay."

I uncapped the lemonade and took a long, hard swig. It was the perfect mixture of sour and sweet, kind of like Pey and me.

I could feel her longing eyes watching me, waiting for my approval. She always was a pleaser, something I could never understand. Peyton was a dog in another life—loyal, loving, affectionate, and craving attention. Me, I was a cat—did my own thing, didn't need others, and didn't give two fucks. I am not sure if I was always that way or if things shifted for me after the accident . . . but I don't talk about that anymore. It's too much. Too deep.

"This is good, Pey. Incredible actually."

She wagged her tail, and I went into the kitchen to lick my paws and ignore the world. She followed, just like a good dog did.

The chicken salad sandwich was wrapped in one of those white paper wrappings that they scribbled your name on with wax pencil. I flipped over the sandwich to make sure this one was indeed mine.

"HER?" I looked at Peyton quizzically.

She giggled. "He told me to do it. Told me to tell you it stood for Hot Erratic Runner. I knew it would confuse you, but he insisted. Kind of weird, I know, but he wouldn't stop bugging me about it, so I did it."

"He?"

"James. My husband's law partner. He stopped into the diner after he finished his run and told me he ran into you out on the trail. I was sure he must have been mistaken since you don't run, but he was sure it was you and insisted on the sandwich name, so I obliged, figuring when I got home we would laugh about the mistaken identity, but then I saw your note and it made sense. He obviously has a thing for you."

She let the words hang there, awaiting my response. Would I blush like a schoolgirl or brush the whole thing off? I let the words hang there, as well, and let my mind wander back to the trail and the brush of his arm against mine. I suddenly felt the need to shake my shoulders and exhale. What was it about this man? I thought it was only me noticing him, but apparently he had observed me, as well, even if just because I made running look painful.

"What a funny guy," was all I could get out at first without letting my face give the whole thing away.

"Funny guy? So you know who I am talking about? You have seen James? What happened out there?" She smiled and placed her face in her hands that were being supported by her elbows on the counter.

"Oh, Pey. It was nothing," I started as I began to unwrap my sandwich. The thought crossed my mind that I should keep the paper, remember the moment he made the first move. Good Lord—who was I becoming? A damn Hallmark fool. I crumpled the paper and set it next to the lemonade.

"Nothing? Your face doesn't look like it was nothing. And those goose bumps on your arms tell a different story!" she kept on.

This was so stupid. We weren't back in high school talking about my latest conquest. We are grown ass adults, and we don't gush over some guy, especially some guy I didn't even know. He knew nothing about me, and that's how it needed to stay.

"Pey, it is really nothing. We met when he showed up here to get me to come in and hear my mother's last wishes. That's about it."

I wasn't even convincing myself.

She shifted her head to one side and leaned on her right hand, resting her porcelain skin against her palm.

"I don't believe you. If that is all, then how does he know you have been running? Are you guys sleeping together?" She smirked.

"Jesus, Pey. No."

"Come on, Finn—give a poor, huge, sexless, pregnant girl the details. I need something to think about. How is he? He surely is cute. Don't tell Will, but I have had a few fantasies about James. But I am not his type. You, on the other hand . . ."

"Oh my God, Pey—you are insatiable. I am not sleeping with him. We have merely bumped into each other while running through Perchman's Path. And that is it. I swear."

She shifted her face over to her other hand and looked a little depleted. She started twisting the huge diamond stud in her ear. "Ugh! I was looking forward to all the exotic details . . . and Perchman's Path nonetheless. Mmmm." She moaned. "The stories those trees could tell, huh?"

"None of my stories," I reminded her.

"Oh right. Finn was too good to frolic in the forest," she said in her singsong way.

"It wasn't even like that, and you know it. The old Finn wasn't too good for anything or anyone. I damn near sat on anything that I could." I laughed.

"Except James." She grinned.

I could feel my cheeks starting to flush at the thought of him doing those kinds of things to me. I took a bite of the sandwich and tried to deflect the conversation to a less arousing topic.

"So . . . you said you got started around here?"

"Oh no, Finn—you are not getting off that easy, but since you swear that there is nothing going on with you and Mr. James, then it shouldn't be a big deal that I invited him over to join us for dinner at Tin 'n' Grits tonight."

"No way in hell am I going to eat at Tin 'n' Grits, Pey. You know I am not ready for that yet. There is too much there. I am not ready to deal."

"Well, it is good to see that it is not James you are opposed to, just the dining facility. Trust me—no one will recognize you. Besides, the place is so different now. You won't believe it. After Jim retired, Tom gutted the place, and with it went the locals and the scum. You will like it—I will get a corner booth. It will be fine."

She was now standing next to me, rubbing my arm as if this was going to get me to say yes.

"Peyton—" I began as I jerked my arm away from her gentle, encouraging strokes.

"Finn! I won't hear it. I went out of my way to make this happen, even got that silly Gavinson girl to babysit my monsters. I need this night out, and you need to reenter society. This house is toxic, and you know it. So . . . dinner! Seven! And that is that!"

She was looking at me in a way I never remember my mother ever doing . . . like someone who cared. I hated myself for it, but I was touched. She really thought she was doing the right thing, and who was I to begrudge her a night out.

"Fine," I succumbed.

"Great! Oh, Finn, it will be so fun!" She clapped her hands together and turned towards the sink to rinse out her empty lemonade bottle.

I took another bite of my sandwich and watched her do her magic at the sink. I have never been attracted to women, but watching Peyton move so gracefully made me envious of her. She had always been so confident in herself. Of course she had nothing to feel self-conscious of. She was the perfection of beauty and elegance. She got perfect grades and had the perfect guy. She never faltered. I would have given anything to feel an ounce of what she felt.

I did well in school (really well), but my skin never felt like mine. I didn't have the perfect boyfriend or perfect life. I settled into an existence of madness and promiscuity. To be honest, I never really enjoyed sex. After each encounter, I would get into the shower and touch all the body parts I hated. I felt so disgusted with myself and so appalled at my behavior, but I couldn't stop. It never felt good or meaningful. I don't know if it was learned behavior, a learned coping mechanism, or if it was just general rebellion, but whatever it was, it wasn't me. There was a time when I was in love and thought for a minute that I could do this forever, be here with him, but instead I was left in a heap on the floor and things had forever changed in me.

Now here we were . . . so much time since those two girls in high school. There were years and a lifetime of pain and transformation in between. So much was different, and yet some things remained the same. She was still the beautiful girl with the perfect blond ponytail who could kill you with her kindness, and I was still the hot mess she catered to.

"You checking out my butt?" She turned and tried to look over her shoulder as if to check it out for herself. "I have been working hard on not letting it get huge while I have baby on board. My trainer makes me do about five hundred squats every day. But if it means you are staring at it, then maybe it is worth it." She turned back and looked at me. "Are you into girls now? Is this another part of the new you?" She twirled her finger as if to put an imaginary circle around me.

"Okay, first off . . . I am not into girls. That part has never changed. But, yes, I was checking out your ass. You could bounce a quarter off that thing. I am crazy jealous. You must spill your secrets. You know I love me a good ass," I quipped.

"Deal. I will trade you—dinner tonight for my butt secrets." She snickered.

"Okay. Back to business, though," she started and then turned to grab a colorful folder sitting on the kitchen table behind me.

"Do you remember these?" she asked, shaking the folder at me. "Lisa Frank!" she shouted before I could answer. "Remember how into these I was, and I had to twist your arm into buying a matching one in fourth grade because what kind of best friends were we if we didn't have matching folders? And you—being the great friend you are—swallowed your pride and bought the colorful folder that made you grit your teeth every time you looked at it."

I couldn't believe her memory, or mine for that matter, because I remembered that folder so distinctly. It was the bane of my existence. Peyton's parents had taken us school shopping together after my mother had become too tired to even make an appearance out of her bedroom. Gramps had given me enough money and sent me on my way with the school list we had grabbed from the folders taped to the school's front doors marked by grade. I had my eye on this great folder with a picture of a black lab puppy on it, the kind my mom would never let me get. I had begged for months for a dog, but surprisingly it was the only thing she ever took a parenting stand on with me. No dog. No more badgering about it.

That black lab on the folder was the epitome of everything this single child wanted and could never have; he was my new, fictional, man's best friend. So you could only imagine my disappointment when my real best friend informed me that we were not getting puppy folders, we were getting Lisa Frank because Lisa was the next big thing, and didn't we want to be cool and matching? It might have been one of the few times that my "cat persona" morphed into her "dog." I gently set down my black lab folder and silently shed a tear for the best friend I would never know. She linked arms with me and shoved my new, bright, and happy folder into my hand.

"Fourth grade is going to be so cool now," she had said.

Fourth grade, as it turned out, was not such a cool year for me. No amount of cheer and brightness coming off that folder could change my outlook on life that year. Fourth grade was the year that my grandmother died, and though she and I were never on the best of terms, it was the first time I saw death. Real death and what that does to those left behind. While Gramps seemed indifferent on her passing, possibly even glad to be rid of the old bag, my mom handled it differently. She became even more distant from me. She would spend days in her room, only coming out to go to the bar or get another drink from the freezer. She seemed weaker, frailer, and quite honestly, she seemed despondent and scared.

While I may have been apathetic regarding my grandmother's death, I was a mix of emotions as my hormones began to rage. Fourth grade was the year I began puberty and feeling a whole mess of things that didn't make sense to me. I needed a mother. I needed *my* mother, but that was one luxury

I wasn't afforded. So instead I wrote. I wrote to my gramps, and I wrote in my journal. I tried to document everything I was thinking and feeling. I am sure it was oh so Dear Diary-esque. I would probably laugh now at what I thought mattered then. I was wise beyond my years, but still thought that what mattered most was fitting in and being just like everyone else . . . which brings us back to the Lisa Frank folder and the death of my innocence.

"Of course I remember Lisa Frank," I responded. "Didn't we have the matching notebooks and pencils that went with that folder? I think your dad even sprung for the pencil case."

"Oh he was a sucker for my smile," she gloated. "I think I may be fully responsible for Lisa's success at Hadleigh Elementary."

"I think you might be right. Anyway, what's in the folder?" I questioned.

"Right . . ." She flipped it open and placed it on the counter next to the sandwich wrapper I was still mildly coveting.

"I went through the whole main level while you were gone. As you can see here." She pointed to a spreadsheet in the folder. "I detailed what each color Post-it means. What can stay. What can go. What you can donate."

"Jesus—how long was I running?" I said, wide-eyed.

"Oh, Finn, you know me. Type A and perfectionist at your service." She raised her hand and saluted me as though I were a ship captain.

"Anyway . . ." she continued, "I think I pretty much nailed it. I am not sure there was much that was sentimental on this level besides the desk and the letters. But of course you should look it over and make the final calls."

"Pey, this is huge. Thank you so much. You have no idea how much this helps. I am speechless."

"No problem. It's what I do. I have the Goodwill people coming day after tomorrow, so we need to get the rest done by then. You are going to have to buckle down and deal with this shit . . . oops . . . pardon my French." She covered her mouth and looked around sheepishly, as if to make sure no little ears heard.

"Oh, you sailor!" I called to her. She started to flush. "Don't you dare cuss in this house. You know better."

She smiled and playfully hit my shoulder. "Stop. You know I am not like that. Being a badass was always your territory."

"True. I did march to the beat of my own drum."

"Indeed you did. Still do, I guess."

"I guess."

"Anyways, go through this and head to the basement. I need to go pick up Champ from school. I'll see you at dinner, yes?" She tilted her head and smiled.

I knew it wasn't a question as much as a statement.

"Yep. See you at seven. I'll work on the basement."

"Okay. Sounds good. Save the upstairs for me. There has to be some stuff in your bedroom that I can't live without." She winked and headed to the door.

"Try to be nice tonight too. I want James to see the Finn that I love, not the disgruntled, cynical writer who hates people, okay?" she said while simultaneously slipping her flats on again.

"I will do my best," I promised . . . and I meant it.

"No, it wasn't really a thing. Maybe it was. I don't know. We have had a few times together, and I think there something there, but I don't know what Finn thinks."

"Oh my! I knew Finny couldn't keep it in the pants when it came to you! Was it good? It's been too long since Finny got some!"

"Too long? Like how long?"

"Oh, I don't know . . . since we moved in together. What is that? Like eight or so years."

"Wow. I didn't know."

"Oh shit. Maybe it wasn't my place to say. Don't mention it to Finn, okay? Shit!"

# 13

One being among many ghosts. Just like that I was alone in this big house again. And while I don't believe in ghosts, if there was a chance they existed, it felt like it would be here.

My eyes wandered over to the crumpled-up sandwich wrapper, and before I could even convince myself otherwise, I was un-crumpling it and smoothing it out, just like I had those notes from Gramps.

I stared at it for a moment and felt the corners of my lips start to curve up and the heat in my chest start to rise. I felt a little like the Grinch when he looked down over Whoville and they were singing, despite his best efforts to stop it. Like it or not, my heart was growing.

I folded the note and stuffed it in the back of the neatly organized Lisa Frank folder that Peyton had left for me to rummage through. I was sure she had done her due diligence, and so I didn't even think twice about what she thought I should throw or keep.

Sandwich in one hand and the folder tucked under the other arm, I opened the freezer with my free pinky and shoved the sandwich in between my teeth so I could utilize my free hand to grab that ice cold bottle of vodka. If I was going to tackle the basement, I was going to need my friend Tito to help me make sense of it.

The envelope nestled in my armpit threatened to fall while I turned the crystal doorknob to the right. For everything this house looked like on the outside, the basement was the only indication that everything inside was not as perfect as you would think. It was the dirty little secret of the house, the one you didn't let the outside world see. Most houses in Hadleigh didn't even have a basement; that was far too fancy for their tastes or wallets. The Amgine farmhouse had a basement, which made it even more interesting to outside folk.

"What would you need a basement for?"

"What does it look like?"

"What do they keep down there?"

"Is it safe to have your house on top of it?"

All these questions around something that a lot of houses throughout the country have without thought. Amgine Farm was going to shake this town up—they knew it back when they dug in the ground to lay the foundation for a basement.

Truly, not much had changed about the basement since then. The two-by-four boards creaked as I gently stepped across the stair treads with nothing between them or covering them. It felt as though one wrong step and you were going to land your ass on the concrete below. I tried to balance everything in my arms and not look down.

I counted the steps as I did in childhood until my stocking feet would touch the ground. Ten . . . eleven . . . twelve . . . and immediately you could feel the wood switch to cool concrete underfoot.

Even in the middle of the afternoon, there was not much light streaming into this cold space. There was one egress window they had installed due to building code, but other than that, it was all cinderblocks and cement.

I set the vodka and folder down on the old washing machine, grabbed the sandwich from my mouth, and reached for the string hanging from a single light bulb overhead. The light did little but cast a warm shadow over the darkness. I took another bite of sandwich and looked around at the space that had been one of my few havens in this house. As a child I would sneak down when no one was looking, move the boxes around, and lay on my stomach on a blanket under the stairs. My mother and grandparents would go about their day, never thinking twice about where I was, and I would lie there daydreaming up stories and penciling them into my matching Lisa Frank notebook.

There were times when my mother would come down to switch a load of laundry, and I would peer out from under the stairs, remaining as quiet as a mouse, and watch her perform her task, then brace herself against the machine and cry. Her hands gripping the edge of the machine as if in shear agony, she would audibly weep, but only if both machines were running so no one would hear her. I wanted to crawl out and ask her why she was so sad, but fear or shame told me it was probably about me and better to let her be. This was not an unusual occurrence when I was in my "writing space," but one that I never got used to witnessing.

Another bite of the sandwich and I was heading over to the boxes to rummage for something to use as a glass for the vodka. I hadn't even begun unearthing anything and already I was unhinged.

I gave the search for a cup a solid two minutes before I just started drinking out of the bottle. There were roughly ten to fifteen cardboard boxes filled with God knows what in this dungeon, and other than that, all that was down here was the old washer and dryer and a few quiet spiders and starving mice. All that pomp and circumstance for the basement no one in town had, and all it did was serve as a large, pseudo closet, a place to store things. Essentially a metaphor for life. We all have a basement, deep in the dark hallows, surrounded by concrete, only accessible by frightening steps that most don't want to risk their lives on. But if you are lucky, there will be a few who are willing to take the risk and venture into the shadowy abyss to find out your truths.

Another swig and I was unfolding the flaps of box one. The dust flew from the folds, causing me to cough a few times before continuing, the vodka on my breath burning the inside of my nose as the coughed breaths lingered in the cold, damp air. Inside the box were tons of old newspapers, mainly the *Hadleigh Gazette*. I flipped through each of them, browsing for significance, but when I couldn't find any, I closed the flaps and set the box aside.

The next box was more of the same, as was the box after that. Why did anyone want to save all these old papers? I took a few more swigs and reached for another box. This one was marked "Grace" and hoped to be more promising that the last few.

Sitting atop the box were a few black-and-white photos of my mother as a child, photos I had never seen. She was the cutest little blond girl with those same ringlets, but tighter then, and her eyes, a piercing green you couldn't see in the black-and-white photos, but I knew all too well. Truth be told, if I didn't know it was her, I would have thought it was me. It was astounding how much we looked alike. Each picture progressed her through the years. Her in the field smiling, holding flowers. Her on the tractor grinning ear to ear. Her holding up the first fish she caught. Her on her mother's lap holding a present. She was one of those girls who stayed beautiful even through the awkward tween years. She was an anomaly, even then. That part of her I could relate to. She still looked happy in her tweens and early teens, but as the pictures faded into high school, her look started to change. Her smile seemed phony, like it was hiding something. As the pictures went from black-and-white to color, strangely the color in her face seemed to fade. She was great at putting on a front, but I could see through it. I had watched her pretend to be a lot of things—happy wasn't one until I saw these pictures. I guess I learned from the best, even though I didn't know what I was watching.

I set the pictures aside and picked up her yearbook, *Cornucopia 1984*. Hadleigh High School was ninth through twelfth grade and housed just over two hundred kids in 1984. Grace was all over the pages of this yearbook. She was the Peyton of '84. There she was on top of the cheerleader pyramid, homecoming queen, and voted most likely to succeed. What they thought she would succeed at was beyond me, but I was sure she never came close to living up to that title.

In the middle of the book were the autograph pages.

Pages upon pages of people telling my mother how great she was. How she would really become something amazing someday. How she was their high school "one that got away." I was flabbergasted. This woman they described was such a stark contrast to the one who raised me (if you could call it that). Had I been the thing that wrecked her? Was I the reason she wasn't this super successful whatever? The loop of my childhood insecurities began to play again on a repeat in my mind.

Another swig. And again.

A few boys had written of their crushes for her, but one in particular had gone further than that. Beau Boyton was the football captain and voted most likely to become rich. His chicken-scratch yearbook letter to my mother was barely legible but was filled with undying love.

My saving Grace—

You are the light of my life. I don't know where I would be without you. You make high school bearable. I love you more each day and am so thankful you decided to date a dud like me. I will love you forever, my Gracy girl.

Heart symbol,
Beau Bear

So it was no Voltaire, but it was as sweet as most teenage boys get. He was clearly smitten with her, yet I had never heard his name.

Another swig.

Was this boy my dad? Was he the strong arm in the picture?

I quickly flipped to his picture in the senior class. He was strong with lighter, almost sandy blond–looking hair in tight curls around his head. He had a megawatt smile and an all-American look. He looked like her perfect match on paper. What happened to them?

Another sip. Another stare. I thought for a moment that I recognized my eyes on him. Beau. Beau bear. A longer swig.

I blinked my eyes shut tightly to try to shake this from my mind. I flipped the page and kept looking. There they were— homecoming king and queen. Then they were smiling at prom. Then his arms were wrapped around her from behind at a pep rally, and she was smiling up at him. It was not the fake smile I saw in the home photos; this smile was genuine, real.

I kept flipping the pages as I entered into the clubs and groups section, assuming that my mother would have been too popular to be part of these. I wanted to get to the back and see if she and Beau looked as happy in the junior class picture when something caught my eye. I flipped the page back and squinted to read the caption below the photo.

"Grace Harper and Lee Knowles work hard at the *HHS Press* to get out the school paper every week."

I blinked again. Was I reading this correctly? My mother was part of the school newspaper? Why had she never told me all these years as I pursued my journalism major and began writing?

I looked through the pictures of the newspaper crew and there she was, writing, editing, helping with layout.

Another caption read, "Grace Harper's work caught the eye of the editor at the *Hadleigh Gazette*, where she will further her writing career once she graduates."

Another drink.

I had spent my life reading the *Hadleigh Gazette*, even trying to intern there in high school, and I had never seen her name on a byline, much less heard her mention being offered a job there. Did she actually write for them?

I turned around and grabbed the stack of papers and began to page through them, looking for her name. Page after page there was nothing. No hint that my mother was a writer. I was beyond confused.

Gulp.

Turning back to the box filled with photos and yearbooks, I caught a glimpse of something behind it. I slid the box over, but not enough to make it fall, and there it was. My old blanket still laying under the steps. All this time had passed and no one had moved it, which meant either no one ever came down here or they hadn't had the heart to.

I shimmied my way between the boxes and ducked under the stair treads. I lay down on the quilt, closed my eyes, innately curled up into the fetal position on my right side, and took a deep inhale of Tommy Girl perfume, which had grown faint with time and dust. My mind was reeling—my mother, a writer. A real writer. Between the vodka and these revelations, sleep seemed to be the only antiserum, and so I let my eyes flutter shut.

"Do you remember when Grace was voted most likely to succeed in our class? What a joke!"

"Yeah. I don't think she ever amounted to anything. I know she mounted a lot, but as far as amounting . . . Ha!"

"I don't know, ladies. I heard that she had a secret or two."

"Who told you that? Was she being paid for sex?"

# 14

I woke up with a jolt and banged my head on the stair treads looming overhead.

"Fuck!" This house was going to be the death of me.

I began to rub the spot where the wood met my skull and looked around to gain my bearings. Basement. Blanket. Box. Writer. My mother was a writer, but I had never seen anything that she had written. There was all this talk of her skill in her yearbook but no proof.

I peeked around the corner to check the time. Peyton would kill me if I were late to dinner. It was only four, so I had some time and a whole basement to get through. I grabbed the bottle and blanket and squeezed out from under the stairs. Setting my two prized possessions on the washer, I turned and looked at the ominous piles of boxes left. This had to get done, and according to Pey, it needed to get done today.

I went to uncap the vodka but thought wiser of it. I needed to get through this.

The next box had no label, nothing marking what I was about to uncover. The flaps were folded in that perfect one-over-the-other way that allows the box to remain shut without taping it. They opened with ease. Inside was a bunch of old pots and pans. I stood there puzzled for a moment, wondering who would want to keep these. Then I slid the box off the top of the stack, marked it with a yellow Post-it to donate, and moved on.

Most of the other boxes contained more of the same: kitchen utensils, old blankets, and childhood clothing. I marked each with that same golden paper and set it aside.

I was down to three boxes but out of time. The clock chimed six, and I knew I still needed to wash off this dried-up running sweat, brush the sleepy vodka from my breath, and make myself semi-presentable for dinner tonight. I tried to convince myself that I didn't care that James would be there, that I didn't have little butterflies in my stomach. I didn't want him to think I was just a hot mess all the time.

I left the three boxes in a pile and made a mental note to go through them first thing tomorrow. I pulled the light string, making the single bulb swing from side to side, as I climbed the darker stairs. Once back upstairs I could feel the temperature rise and turned to shut the door, immediately realizing I had left my vodka and blanket down there. *I'll get it tomorrow—more incentive to actually go back down,* I thought and headed up the main staircase to shower.

A few steps up, it dawned on me that this was the first time I was going up to the top level. The carpet running up the middle of the steps was so worn that you could barely make out the faded paisley pattern. Grandma was a huge fan of paisley. There was paisley on the stairs, on the walls in every bathroom, and on every gift she ever gave. I secretly always really liked it, still incorporating it into my current wardrobe.

The boards moaned under the carpet as I ascended the stairs. The wall was flanked with painting after painting by Terry Redlin. My favorites were always the ones where the farmhouse was covered in snow and the kids were making snowmen. I had never seen snow until I moved to Boston, and so those paintings always struck a chord with me, left me with a longing. Now, having lived through shoveling out your driveway after a blizzard and trying to get to work when flurries hit during rush hour, these paintings made me a little anxious and thankful to be in a place with no snow.

Grandma used to give Gramps one of Terry's paintings every year for his birthday, and so they were littered all over the house. He was the Norman Rockwell of Amgine Farm.

At the top of the stairs, I instinctively turned right to head towards my room and the tiny bathroom it shared, but stopped once I realized I could use the much larger master shower.

I turned and headed to the master that once housed my grandparents, and then my mother. She had taken over it once the house became hers. A day that is burned into the furrows on my memory. She was in one of her spells. She began by throwing all the smaller items out the window. My gramps's clothes, books, and toiletries. In between the throwing and drinking, she had managed to call Goodwill to come and pick up all the furniture in the room. By day's end, the room was completely empty, and when I finally mustered up the courage to crack the door open slightly, I saw her standing there with a do-rag covering her recently box-dyed blond hair and a paint roller in her hands. She was furiously rolling the fresh new paint on to the walls and crying. She didn't see me standing there, but I watched for a while. She kept up this incredible pace with the roller and tears. After what seemed like hours, she collapsed on to the floor and threw her head into her hands. I sat on the floor in the hallway, barely peeking into the room.

"Fuck all this shit!" she yelled, then lifted her head, wiped her tears with her paint-stained hand, looked over, and caught me watching her.

"Oh, Finny. I am so sorry," she mustered through her raspy voice.

"Things are going to be so different now," she stated and rose to her feet. "This is a new beginning. First this room and then in life!"

She walked towards me, pulled the door wide open, and reached for my hands. I reluctantly and semi-obediently grasped her hands and let her pull me to my feet and embrace me in a tight hug.

"It's over now. It will be better. I promise," she whispered.

I didn't react. I didn't know what to do or say. She had just vandalized everything the most important man in my life had left behind. How were things going to better now that he was gone? What was so wrong before? And why would she ruin all my memories of him? What the hell was wrong with her?

I reached for the doorknob and entered into the bright, peach-colored room. It might have been the only room in the house that she didn't smoke in because the paint still looked the same as it did all those years ago when she went on her tirade.

The four-poster bed was still made with throw pillows she had collected at garage sales she sometimes dragged me to. Next to the bed on the nightstand was a knock-off Tiffany lamp and a copy of a book . . . my book . . . *A Light in the Dark* by Finnegan Hadleigh. I stood frozen for a moment. Did she know it was me? How could she have known?

I picked up the book; the pages were well worn and dog eared. This book had been loved, and I knew a thing or two about loving a book. I opened the cover and began to page through a book I knew by heart, and just about every page was highlighted, underlined, or had notes in the margins in the tiniest of print.

There was no way to know what it all meant; the ink had blurred and blended into the paper leaving it unrecognizable. Was it good or bad? One thing was for sure—I wasn't the only one who knew this book by heart.

I absentmindedly closed the book and held it close to my chest, borderline hugging it. I wasn't sure what I was wanting from it, but it just felt right. I walked through the bathroom door and set the book on the vanity next to the sink. I looked at it once more and cracked the smallest smile. She knew it was me. I just knew she did.

I turned the shower on, and while I waited for it to heat up, I opened the medicine cabinet that hung above the sink. My mother had left behind a plethora of drugs, enough to make anyone forget any physical or emotional ailment. Towards the end I had gotten a phone call from someone I assumed was her doctor informing me that my mother had cancer, stage 4, and so they were going to do their best to make her comfortable, basically drug her into the afterlife.

I shut the cabinet and made a mental note that all those goodies were there should the situation arise (a note that would have thrilled me in my younger years) and jumped into the shower.

The steam began to rise over the white subway tile that lined the walls that had recently come back into style, as everything seems to do. I tried to clean my body and clear my mind. All these revelations had me reeling. My mom was supposedly some kind of a writer. She knew my pseudonym. What did she think of my books? Why did I care? My mind raced as I absentmindedly went through my regular shower process. I was never a fan of the bath. Something about bathing in your own filth really rubbed me the wrong way, so as long back as I can remember, I had been an enthusiast of the place where the water washed all your sins away down the drain and you didn't have to look at yourself any longer than you needed to get clean.

With a towel wrapped around me, I headed back through her bedroom, noting the picture frame on the dresser. It was a four-by-six gold frame with a photo of her and me at my college graduation. I was holding my newly acquired Frye bag and faux smiling with the best of them. My mother had her arm around me and was sincerely smiling. I bent over and looked closer at the picture. She had a kind of sadness in her smile, almost as if she was so proud but knew the moment was fleeting. It broke my heart a little to see. Two people united together by blood but forced apart by secrets and resentment. Maybe it wasn't all her. Maybe I was part of the problem in our dysfunctional relationship.

Truth can hit harder than you mean it to and definitely harder than you expect. I found myself sitting on the edge of the bed, trying to force my breath to slow while my heart began to speed. I had spent so long trying to forget everything about this place and the girl I was here that maybe I had lumped her in with all that baggage I had left on the curb, waiting for a garbage day that never arrived. I had watched her try to do it one time: pack a bag and leave. Her eyes had met mine as I sat on the floor with Grandpa playing cards, his back to her, and with suitcase in hand, she tiptoed toward the front door. She had stopped, only for a second, my eyes veering from the game up to her, Grandpa getting upset that my focus wasn't on him and this game. It was the first time I remembered him hollering at me, telling me that I needed to focus on him or he was going to get really angry.

His outburst had caught me off guard enough to focus my eyes back to him, trying to gauge what had just transpired, and by the time I had calmed him and convinced myself that he must have just been having a bad day, I looked up and she was gone. It was fair of me to assume she was gone for good, but the next morning, she was sitting at the breakfast table as if I had not witnessed her trying to escape. When I walked into the kitchen, she looked up at me, and for the first time in my entire life, I could swear I saw her smile.

The edges of the comforter were now intertwined in my fists that had balled up, remembering that day and what came after. I stood up, feeling a little dizzy, though I had not drank for hours now, and headed back down the steps to find my suitcase and some decent clothes. What does one wear when they are about to come face-to-face with a man they barely know who gives them goose bumps but doesn't really want to be there at all?

*I could still bail,* I thought as I pulled my J. Crew V neck over my wet hair. I am an adult and don't have to do everything Peyton says anymore.

*I should have shaved,* I told myself as I pulled on my favorite pair of jeans.

Where were my Converse?

*This is going to be a mess,* I thought as I slipped on my shoes and shut the door behind me.

"Did you see that Beau is here? That man looks as good as he did in high school!"

"What ever happened with him and Grace? Is he Finn's daddy?"

"I heard that she broke his heart, and he spent the next few years trying to win her back. What he saw in her is beyond me."

"Oh let's be honest. Grace was different than us, but she certainly was beautiful, and she softened and mellowed as she aged."

"I heard that Beau married a model, but they divorced after she left him for Gary Busey."

## 15

I reached for the same door handle that had given me the cold sweats a few days before as I debated whether to reenter my "glory days." I pulled the heavy, wooden door open, and immediately light poured out onto the street. The front door was the only thing about my old stomping ground that hadn't changed. Tin 'n' Grits was nothing like I remembered it. The walls were a bright, yet calming, white with beautiful, artistic crown molding that blended into the reclaimed wood ceiling. Covering the white walls in perfectly placed spots were different black-and-white photographs of old Hadleigh. I began to wonder if there was a picture of Amgine farmhouse on one of these walls.

The once dingy, grimy, and dark bar that used to be covered in peanut shells, beer stains, and tall tales was a sleek slab of concrete flanked by beautiful wood beams and topped with a stunning and perfectly aged metal countertop. Resting on top of coasters engraved with the new "TnG" cursive logo were fancy cocktails that would have offended every bone in the old townies' bodies. These cocktails would have made Carrie Bradshaw blush.

The tables were family-style, huge tables running through the middle of the room, and made from some sort of reclaimed wood and skirted by mismatched but charming chairs. Along the side walls sat the booths that were all covered in a worn honey leather that looked elegant yet homey. The floors were made of wood painted black and worn perfectly by foot traffic. Overall, the place was stunning and exactly the type of spot that was popular in the Bostons or Austins of the world. Yet here in the middle of this small town, this space was happening.

I made my way through the crowd of people, none who looked familiar, and looked for Peyton. I scanned the crowd, silently praying that I didn't see anyone I would recognize, and then glanced at my watch: 7:02 p.m. There was no way I was the first one to arrive—Peyton was too type A to be late . . . ever. It dawned on me that maybe this town was capable of change after all. If Tin 'n' Grits can have this kind of facelift and maintain a waitlist, then maybe this town was capable of change. I mean, it did have a damn goat's milk soap shop, after all. Maybe I wasn't the only one who changed.

"Finn!" I heard her yell, and it made me cringe a little realizing that I was exposed now that my name had been broadcasted.

She was in the corner booth as promised and was waving her perfectly toned arm in the air. "Over here!"

I looked over my shoulder to make sure no one was looking at me and made my way to the table.

She and Will were on one side of the booth, and across from them sat two chairs: one empty and one where James was sitting and watching me as I walked over to them. I felt my heart in my throat and tried to swallow it down as I approached the table.

Pey looked up at me. "I would get up and hug you, but . . ." she rubbed her belly as to imply her pregnant belly had wedged her into the booth with no wiggle room. Will, on the other hand, stood and reached out his right hand, hoping to go for that handshake-into-a-hug move that men often employ. It felt forced and uneasy.

"Hey, Finn. Long time. You look good," he said as he eyed me up and down.

"Thanks, Will. You too." I was able to get out before turning to James, whose eyes I could feel burning a hole through me.

He was pushing his chair back from the table and was about to stand to greet me when I began to sit down. "Oh, you don't have to get up," I began and innately reached for his arm as a comforting gesture, as though we were longtime friends.

I felt my heart climbing back up to my throat as I made a mental note of how strong and sculpted his arm felt under his button-down, cotton, thin dress shirt. Damn this boy.

He sat back down in his chair. "It is good to see you again, Finn." He smiled.

I realized my hand was still on his bicep and quickly removed it, looking sheepishly back at the table.

"Drink?" Peyton asked.

"Yes, please," I responded and began to flip through the cocktail menu.

Will and James returned to their talks about work, while Peyton leaned across the table to me and whispered, "Isn't he the cutest?" with a wink.

I could feel my face flush and figured I didn't need to answer—she already knew.

"What's good here?" I looked up and asked to the table at large.

Everyone began to throw ideas my way, but I could not

look away from James. The way he tried to hide his southern accent under his intelligent exterior. The way his penetrating blue eyes twinkled when he cracked a slight smile and let a hint of his dimples show. His jawline and cheekbones completed the package. I was sure I looked like an awestruck, silly child, but I couldn't look away.

When it became obvious to even me that no one was speaking, I shook my head ever so slightly, stirring myself out of this trance, and looked across the table to Peyton, who was beaming, proud of her set-up abilities.

In perfect, dramatic timing, the waitress appeared.

"You guys ready to order?"

After, with the menus gone and niceties out of the way, Will broke the silence. "So . . . Finn . . . Pey tells me you are an author out in Boston now?"

"A writer, huh?" James reacted. "Here I just thought you were a runner." He flashed those dimples at me and winked.

"Oh." I felt my cheeks heating up again, thinking about that touch in the woods. "No. The running is a new thing. I am still learning. Maybe you could teach me a thing or two—you seem like a natural out there," I retorted.

Maybe you could teach me a thing or two? What the hell was I saying? *Don't come off desperate,* I thought. *Geez, what a moron.*

"I am sure we could make that happen." He smiled.

I looked away before I said something even more juvenile that made me look like I was an even worse flirt than I was a runner.

"Yeah. I have been writing in Boston. I write for the *Herald,*" I responded.

"I thought Pey said you had written a few books," Will countered.

I froze, not knowing how to respond to this. I had written a few books, but only under a pseudonym, one I still wasn't sure how my mother figured out, so there was no way Peyton knew.

I decided to keep it vague and lie. "Nope. Just the paper."

"Finn . . ." Peyton said as if baiting me for more. More . . . give them more . . . be more.

I cocked my head and felt myself squirm a little in my seat. Where was my cocktail? Where was this conversation going?

When I said nothing, she continued, "*A Light in the Dark?*" She looked at me quizzically.

I felt my heart fall from its place in my throat all the way to my feet, and I tried to catch my breath. How in the hell did she know? How was I supposed to react?

Everyone at the table was looking at me now, waiting, curious. I looked down, put my elbows on the table, put my fingertips to my forehead and began to gently rub. I focused on breathing in and out and tried to figure out what in the hell my next move would be.

"You okay, Finn?" James's voice broke into my mild panic attack.

I looked up and met his eyes and felt an immediate calm. "Ya. Just surprised," I managed.

"Surprised that you wrote a book?" He looked confused.

"No. She is surprised I knew," Peyton cut in.

"I am so confused," Will interjected and looked at me.

I wanted to say something, but I couldn't get my mouth to move. I could feel the color draining from my face.

Again it was James who snapped me back. He placed his hand on my leg, and I immediately felt every synapse in my body fire.

"Finn? What is going on?" He looked at me, and I had this immediate reaction to kiss him but refrained and instead took a deep breath.

"I did write a book or two," I began as all eyes were on me. "I just didn't use my real name. I wrote under a pseudonym." I paused and swallowed.

"Finnegan Hadleigh," Peyton chimed in, smiling and again looking pleased with herself.

"Right," I said, feeling like a part of me was dying.

I finally looked up at her, and for the first time she could see that this was not a welcome surprise, and her smile faded to a grimace.

"Oh dear!" she exclaimed. "Finn, I am so sorry! I just figured you were done keeping secrets, and so I thought the cat was out of the bag."

"It's fine," I said under my breath, not really sure that it was.

"Oh, Finn, I am just so—" Pey began.

"Wait . . . you are Finnegan Hadleigh?" Will asked.

I nodded my head yes and looked down at the table, willing that damn drink to come.

"I read your books. They were good," Will remarked, sounding surprised. "Dark, but good."

"Thanks," I muttered.

"Why not write as yourself?" James finally chimed in with his hand still on my leg, the only thing keeping me from walking out at this point.

"To be honest, I am not sure there is a simple answer to that question." I made eye contact with him and quickly looked away before getting sucked back in. "I guess I just never felt comfortable enough in my own skin before to allow my full self to come through, including in my writing. This whole thing has been such a process for me, and I guess I was more secure being someone else. I have spent a lot of time since leaving here working on feeling like myself in my body, but this seems to be the final holdout."

More . . . I had given them more than I ever intended.

His hand rubbed ever so slightly up and down my leg and gave it a little squeeze.

"No shame in that," he began. "A lot of writers use fake names. Hell, most creative people in Hollywood have fake names. Whatever works, right?" He squeezed my leg again.

"I am not ashamed. I guess I just feel exposed for the first time in a while. Actually, coming back here exposed me in a way I hadn't expected, and now this." I trailed off.

"Finn, again I am so sorry," Pey pleaded for my forgiveness.

I looked her straight in the eyes. "Pey, it is fine," I reassured her, trying to convince myself. "But how did you know it was me?" I squinted faintly and waited.

"Your mother told me," she said as if I should have already known.

"My mother?" I asked. "You spoke to my mother?" I couldn't help but choke on the words.

"Yes," she began, "After you left, she was lonely, and so I would check in on her from time to time. We would talk about you. It seemed to be the one thing that made her smile."

I closed my eyes, dumfounded. My mother smiled when she thought of me? She had my book on her nightstand? Peyton and my mother were "friends"?

"She was so proud of you when that book came out. I don't think a day went by that she didn't read it," Peyton added.

"I don't know how she knew," I said.

"She said it was the name that caught her eye. Something about how it resonated with her. Then when she read it, she said she could hear you in the pages," Peyton responded.

"She could hear me in the pages?" I half-laughed. "She didn't even know me! For God's sake, I didn't even know her either!" I nearly shouted and felt James's hand tighten on my leg again.

"That damn house is full of so many secrets. . . . My mother was a writer! Did you know that?" I directed at Peyton.

But before she could answer, James chimed in, "I did."

My darting, accusatory eyes moved from Peyton to James. "What?" I managed.

"I knew your mother was a writer." He met my eyes. "We really need to talk, Finn."

Dinner was starting to feel like an ambush when the waitress finally appeared. "Sorry about the wait. The bar got slammed all of a sudden." She set the drink on top of one of those fancy coasters and looked at me again. "This one is on the house for your trouble." She smiled and left.

I picked up the drink and began to slam it, hoping it would make me forget the last twenty minutes. It was the first time since I had been in Hadleigh that I wished I could go back in time.

"Peyton once told me that Finn was a famous author now, but I never saw a book written by her. I am sure Pey just wants us to think her friend was a success."

"Poor girl. I am sure it was hard being raised in that house. It was a beautiful house, though. What do you think she will do with it?"

"I think Peyton is trying to get her to stay. I wish my daughter would learn to see people for who they really are and let Finn go."

"I know. Peyton has it all. She doesn't need someone like that hanging around and bringing her down."

# 16

The rest of dinner went fairly smoothly, especially since it was fueled by large amounts of gin and vodka. I had decided to drown my frustration and anger in booze and fake conversation. Peyton spent the rest of the evening shooting me frowny faces with puppy eyes and mouthing, "I'm sorry" over and over again. Will spent his time talking about himself (just like high school), and occasionally he would throw in an "I can't believe you are Finnegan Hadleigh" whenever the conversation lulled. I didn't know if this was a compliment or a slam. I decided to take it as the former but was sure coming from Will it was the latter. Will and I always had a tense relationship; fighting over the same girl can do that to two people. He wanted her by his side, and I wanted my friend around. For a long time, I was the winner in the brawl, but now it seemed he was, whether she liked it or not. Every time Will would mention Finnegan Hadleigh, Peyton would try her very best to change the topic, usually back to something that would interest Will and distract him from her mistake. It was obvious that she felt bad and was used to dealing with toddlers.

James, on the other hand, spent the night with his hand firmly on my thigh and shooting me comforting glances any time he could sense the tension or hear me order yet another cocktail. He did his best to engage me in light conversation, trying to figure out my story. I wondered if he would remove his hand once the mystery of me was gone. Once he knew all my secrets, would he still look at me like this?

Will had begrudgingly paid for dinner after Peyton reached for the bill from the waitress and contended that it was their treat. She looked at me and winked as she said this as if to imply that her credit card was about to make up for her mouth. While Pey insisted on paying the bill, James insisted on walking me home. I informed him through my tipsy slur that I was fully capable of walking myself home, but he persisted. So now here we were walking down old main street that wasn't old main street anymore, sauntering towards a house that was no longer my home.

The streetlamps casted a warm haze over the dark sidewalk as we strolled along, him trying to get to know me, and me trying to act sober.

"So you and Peyton were close back in the day?" he started.

"Yeah. Two peas in a pod," I responded and did the same fist-pump motion I had done on the plane. What the hell had gotten into me?

He smiled. "And you lost touch?"

"I suppose. I mean there was Facebook, but when I left here, I left everything and everyone behind. I really only spoke to my mother sparingly, just to maintain my offspring duties. In order to really be me, I needed to leave all this behind. This place was toxic," I spewed and looked over at him to see if I had overshared.

"Toxic?" He looked at my quizzically.

Jesus. Why did this guy care? Why didn't we just go home and screw so he could stop with the questions?

I started to blush at the thought of us coiled up in bed together. But what bed would we use? My mother's? My childhood bed? The guest bed? All felt strange and made my face twist up a little at the thought.

"Forget I asked," he said.

He was staring straight at me, my grimaced face obviously projecting an uncomfortable quality that was not directed at him in any way, but he clearly thought it was. And while this town and my life did make me a little queasy, I was different now, and the new me was trying to be more open to sharing with others. I was going to answer his questions, even if it made me want to throw up.

"Honestly . . . I don't really ever talk about it, but I didn't have the greatest life here. My grandma died when I was ten. My mother was moody, distant, uninvolved, and probably some form of bipolar. I was always struggling, never fitting in, never feeling like myself. My gramps and high school boyfriend, Nick, died my sophomore year of high school. And I spent the last couple years trying to drink my way out of feeling anything until I could get the hell out of here. But now I am back, so that's super fun!" I finished sarcastically. I took a deep breath before I looked over at him; there it was . . . verbal diarrhea directed straight at him. Most of the shit I went through before I left here. Not all. Everyone has a chapter they don't read out loud.

I couldn't tell if the look on his face was one of shock or sympathy. I didn't want his sympathy, so I guess I was settling with shock.

He reached over and in one quick motion grabbed my hand and squeezed it tightly. I felt my breath catch in my chest and had to remind myself again to "Act cool. Act sober."

"Finn, I had no idea," he started. "Your mother spoke of you as though you were her prized possession. She would come into the office and read me your stories in the *Herald* or leave me emails with quotes from your book in them. She would tell me over and over again how she couldn't believe that such a talented writer had come from her gene pool. She had always fancied herself more of a small-time pencil pusher, but you—you were an author, and she never missed a chance to tell me that."

I looked at him, still keenly aware that he was firmly holding my hand. But I hadn't realized that we had stopped walking and I was standing with my whole body facing him, the body that never felt fully like me. I was hanging on his every word, partially because I always wanted to hang on his every word, but also because what he was saying was blowing me away.

"I assumed by the way she spoke of you that you two were close until she told me otherwise when she brought in the box," he continued.

I stood there, frozen; so many questions swirled. How did this guy know more about my mom than I did, and what did she tell him about me?

"So . . ." I cut him off, trying to break the tension and prevent him from asking me more. "How much do you know about the old me and this place? What did my mother and Pey tell you?"

"Honestly, not much. I knew you went to high school with Will and Pey and that you and she used to be close. And as far as your mother goes . . . all she ever told me was that you lived in Boston and were a writer, an incredible one, according to her. She never did mention the pseudonym thing though, which is interesting considering she told Peyton," he said.

"Oh, and she mentioned that she hoped you would end up with a nice guy like me one day." He smiled and squeezed my hand again.

I blushed but hoped he couldn't see under the streetlights. I tried to hold back my smile as I turned and began walking again. Holding hands is not something the old me would have ever done with a guy down main street. The new me kind of liked it but was worried about being seen. People in this town could talk, and while they may have given it a facelift, I knew deep down people were itching to catch a glimpse of me roaming these streets again. Oh and wouldn't they love it if it were with a man. . . . "Just like in the old days," they would all say.

I kept my head down as we ventured off main street and onto the dirt roads that would lead to Amgine farmhouse.

"A small-time pencil pusher, what did she mean by that?" I asked him.

"Well, I am not 100 percent sure, but I do know that your mother had a part in the *Hadleigh Gazette*," he answered.

"No. I found a few boxes full of the *Gazette*, and after discovering in her yearbook that she was a writer, I scoured through them looking for her name anywhere but came up empty handed."

"Well, I am not sure what to make of that," he started. "She has been getting checks from them as long as I have been working with her. I never asked for more information, though. Sorry," he said with a slight, woeful look in his eyes.. "Maybe she wrote under a fake name," he said with a little smirk, as if he was kidding.

"Maybe," I said, feeling the possibility. "And this box?"

"Yeah. If you would have called, we could have discussed it." He squeezed my hand.

I looked away, preparing to come up with an excuse.

"Come to the office tomorrow and I will give it to you. Your mother says it will explain everything."

"Everything?" I said aloud, wondering what the hell that meant.

We walked quietly the rest of the way to the front porch of Amgine Farm. He walked me up the steps with his hand still encompassing mine and stopped in front of the door as I reached to open it.

He stood firm, not willing to follow my lead into the house. I was taken aback for a moment that he wasn't following me in. I had performed this dance so many times before, and no one had ever stopped on the stoop, refusing to go in.

I realized this might make me seem like a slut, assuming that we were just going to go inside and go for it. I am not sure if it was the fact that this was my old MO with men on this porch or the fact that I really wanted him that led me to just reach for the handle without even thinking.

I turned to face him, reminding myself once again that I was not that girl anymore, and was about to explain to him that I don't know what I was thinking when he reached his hand up to my face, right where my jawbone met my ear, and pulled me close to him and kissed me.

His lips felt smooth and yet manly. He tilted my head slightly with his hand and pulled me even closer and slipped his tongue in my mouth. I hadn't been kissed like this since high school. The kind of kiss that makes you want someone so badly you can barely contain yourself.

We stayed like this for a few minutes on the porch, our lips locked and tongues navigating. I could feel my body start to quiver with anticipation, hoping he would head farther south with his free hand. I reached around and placed my hand on his lower back, angled perfectly so it was also touching the top of that ass that I had been coveting for days.

I took in deep breaths of his cologne that was distinctly

unique with a rugged authenticity and enduring appeal. He smelled exactly like I had imagined when I wasn't supposed to be thinking about him. He let go of my hand and brought it up the other side of my face and managed to pull me even closer. I reached around and pulled his body closer to mine. I could feel him growing harder against his jeans that were now pressing against my hip. I wanted him and I wanted him now. I tried to pull him back towards to door, releasing one hand from his lower back to frantically try to open the door but then he stopped, pulled his face back from mine and looked at me.

It took a second to catch my breath as we stood there, inches apart, eyes locked, my hand resting on the door handle.

"Finn," he began, "I want nothing more than to follow you into that house, but I can't. Not now. Not like this."

"Not like this?" I countered.

"I just . . . this is all so new to me, and I don't want to start it off while you have drank your weight in vodka." He smiled and flashed those damn dimples.

He reached out and took my hand and pulled me back to him. "I want this, I do. Just not here. Not now. Okay?"

I couldn't put my finger on what feeling was more overcoming in this moment: embarrassment or lust. Here I was being all kinds of sexually aggressive, and he wanted to press pause. I understood where he was coming from, but every bone in my body wanted him right this minute.

He lifted my chin with his fingertips; at six three, he was one of the men who actually towered over me.

"You and me, this is going to happen," was all he said, and then he kissed me on the cheek. "Call me tomorrow. We can grab coffee and chat about your mother."

He turned and walked down the steps and into the darkness, looking back once and flashing me a crafty grin that was visible only by the moonlight. I leaned back on the door and gently banged my head against it. What was I thinking? I can't get wrapped up with someone in this town. I can't have to worry about leaving someone behind when I disappear. Maybe it was better that he didn't come in and things didn't get complicated. Maybe he was smart to stop it now. I have never been one to make things easy, and this was no different. He had no idea what he was getting into. I should stop this now. . . . If only he didn't have those dimples and that ass.

Once back inside, the house hit me like the cold shower I needed. Nothing in here screamed sex, or even fun for that matter. My eyes fixated up on the patched ceiling hole that my gramps told me was the product of a bad night and some bad decisions only adults would understand. Now, being an adult myself, I couldn't help but wonder what the true story was behind the mismatched color patch lying among the popcorn ceiling. I was exhausted from an evening of interrogation and revelations. I was beginning to wonder if everything I ever knew and everything I ever was was a lie. I wrote under a lie, my mother was full of lies, and I lied about myself for years.

I didn't know where I should sleep, so after weighing my options, I remembered that I had left my booze and blanket in the basement and decided to venture down there to retrieve them. Both would help me sleep.

The basement had dropped a few degrees while I was out, but my two favorite items sat untouched. I was about to grab them off the washer and head back up, but I saw the boxes full of newspapers, and it got my mind pondering again. James had mentioned that maybe my mother had written under a pseudonym like I had. I scrunched my nose up a little at the thought. Why on earth didn't she didn't use her name if she was writing? It certainly didn't seem like she had much to hide in her life; she seemed to put all her shit out in the open. A fake name didn't seem like her, not that I really knew her.

I flipped open the top of the box and grabbed a *Gazette* from 1986. I carefully paged through, analyzing each byline and trying to see if anything jogged my memory or seemed feasible.

The front page had pictures from senior night at the high-school football game. Eighteen-year-old boys/men standing next to their parents, trying to not look embarrassed, while the parents tried to not look like they were placing all their hopes and dreams on an NFL career. Beside the pictures were notes about the chamber meeting and the community blood drive information. The next page had a large article by Bob Darlin about whether chickens should be allowed in the city limits. The subsequent page was obituaries, engagements, and birthdays, followed by public notices and letters to the editor.

The page following had all the information on the Hadleigh High Hawks sports teams, the police log, and school lunch menu. I couldn't help but smile, thinking about the random and seemingly ironic grouping of these articles. Layout was not the *Gazette's* specialty. The last few pages were opinion pieces and classifieds. The back page had the weekly poem, a cartoon called *The Gullible Goat,* which I loved as a child, and a weekly piece called "Yes & Know from So and So" by Hadley Finnegan.

I traced over the name with the fingers of my right hand, my left hand flung up to cover my mouth as I gasped. How had I missed it before? Hadley Finnegan. Peyton had said it was something in the author's name on my book that caught my mother's eye, something that seemed familiar to her. Here it was, staring me in the face. Hadley Finnegan was my mother, and my mother really was a writer.

I tossed the newspaper hastily back into the box, flopped the top back over the box, and picked the whole thing up under my arm. I grabbed the blanket and threw it over my shoulder, liquor in my hand, and headed back up the stairs. I needed to get some sleep, but I also needed to know exactly who Hadley Finnegan was.

I plopped the box on the coffee table and placed the bottle next to it. I grabbed a single glass from the kitchen sink where Peyton had done my few dishes like a good little wife does and sank back down onto the davenport. I threw the blanket over my legs to fight the chill that had cut the air, poured myself a large drink, and leaned back, ready to spend the evening with Hadley Finnegan, not exactly who I had planned to sleep with when the evening began.

"I heard that a few people in town have actually seen Finn out, and with that super cute lawyer over at Samson & Brown . . . you know . . . Will Samson's partner?"

"What would he want with Finn? I heard that he was gay."

"I don't know, but the people who saw them said they seemed pretty cozy."

# 17

The sun was rising over the horizon as I still sat surrounded by multiple newspaper pages, an empty bottle, and a worn blanket. I had no concept of time or the fact that I had yet to close my eyes when in the distance, as if in another world completely, I heard Prince begin to sing "I Would Die 4 U." The lack of sleep and overflow of booze created a state where it took longer than it should have for me to realize that my cell phone was ringing again.

I tried to rub the sleep from my eyes as I wrapped the blanket over my shoulders and headed into the entryway, where I had left my phone on the bench the night before after my make-out session on the porch. The caller ID was blinking "Letty," and behind it flashed a picture of Letty yelling with her tongue hanging out one side of her mouth and arms up in the air. She was obviously really excited in the picture or really drunk. Either way, it encompassed her perfectly and made me smile as I slid the box.

"Hello," I said, much groggier than I expected.

"Hey, babe," she came back. "Did I wake you?"

I tried to clear my throat a little. "No actually. To be honest, I never went to bed last night."

"Ohhh! Who's the guy? How was it? It's about time you got back on the horse!" she exclaimed.

"No guy, although I did make out a little with that lawyer I mentioned earlier, but he left me high and dry on the front porch. He was being a gentleman, and yet it made me feel like a slut." I frowned a little, thinking about how badly I wanted that make out to continue into the night.

"Make out? Who makes out anymore?" she asked before taking a sip of coffee

"But I guess it is better than the nothing that you have been getting lately."

The sound of her slurping made me need coffee ASAP, and so I headed into the kitchen to start a pot.

"So," she continued, "if it wasn't a man who kept you up all night, then what the hell were you doing, babe?"

"Honestly, the whole story is a little long and twisted and best told after I get some coffee in my veins," I responded.

"Okay, babe, FaceTime me after you IV a cup in," she said.

"Deal."

I hung up, grabbed a mug, and filled it to the brim. I promised myself I would read a little more, sneak in a nap, and then call James. Not only did I secretly long to see him, but I had spent the evening discovering more about my mother than I had ever known in the last God knows how many years, and I wanted to know more. What had she left for me in that box? What other secrets lie hidden?

The coffee splashed a little on the table as I set it down and repositioned myself on the couch to read more. My mother's column had seemingly ran my entire lifetime. I didn't have everything she had ever written, far from it, but from what I could gather, she started right after high school, just as the yearbook had mentioned, and kept going well into the 2000s, stopping abruptly a few months before her death. I had gone downstairs a few times throughout the night to grab another box and keep reading. She was witty and funny, two things I don't ever remember seeing in her. She was also smart and insightful. She seemed to see things differently than others in town, almost as if she could see through people and situations and find the honesty there.

She wrote about local happenings in a deep way. She wrote about moments that struck her in society, or about the world according to Grace (or Hadley I guess). I couldn't help but wonder what it was about her that made the editor trust such a young girl with this kind of freedom in her writing, but whatever it was, they were onto something. She was fresh, insightful, and provocative. I loved the person who wrote these words, so why did I have such a hard time loving her? Why didn't she ever show this person to me? I guess we all have our secrets. I sure as shit did for a long time.

I went on reading until my eyes forced themselves shut despite my best efforts to the contrary. I nestled up on the davenport, covered in a blanket of newspaper over my basement blanket, and an old corn feed bag pillow under my head that would have made Joanna Gaines jealous. I drifted off to sleep, trying to fight the whirling of questions in my head.

· · · · · · · · · · · ·

"I am not a woman. I am not a man. I am something that you'll never understand . . ." began again from the kitchen counter. I sat up and shook the newspapers to the floor as I walked across the creaky floor to retrieve my damn phone again.

I slid the bar across again without even looking at the screen and suddenly Letty's face was staring back at me.

"Okay, you must have had enough coffee by now. It's been three hours, babe!" she began. "Oh my, you look like hell."

"Jeez, Letty, thanks for the vote of confidence," I retorted.

"No, babe, I just mean . . . are you getting enough sleep?" she responded.

"I came here to bury my mother, not get another one," I barked, only half joking.

"Okay, okay. Give me the grand tour. Flip the camera."

I did as was requested, disappearing my apparently rough-looking expression off the screen and showing her Amgine Farm.

"This is the living room. Dining Room." I turned around. "And the kitchen."

"Wow! I feel like I'm in *The Notebook* house!" she exclaimed.

"I guess it does kind of feel like that."

"Anyways, here is the entry, and the guest room where my mother used to stay before my grandparents died." I walked her through the main level and out onto the back porch. "And here is the porch—"

"Where you lost your V card!" she chimed in between chomps of frosted flakes she was spooning in and crunching along.

I laughed. "Yep. Every kid's dream first sexual encounter."

I walked back into the house and up the stairs to finish the tour. "This is my mother's room and bathroom." I walked down the hallway, and for the first time in twelve years, I opened the door to my childhood bedroom.

"And this is my old room," I said and paused.

The room was exactly how I had left it. It felt slightly eerie that not a thing had seemingly been touched or moved, almost like a shrine to a dead child. Maybe that was how my mother thought of me . . . dead.

The walls were a light blue and lined with posters of Prince, George Michael, and Madonna. I was born in the mid-eighties but stay enamored with the music for decades after. The bed rested against a wall in the middle of the room. A simple twin mattress atop a modest metal frame, adorned with a black-and-white paisley comforter (which my grandmother must have picked out) and two matching pillows. There were no throw pillows to top off the look. I had always thrown them on the floor, so eventually I just stuffed them in the closet, and I am sure that is where they remained.

There was a nightstand next to the bed. A simple, cheap, white wood one with a drawer where I hid my cigarettes and condoms (not that anyone looked or cared), a lamp, and a picture of my gramps and me on top. The window above the bed overlooked the backyard and our acres of corn and hay. I remember sitting crisscross applesauce in my bed, eating Twizzlers and watching my gramps bale the hay with his huge John Deere.

Across from the bed was a dresser that used to house all my childhood clothing, and the occasional joint rolled up in the back of my sock drawer. On top of it sat my old computer, an original Macintosh classic that I had begged my mother for years for. She finally caved one birthday, and I came home to find this gem of a machine on my dresser, complete with Crystal Quest and AppleWorks. Some of my earliest stories were written on that beauty. I felt a little nostalgia looking at that beast now. At this computer I was the future Ann Martin or R. L. Stine; thinking now of my high aspirations back in the day made me smile.

I flipped the camera back to me as I took a seat on the paisley comforter.

"Well, there you have it. Amgine Farm," I said.

"It is so charming and retro. I just *love* it! I know you don't want me to, but I do!" Letty said.

"No. It's fine to like it. I like parts of it too. It's a love/hate thing, you know?" I asked.

"Totally, babe! So back to what kept you up all night. You were going to dish!"

"Right . . ." I said and went on to tell her all about what I had discovered about my mother in the basement boxes. I tried to fill in every detail I knew to convey just how much I didn't know about a woman I spent my entire childhood with. I thought about telling her about the pseudonym reveal at dinner but decided that my secret needed to stay in Hadleigh for now. If I had learned anything in my short time back here, it was that this town was full of secrets, so I was sure one more wouldn't hurt.

"Finny! What the hell is happening at that house? You poor thing! What are you thinking? How are you dealing? Are you drinking?"

"I am fine, Letty. Just confused. I think I am finally going to go talk with James today. Apparently there is a box that my mother left behind for me that will explain everything . . . whatever that means."

"Oh, James! Try to keep it in your pants." She giggled.

"Are you ever not thinking about sex?" I asked her.

"Not really. Life is too short to not have fun," she started. "When was the last time you got your head out of a book or eyes off the computer long enough to have fun, Finny?"

"I will work on it once I get the hell out of here," I retorted.

"Or you could have a little fun while you are there. Re-christen your old room as the new you," she said.

"I'll think about it." I smiled, thinking about last night on the front porch and feeling James pressed against my hip.

"Do you want me to fly out and help you?" she asked. "You know I totally can. I can be your drink bitch while you vent and reveal secrets. We could be a modern day Watson and Holmes. You would be Holmes, obviously, and I could be a drunker version of Watson." She giggled again.

"Elementary, my dear Watson," I responded.

She laughed. "No seriously though . . . do you need me, babe?"

"Letty, you are the best. I will be fine. Pey is helping me get through the material things, and the rest I need to process on my own. Thank you though, truly."

"Okay, well I am just a call away. I'd be on the next plane. Okay?"

"I know."

"When is the service, by the way?"

"Sunday. In a church no less," I said.

"You going to speak?"

"I think so. If I don't, who will?"

"You have any idea what you will say?"

"Honestly, I had planned on keeping it simple and vague, but now I don't know. I feel like I am seeing her differently. I don't know if it is the revelation in the writing or the way people look at others through rose-colored glasses once they are dead, but I feel like I have so much to say to her now. But maybe the funeral isn't the time or place. I don't know. This town has me all twisted."

"Well, you only have a few days to figure it out, babe."

"Yeah, I know. It's daunting."

"Well, do what you do best . . . sit down and write. Words seem to flow like honey when you put pen to paper," Letty suggested.

The idea was brilliant and had somehow escaped me thus far. Between the revelations and the sorting, I had forgotten about my own secret power . . . writing. I didn't want to give Letty a bigger head than she already had, so I made a mental note and played it off.

"That's a thought. Anyways . . . I should probably get my act together and call James."

"Ohhhh Jammmmessss," she singsonged.

"Right . . . I forgot we were twelve," I snapped.

"Call me later, babe. After you go through your mom's box." She laughed

"It never ends with you," I replied. "Bye, Letty."

"Bye, babe."

"That Finn girl used to get around like her mother. I would be surprised if there was a man in town that one or the other didn't sleep with. Such a sad existence."

"I don't know. I think a lot of those stories were fabricated. I thought I used to see Grace coming and going out of the *Hadleigh Gazette* a few times. I am sure she wasn't sleeping with people there. Maybe there was more to her than we knew."

"You are always a half-full gal. I am more of a realist, and I am really sure she was probably screwing the editor. What was his name again? Paul something?"

# 18

Boxes in the elusive basement of town lore had sparked my intrigue enough to finally call James and find out more about this mother of mine who apparently I never really knew. I was nearly there, but first I needed to get out for a bit. Out of this house, out of my mind, and out of my old bed.

Ruffling through my suitcase, I found a clean pair of socks. I threw on my old, and still unwashed, running clothes from the other day, making a mental note to use that old washer in the basement after this run. I threw on the slightly stiff clothes and ironically clean socks. Somehow I had made amends with my needing the socks to be clean but ignored that the rest was dirty. I was used to feeling like I was covered in filth.

I laced up the bright running shoes and searched through my Frye bag for a pair of headphones that I could plug into my phone so I could listen to one of my Prince playlists while I ran. I may not have all the right gear, but I was heading in that direction as I pushed in one ear bud after another and clicked to "The Hits." And as "When Doves Cry" started to play, I bounded off the front porch and headed out on what was starting to feel like a familiar route, yet an unfamiliar feeling. I had crossed over from virgin to slightly seasoned . . . not quite a veteran by any means, but here in Hadleigh I had lost my "V" card again, and I was beginning to actually like what came next this time around.

The breeze blew my hair back off my face as I ran through the dirt roads, downtown, and eventually heading onto Perchman's, and for the first time since I had gotten here, I didn't care who saw me. I didn't duck my head while I ran down Main Street; I didn't look over my shoulder as I ran towards the path. I just ran. I listened to Prince sing about his "Little Red Corvette," and I aimlessly ran. I didn't think about my mother or her writing. I didn't think about my funeral speech or my cover being blown. I didn't think about Nick or James. I didn't think at all, and it was glorious.

It wasn't until I was through the path that I realized I didn't see James on this run. This was the first time we hadn't grazed by one another. I felt a pang in my chest, an instant of sadness that I didn't get to see him in his glistening glory. There would be no step-quickening end to this run, just the mind-numbing monotony that I was loving and a little "Kiss."

It seemed like I got back to the front porch and the shoe removal faster than before, but I was sure it was just blind optimism mixed with a runner's high. Once inside, I stripped by the basement door as a reminder to actually go downstairs and wash my running clothes. I turned to head up the stairs to shower and stood for a moment, naked, and smiled, realizing I actually had "running clothes" that needed washing. I was definitely not that girl anymore.

The shower was refreshing and gave me the final oomph I needed to call James.

The phone rang twice before his wonderfully deep voice answered. "James Brown," he said.

It always baffled me when people answered their phone by just stating their name. It usually seemed rude, self-centered, and off-putting, but in this case, it suddenly seemed sexy and powerful.

"Hi, James. It's Finn Harper."

"Finn. I was beginning to wonder if I was actually going to hear from you."

I could hear him smile through the phone.

"Yeah. Busy day," I lied.

"I am sure you have a lot on your plate," he politely responded as though we were simply acquaintances and not two people who spent time making out on my front porch the night before.

"Yeah" was all I could get out while telling myself to say more . . . be more . . . give more.

"So . . . you want to stop in and we can chat?" he said before I could give more.

"Sure. When works?"

"How about five today? Then maybe you will let me buy you dinner after?"

His tone quickly switched from acquaintance to someone I might hopefully have sex with later that night. Put those old condoms in the drawer to use. Do condoms expire?

"Sure. I will see you then," I said.

"I am looking forward to it," he finished.

Then it was over. A mere three minutes, and I had plans to hear my dead mother out and then get laid, almost like a poetic tribute to the woman who had shown me everything I needed to know about being a floozy. Or maybe it was just dinner. Either way, I figured I better go back upstairs and shave. Better to not be caught off guard this time.

"I sometimes feel like I may have been the only person to have known the real Grace. I am really glad to know that she shared her final days with you who cared about her as much as I did. It is nice to finally put a face to a name, Beau."

"You too, Paul. I know she truly loved working with you."

"Well, Beau, I was a friend and a fan. She was an incredible writer with a tough life, although we never really talked about personal lives. It was just a feeling I got from her. Things didn't come easy for her. I am glad to know she found her happy ending in you."

# 19

The law offices of Samson & Brown were the perfect mix of small-town charm and pomp and circumstance. The leather chairs that sat in the waiting room looked expensive but worn, and the chair rail that separated the white beadboard from the warm, gray walls helped soften the masculine furniture and trim.

I sat there aimlessly flipping through the latest copy of *Better Homes & Gardens*, trying to feign a person who wasn't freaking out about coming face-to-face with their crush again, when a young woman dressed in a floral pencil skirt and button-down top with her hair pulled back into the perfect blond bun peered into the waiting room over her large, dark, wooden desk.

"Um . . . Finn Harper," she called.

I raised my hand and set the magazine back on the coffee table, realizing that I was the only one left in the waiting room and immediately feeling dumb for having raised my hand as if she didn't know it was me.

"You can go in. James is ready for you," she murmured.

"Thank you," I said and walked down the brick floor hallway to his office at the end.

He sat behind a similar dark wooden desk, but his appeared bigger and more expensive. He was typing on his desktop and had the sweetest wrinkle between his eyebrows as he focused under his glasses. This was the first time I had seen him wear glasses, and it did nothing but fan the flames I could feel heating up my cheeks as I watched him for a moment outside his door. He looked so sharp, so commanding.

I gently tapped the back of my knuckles on the door and slowly pushed it open.

His brow went from focused and furrowed to pleased and delighted the instant he laid eyes on me.

"Finn!" he said, sounding happier than I am sure he wanted to let on.

"Hi. Am I interrupting? Your receptionist said I—"

"No. No. I was just trying to fire off some emails before we head out."

We. He said "we." We as in he and I. He and I were a "we." I tried to hide my smile.

"So, should we just cut straight to the chase and rip off the Band-Aid?" I asked.

He looked at me a little confused. "My mother. The box. Her wishes," I said, trying to help.

"Right. Sorry. Straight to the point. I like it," he stammered.

He reached into his desk and pulled out a simple shoebox-type box, one of the ones you buy at Hobby Lobby to store photos in. The outside of the box was a simple white with gray paisley, paying homage to my grandma, I thought, but I wasn't sure why my mother felt the need to do that.

On top of the box was an envelope with "Finn" written in perfect cursive, the kind you were supposed to learn back in fourth grade, the year my life began to fall apart.

He slid the box across the table to me, patted it as if reiterating that this was indeed "the box" we had discussed.

Then he looked up at me. "I am supposed to tell you the funeral is planned all to your mother's wishes, and that everything else you need is in the box. You may not like it, but you need to know all of it. The house is yours, willed to you by your mother, along with all her assets, and this box."

"Her assets?" I looked at him, confused. "My mother had assets?"

He looked over to his computer, clicked around a little, and, still staring at the screen, said, "Yeah, it looks like your mother had a little over a half a million in savings and is a part owner in the *Hadleigh Gazette*. Actually it looks like she is 51 percent owner, so majority owner of the newspaper."

"What the fuck?" I exclaimed. "Is this some kind of joke?"

James looked up from his computer, a little taken aback.

"No. No joke," he stated.

"I am sorry. I just don't understand what is going on. My mother is a secret half millionaire and owns a fucking newspaper? I feel like I am being punked.

"I mean, if you knew my mother, this would confuse the hell out of you too. I just don't get it. Who the hell was this woman?" I took a deep breath and placed my hand on the chair in front of James's desk, realizing I was now standing in the midst of my fit.

"I did know your mother," James muttered. "I saw her fairly frequently in the last two or so years of her life."

His eyes met mine, and in that moment, I realized that maybe I was the one who was hiding in all of this. Maybe I was the dick who didn't bother to get to know their own mother.

I stood silent, feeling slightly ashamed, but mostly angry, afraid of what I would say next.

He placed his hand on the box and lightly patted it again. "I hope this brings some explanation," he said and slid it closer to me.

I sheepishly sat back down in the chair and reached for the box, sliding it off the desk and onto my lap. I sat there with my hands resting on top, my gaze fixed on my name written so impeccably on top.

"Finn . . ." he broke into my trance. "Are you okay?"

"Yeah. I'll be fine. It is just a lot."

"We still on for dinner?"

"Yes. Of course. Sorry. Let's go." I began to rise.

"Before we head out, let's quickly sign all this paperwork and officially get you the keys to Amgine."

"Right."

I wondered for a brief second while uncapping the pen why I needed keys to a house that was supposed to be eternally unlocked. Wasn't that part of this town's motto?

I signed my name way less neatly than it was written on the box and received the keys to a house that I wasn't even sure I wanted and the account number and passwords to my mother's savings. Just like that I became a homeowner and person with money in the bank- both firsts for me.

We hopped into James's sleek black Lincoln MKX, and it dawned on me that this was the first time in my life that I could afford a luxury vehicle if I wanted—I wasn't sure I did, but the option felt strange. Kind of like the realization when you turn twenty-one and can drink legally. Somehow the intrigue fades slightly just in knowing that it is no longer out of reach, no longer a rebellious act. I slid in the passenger seat with my box still on my lap, holding it tight like a child with their blankie. We drove outside of Hadleigh and into the neighboring town of Wiley Bluffs. I had a slight moment of panic when I realized that I had no idea where I was going and no one knew where I was. What if he actually had been stalking me on my runs to kill me and take the money? Oddly, now the money part of the equation was real, and he was the only one who knew it was coming. I couldn't help but peer over at him and wonder.

James was staring straight ahead and singing under his breath to the Johnnyswim album playing through the speakers. He glanced over at me and caught me staring. He smiled, flashed his dimples, and said, "Almost there."

I smiled in return and reassured myself that this man wasn't a serial killer; he was a lawyer in Hadleigh, for God's sake. Any person who works there has to be too antiquated to be a killer . . . Right?!

He turned down a dirt road and the car gently bumped along until we reached a dead end. In front of us was a hay field, the stalks gently blowing in the sunset breeze. Just beyond the hay was a clearing with bright, lush grass and a huge willow tree that loomed over a small pond. You could not have painted a more beautiful setting if you tried.

James hopped out of the car, popped the trunk, and pulled out a picnic basket and old flannel blanket. He peered back into the car, arms full, and called, "You coming or what?" Then he smiled and walked towards the tree.

I unbuckled my seatbelt and opened the car door. I panicked for a moment, thinking about leaving my box in the car unattended, but reluctantly set it down and shut the door behind me. The hay swayed gracefully around my legs as I walked towards the pond. James was smoothing out the edges of the blanket as I approached.

I was watching him. What an amazing man he was, all this time and thought for someone he barely knew and I wasn't sure he would like once he actually did. He sat down on the blanket with the basket and patted the area next to him, motioning me to join him. The warm sunset created the perfect glow behind him, in turn forcing my stare to not break from his glow as I sat. He reached into the basket and pulled out two beers. I was a little surprised. Nothing quite screamed "romantic picnic" like two beers, I thought, but it was a perfectly odd pairing, kind of like us, and so decidedly brilliant.

"I realize these are not the fanciest of beverages," he began as though reading my mind, "but I do just love a good beer, ya know?" He smiled.

"It's perfect!" I said.

He pulled out two turkey sandwiches, some chips, and fruit—almost like we were at a picnic meant for children—and it made me smile at the clumsy effort. He clearly did not do this on the regular and either didn't know what romantic food was or was all about comfort and ease. Either way, it was exactly what I wanted but didn't know I needed.

We sat on the blanket, munching on our sandwiches and chips, washing it all down with sips of lukewarm beer and watching the sun fully set. We talked and covered surface subjects: favorite movie, sports teams, type of food. We talked current events and Peyton and Will until the moon had replaced the sun.

"Tell me a secret, Finn Harper," he said out of nowhere.

I took a swig of beer and looked up at the stars, contemplating which secret to tell, or whether to make one up completely. I could feel him waiting, looking at me. I took one more gulp and braced myself for blowback.

"I am not who you think I am," I finally said.

He looked at me for a moment, tipped his head slightly to the side, and said, "What does that mean exactly?"

"The Finn Harper you know is not the Finn I have always been" was all I could get out. I didn't feel the need to divulge it all in one evening. My secrets were mine, and I would tell them when I was ready. No amount of beer on a blanket under the stars would force my hand.

He smiled. "Whoever you are, and whoever you were, doesn't matter. I like you, Finn."

"You like the part of me you barely know," I countered.

"I am trying to change that," he said. "I want to know you, all of you."

"It's not that simple," I started. "I won't be here that long, and I don't want to lead you on. I like you, too, but I am not sure this can go anywhere"

"Oh, Finn. People have conquered worse things than distance, and who knows . . . maybe I can get you to stay in Hadleigh." He winked.

"Maybe . . ." I said, allowing the slightest shred of hope to float in the air between us.

"If it helps ease your mind," he started and looked at me sheepishly, "Will told me about you in high school. Told me about who you used to be."

There it was. The bombshell I had been trying to hide, the person I used to be rearing her ugly and slutty head. I wasn't sure if I was relieved or embarrassed.

He moved closer to me on the blanket and reached for my hand.

"Finn, we all have a past. We all were different people at one time or another. People change. Things change, but who you are deep down has always been there. I don't care about the rest of it. I am not a simple-minded guy. I know that transitions can be incredibly tough, and I respect the hell out of you for getting out of here and becoming who you are now. I want you, as you are now." He squeezed my hand.

I felt the lump in my throat start to drop as a tear began to form in the corner of my eye. Here was a man who knew my whole story and wanted me in spite of it. It had been so long since I thought someone could know all of me and still want me. I tried to look away, hoping the darkness would hide the tear, but he reached out and turned my cheek towards him and kissed me, softly at first as if to reassure me, and then more passionately to turn me on.

We spent the next hour with our bodies intertwined, but when it came time to actually seal the deal (so to speak), I was the one who stopped this time. I am not sure what it was exactly that made me pause, but he seemed fine with the decision. He would be the first guy I had been with since I left Hadleigh and the old me behind. As much as I wanted him, the fear of going down this road again and knowing how I used to feel after, forced me to take an exciting experience and make it about something it wasn't; doubt.

Once we had regained our composure and clothing articles, we lay there on the blanket, my head in the crook of his shoulder, just watching the stars. We didn't need to talk; most things had already been said. Slowly, almost naturally, I closed my eyes and fell asleep cuddled next to a man who I could see something with for the first time in a long time.

• • • • • • • • • • • •

He lightly shook me awake and kissed my forehead. The dawn was about to break, and we were still on the blanket nestled into each other like two lovestruck teens. I looked up at him from my spot on his shoulder and smiled. He kissed my forehead again and gently began to sit up.

I am not really the outdoorsy type . . . I love not camping, but it must have been the mixture of beer, making out, and lust that had thrown my better judgment to the wind and allowed me to relax enough to fall asleep next to him out in the wild. He looked even hotter with the sun barely illuminating his five o'clock shadow and his hair all ruffled and adorable. I was certain that I did not look as perfect, nor did my breath do me any favors. I reached into my pocket, searching for a stick of gum, a mint, anything, but was left empty handed, until he stood up and reached for my hand.

He pulled me up close to him and kissed me again. I felt every muscle in my body quiver. Why the hell didn't I sleep with him last night? It was more romantic and perfect than any Hallmark movie I had ever watched, and yet I withdrew. The truth was that I hadn't had sex since I left Hadleigh. I left in search of the me I felt was always suppressed back home, and while focusing on that, I had neglected my sexual desires. So, though I knew all the moves by heart from my days back at the Tin 'n' Grits of old, it felt weirdly like I was a virgin again . . . all nervous and excited to let a man have his way with me.

He let go of my hand and began to fold up the blanket. I bent down and tried to stuff everything back into the picnic basket. The beer bottles clanged around as I carried it back to the car.

"Back to the real world," he said, frowning. "But first, coffee!" which he followed with a smile.

I nodded, hoping to not let my breath ruin this moment. I opened the passenger door, and there sat my box, the box full of everything I needed to know. I was back in the real world in an instant. Guess the coffee would just have to soften the blow.

"Oh, I hate that Finn has to go through this. I know this must be awful. Part of me wants this over for Finn's sake, but part of me wants it to last forever so we don't have to say goodbye."

"Oh Jesus, Pey, don't tell me you are actually besties again? You knew this wouldn't last. Finn left once and will do it again. Don't get all sappy. Plus—maybe we can get the Amgine farmhouse out of it."

"Will, don't be a dick. Finn has always been my friend, and sorry if I don't want to go through losing that again. Gosh, you are so insensitive."

## 20

The ride back into town was a quiet one, in part because I was über focused on the box and partially because I didn't want my breath to waft. The bumps under the car gave the alert that we were already back on the dirt road to Amgine Farm. I tried my best to act as if the box wasn't a big deal and keep up the minimal small talk as best I could.

"You nervous to open it?" he finally asked. I was obviously not doing the bang-up cover job that I thought I was.

"Nah. I am sure it is nothing." I tried to play it cool.

"I don't know," he said. "She seemed pretty protective of it and adamant that you read everything in there. Must have been pretty important to her."

"We will see, I guess." I again tried to fake laissez-faire.

"Do you want me to stay and go through it with you?" he asked.

*How incredibly sweet and chivalrous,* I thought. I am sure that is just how he wants to spend his day, going through the diaries of a dead woman.

"That is very kind, but I think it is something I have to do on my own."

He put the car in park as I looked up from the box to see we were at my front porch.

"Well, call me if you need me. I am happy to bring food, drinks, or a sexual tryst." He flashed his dimples again and squeezed my thigh.

I smiled back. "I will."

"I'll call you later." He kissed me on the cheek.

"Thank you again for last night," I said. "It was amazing."

"Anytime, Finn Harper."

I opened the car door and, grasping my box, walked up the porch. I turned back to see him watching me and wave as he put it in reverse.

Dust kicked up from his tires as he drove off and left me standing on the front porch grinning like an idiot, half falling, and half trying to talk myself out of it . . . just like Nick had once done.

I set the box on the kitchen counter and went to fish in the cabinets for some booze to offset the distress of whatever my mother thought was "everything." I quickly realized I had damn near drank us out of house and home except for an old, half-full bottle of some moonshine-type spirit that some neighbor had made and given to my gramps as a harvest gift. I wasn't sure how old it was or what it would taste like, but it would have to do. The clock reminded me that it was only six a.m., and so I decided to chug a cup of coffee before hitting it hard . . . the booze and the box.

Alcohol wasn't the only thing I was almost out of. I was down to my last coffee grounds, as well. I was going to have to call Pey or James later, if for no other reason than to bring reinforcements.

I tucked the moonshine under my arm, grabbed the box with the other, held the coffee in my hand, and headed out to the back porch. I walked past the davenport where my blanket was and thought twice about catching a few more z's before hearing my mother out. But instead I kept walking, pushed the screen door open with my hipbone, and set the box and beverages on the coffee table. I lay down on the swing and could feel my back was a little sore from sleeping on the ground the night before, reminding me yet again that I was, in fact, no longer that young girl who lived in this house. I tried to reposition myself on the swing, rested my head against a pillow, ripped the envelope off the top of the box, tore it open, and let the bleeding begin.

Dear Finn,

In this box are several journals I kept to tell you my story, the story I never told a soul. We all have our secrets, and I am not proud of mine, nor the fact that I never shared them with you until now. I wish I could have been the kind of mother you deserved, the kind I wanted to be deep down, but I was too busy trying to survive to focus on anyone but me. I hope this journal helps you to see me in a different light and understand why I was the way I was. If nothing else, I hope it brings you peace. It is not going to be easy to hear, pretty, or painless, but it is going to be true. As you know, I was not a good mom, but by now I am guessing you have found out that I was a decent writer. So this is my final piece of work, my one and only book, written just for you, sweet child. I hope you find every happiness and live life on your terms. Don't let fear determine your future, and don't let the past define you. I love you.

Love,
Mom (G. E. H.)
PS: How cute is James, right?

# PART 2

"So I heard that her mother left her some kind of box. Did you ever open it? Do you know what is in it?"

"No. Her mother was very specific that it was only for Finn's eyes. There were things inside only they would understand, and she wanted Finn to decide which secrets to keep and which to tell."

"Oh come on, babe . . . You didn't sneak one peek? I won't tell Finny!"

**21**

# grace

Grace Harper lay on her side in the queen bed. She could feel her hip digging into the old mattress, almost touching the springs. Her paisley comforter still pulled up over her bare shoulders, her box-dyed blond, frizzy curls resting on the pillow under her head. She looked out the window flanked by yellow walls and realized for the first time that she would never again see her mother come down that dirt driveway again. She wasn't exactly sure how she was supposed to feel. Her mother had passed away last night shortly after dinner. It was a moderately quick death after a painful battle with breast cancer. Elizabeth Harper was not the warm and cuddly type of mother. She never held Grace's hand or ran her fingers through her hair. For as long as Grace could remember, her mother had been there but not all there. One couldn't blame her; things hadn't been easy for her. She probably secretly blamed Grace for a lot of it. Grace just assumed this, of course. She didn't know for sure . . . that would require her mother actually talking to her, which did not happen.

Grace had always been the golden child in her father's eyes.

She was beautiful from the day she was a born. She was funny, sweet, and smart as a whip. People used to tell Elizabeth that Grace should model, which probably didn't sit well with her to begin with. Elizabeth was far from a looker. She was a shorter woman, five feet on a good day, thin hair that began to gray too early in life, and oddly large hands and feet. She never lost the baby weight after Grace and was now plump, bordering on overweight. This of course was before the cancer took over and made her rail thin. Grace wasn't sure which was a worse look on her.

Everyone in Hadleigh said that the only reason Al married her was for her family money. The Elderman family was known for their wealth, not just in Hadleigh, but across the five-county region. Elizabeth, their only daughter, had two brothers who would all share the wealth equally, and so it was assumed that Al hitched his wagon to the money train and went along for the ride. Al was that kind of man, the trouble-maker from the town over. He was a bad boy with a passion for booze and farming, a combo that suited him just fine after marrying Elizabeth.

They hadn't been married long before Elizabeth got pregnant with Grace. Al wasn't sure that he wanted kids, but the minute he saw Grace, that all changed. She was the apple of his eye, in turn driving Elizabeth mad. She began drinking heavily after Grace was born, eventually dabbling in prescription drugs after being misdiagnosed with schizophrenia and given a cocktail of meds that she thought paired well with vodka. She would spend her days sleeping or wandering around the house, mumbling incoherently. It wasn't until she started chemo that they finally regulated her meds, correctly rendering her more lucid.

By the time they had discovered the cancer, she was stage

four and too far gone. They tried to contain it, but to no avail. From diagnosis to death, she lasted a quick three months. During those months, she and Grace had several meaningful conversations that left Grace feeling like she might actually love her mother for the first time in her life.

As Grace rolled over on her pillow to shun the sunlight that was beginning to peek through the window, she closed her eyes and realized that her relationship with Finn was becoming not unlike the one she had with Elizabeth, tortured and distant. She didn't want to wait until she was dying to get to know her daughter and tell her the truth, but right now she couldn't bring herself to change. It was taking everything in her not to end it all.

She squinted her eyes a little tighter, thinking and trying to further block out the sun that was trying to shine into her eyes and brighten her life. Lost in the darkness of her own making, she wondered how she would do it. A mixture of pills her mother had left behind? One of the shotguns her father kept in the barn? Hang herself by the rope over the tractor he used so he would have to see her, really look at her.

She opened her eyes and caught a glimpse of herself in the mirror. She used to be the homecoming queen, one of the popular girls, voted most likely to succeed. *What a joke,* she thought to herself now. She was a shell of that girl. Sure she still had her beautiful blond hair, thin physique, and nice smile when she let it show, but time and the Winstons had done their fair share to her skin and health. Time, cigarettes, and him.

She spent most of her time in this room now, the yellow walls surrounding her, the pain engulfing her. She went out from time to time to fill her glass, trying to numb the pain, or to let a man in the front door. She had gotten used to disconnecting from men by now and would simply use them to get what she wanted and then send them on their merry way.

People in town talked about her and she knew it, but deep down she was simply using her body to render her mind co-matose. She was the one using these men, not the other way around. She would disassociate herself from Grace Harper. To her she had always been Hadley Finnegan deep down, though no one knew it but her and her editor.

Grace had become immensely good at not letting people get too close. Beau was the last one to really know her and after how that ended, she didn't have the heart to try to connect to anyone again, not even her own daughter. This made connecting with her mother days before her death hurt even more. She was good at keeping people at arm's length, not getting too close to have to actually be real, honest. It was easier to live a lie than tell the truth. Her life had become a series of lies, and breaking that cycle at this point seemed too difficult and honestly futile. There were people in her life, each who knew one or two of the truths, but no one who knew it all, the real Grace.

Against her better judgment, she rolled back over and let the sun warm her face a little. She missed her mother and hated herself for it. No one else in the house seemed upset that Elizabeth was gone. She could hear Finn laughing from the back porch and her father's tractor already at work in the field. She knew she should get up and be a parent, be the parent her mother wasn't. Instead she closed her eyes as a tear rolled down and fell on her pillow. It was just her now, one less person in the world who knew her secrets.

Grace lay there for a while, shifting from side to side, trying to fight back the tears and struggling to stop the storm brewing in her mind. Finally, she sat up, swung her legs over the bed, and stood up. She was putting on her robe, ready to head out of her room, not for the reason that she should, but because she was jonesing for a Winston. Smoking was her only vice, other than the men and vodka. She didn't last more than a couple hours without a nicotine hit, and every time she thought about quitting, it only made her want it more. She knew it would kill her someday, and she hoped that day was sooner than later.

She pushed open the front porch door and stepped out into the morning sun. The wood on the deck felt warm under her bare feet as she walked over and took a seat in one of the rocking chairs her father had made. He was handy like that, one of the few traits she actually admired in him.

The matchstick struck against the wooden chair arm and brightly sprung alive. She held it up, the cigarette dangling from her mouth, knowing it was not a good look but not caring in the least. *I should go into the newspaper office today,* she thought. Paul would want her to wrap up her column for the week and people would want her to show her face. People in town loved that shit, acting like they cared about things that merely gave them something to talk about. She knew they would fawn over her and tell her how sorry they were, but they wouldn't mean a word. They would leave feeling good about themselves for doing the "right thing" and then go home and bitch about her deceased mother to their spouses and friends. That's what people in these small towns do. She never quite fit in, just like her little Finn.

*Poor Finn,* she thought, *only left with me and him now.* She wasn't really sure that Finn cared too much about her grandma, but it felt odd knowing it was just the two of them now. She would have rather he died than her.

She puffed a few more times and tried to think about Beau. She liked to do this when she was feeling down. She liked to think about where he was, what he was doing, and fantasize about him coming back into her life again. This, of course, would never happen as long as Al was alive, but he couldn't live forever, the old bastard. So she puffed and ruminated.

When her cigarette was down to the butt, she put it out on the chair arm, rubbing it in a little extra hard as a gesture towards her father. She rocked back and forth a few more times, deciding if she needed another one or if she should compose herself and get out of the house before he came in from the fields. He would be in a mood today, she was sure of it, and she didn't want to be around when he was.

Walking back into the house, she caught a glimpse of Finn lying on the back porch swing, reading and giggling. She seemed so innocent at times, but Grace could tell that something was off about her. Finn was at the very beginning stages of puberty, and her hormones were beginning to flare. At times it seemed like Finn was going through "normal" puberty issues: anger, oversensitivity, seeming uncomfortable in her body, and searching for her identity. But there were times when Grace could almost sense something else. She couldn't quite put her finger on it, but something was there. In all reality, she should just ask Finn, but that would require her actually acting like a mother, and she wasn't sure either of them were ready for that yet.

She shut the door to her room behind her and began to rifle through her closet, trying to find the appropriate "I'm at work though my mother is dead" outfit. She settled on a denim button-down and a khaki pencil skirt. Then she slipped on her white converse and threw her hair up in a scrunchie. She opened her bedroom door and peered out, making sure the coast was clear before scurrying as quickly as possible out the front door and into the Chevy Celebrity she had shared with her mother. As she fiddled to get the key into the ignition, it dawned on her that she no longer shared the car with anyone.

She could feel her breath start to catch, but she willed it down as the car revved up. She put the car in drive and headed to the *Gazette*, never bothering to look back and see Finn standing on the front porch, wondering where she was going yet again.

"You remember how that little Finn used to run around town with her grandpa. She always looked so happy, but Grace was never in sight. I always felt bad for the little girl."

"I know, right? A distant mother and a crazy grandma . . . you remember Elizabeth, right? She was the town nut!"

"You know that Al just married her for her money. He was a looker back in the day. No way he saw anything else in her. Didn't she die of breast cancer too?"

# grace

The *Hadleigh Gazette* was housed in an old flour mill on the edge of town. The only way one would know the paper was operated out of there was a small, round, wooden sign that hung by chains from the metal rod above the door. The sign read: "Hadleigh Gazette Est. 1953."

Grace parked the car and pulled down the visor to take one more look at herself in the mirror. People would be expecting her to look ragged after the events of yesterday, but she was determined to undermine them all and come in looking like the Grace of old. She pinched her cheeks to bring a little color to them and ran her teeth over her lips to pinken them up. She put the visor up and her game face on.

Everyone inside the *Gazette* office worked busily as she entered. A few raised their heads and began to whisper. She walked towards her desk near the back of the room and tried her best to ignore their hushed voices. She held her head up and smiled politely as she passed. Very few people at the paper even knew what she did there. Most were told she was working on the classifieds; others assumed she was just there to bang the editor. Truthfully, it was only Grace and Paul who knew that she was Hadley Finnegan, author of the "Yes & Know from So and So" column. Grace needed it to stay a secret, and so it did. Al didn't approve of women being anything beside wives and mothers, and Grace knew all too well what happened when you didn't follow Al's rules, as absurd as they may be. Those were the conditions when she came aboard eleven years before—she needed to come and go as she pleased, and he needed to keep his mouth shut.

Grace sat down at her desk and began to click the computer alive when there was a gentle rapping on her door trim.

She looked up and saw Paul standing there, and she knew the apologies were about to commence.

"Hey, Grace, I am so sorry to hear about your mother. How are you doing? You don't need to be here. You should go home and be with your family," he said.

She shuddered inside a little at the thought of spending the day with Al and Finn. Home was the last place she wanted to be.

"Oh, thank you. Honestly, I could use the distraction. Thank you, though," she muttered back.

"Okay, well if you need to go, then go. And if you need a few days off, please take them. Let me know if you need anything, okay?" He cocked his head and gave her a sad puppy expression.

"Thanks, Paul." She smiled and looked back at the computer screen that was still booting up.

Paul began to head back to his desk when she called to him. "Hey, Paul . . ."

He popped his head back in the doorway. "Yeah?"

"I thought of something I do need."

"Anything."

"I need you to pony up and get some new computers." She smiled. "And I need you to tell all of them to stop looking at me and get back to work."

He smirked. "On it . . . the people that is. The computers, well, that is out my hands."

He turned and barked, "Show's over! Back to work, people. Leave the lady alone!" Then he headed back towards his desk.

Word travels in a small town faster than a melting snow cone on a hot summer day. Grace smiled and turned back to the computer once more, praying it had finally woken itself up from the 1980s. The damn thing was still spinning, making no progress from before. Frustrated but not wanting to give up and go home just yet, she rummaged through her desk, deciding she would write the whole thing by hand instead.

In the bottom drawer of her old cedar desk that reeked of cigarettes and writer's block, she found an old green leather journal with her initials engraved on the bottom. She picked it up and ran her fingers over the G. E. H. that was embossed in a silver color, making it almost hard to see but still somehow noticeable. A gift from Beau after she had first accepted the job at the *Gazette*. He told her he wanted her to have a place to write her own story, a place all her own.

She flipped open the soft, worn cover and lightly paged through the empty pages. She had thrown the journal into the back of that drawer right after she had ended things with Beau. Taken it out time and again when she missed him, flipped through the pages, looking for answers to a life she wished she could wipe as blank as the sheets before her. She so badly had wanted them to stay together, but she had to end it. He didn't understand, told her they were soul mates and they were meant to be together forever, and even though she knew he was right, she couldn't put him through what was to come.

Here, in her hands, was one of the few pieces left after she was broken. One of the last remaining artifacts of the girl she was then, and the man she still loved now. She knew he wanted big things for her, and she felt bad that she never achieved them. She wanted to do right by him. He had been the only one she ever wanted to make proud.

She set the journal on her desk, creased the front cover open, and dug in her top drawer for a pen. This was not the kind of thing you did in pencil. This was a "screw-ups are okay"; "things happen"; "real-deal honest" pen-type of story.

Grace uncapped the blue pen and began in her best cursive writing.

Dear . . .

At first she thought she was going to write to Beau, share the real her—even the shit that had happened when they were apart. But then it dawned on her—her story was not for a man, not even one as amazing as Beau. Her story, her true story, was meant for one person only.

And so she wrote . . .

Dear Finn . . .

You will read this one day, and I am not sure what you will think of it. I hope you are old enough to understand but young enough to learn the lessons. Today is the day after your Grandma Elizabeth passed away. I am sitting at my desk in my office at the *Hadleigh Gazette*, where I have worked since before you were born. The thing is that no one here knows what I do here. Hell, even your grandpa doesn't know what I do. I had to keep it a secret, for reasons I will explain later in this story, my story.

You see, Finn, the thing is that I am a writer, in life, and here at the *Gazette*. I write a column called "Yes & Know from So and So," where I have creative freedom to say or write whatever I please. I was blessed that my editor, Paul, saw my raw talent even in high school and trusted me enough to let me be me, at least on paper anyways. It has been Paul's and my secret all these years.

But the one story I have never told, the one I piecemeal out to only a few people, is my story. The real story of Grace Harper, or Hadley Finnegan, as I go by in the paper.

Here, in this journal, a gift from the only man I have ever loved, I want to tell you the whole truth, Finn. I know I am not the mother you needed or deserved, but I can promise you that was not all of my own volition. I am not trying to place blame or not own up to my doing in all of this. I just want you to have all the facts so hopefully you can better understand why I was the way I was.

Deep down, Finn, I love you more than you know. It's just not that simple all the time. You bring back a lot of tough feelings, and I am not good at separating you from them.

I am sorry, truly.

Love,
G. E. H.

"I think that is the editor of the *Hadleigh Gazette*. What is his name again?"

"Pete or Paul or something. I heard that he and Grace were sleeping together. People used to see her there all the time, but they never knew what she was doing."

"I heard that she runs the place now. I bet she blackmailed him into giving her the reins."

"I bet. Isn't he married? I am sure he didn't want his wife to know about the affair so he gave her whatever she wanted."

# finn

It truly wasn't that simple all the time. I spent the next several hours reading bits and pieces of a life I never knew. The moonshine went down a little rough, but it was a good burn, kind of like my mother's story thus far. The journal appeared to have been a green hue at one point, but time and dust had rendered it more of an olivey-brown now. I loved the feeling of it in my hands. It felt like an old book—the one you had read so many times, but yet here I was actually reading it for the first time.

I could tell by the way that it started and the few entries after that she was holding back, nervous to actually follow through with her story. A lot of the entries were simple musings about the farm, or life after my grandmother had died. She never went too deep, except to hint at a lot of negative feelings about herself, and suicidal thoughts seemed to creep into the text now and again. She never flat out said she wanted to kill herself, but there were a lot of telltale sentences.

It was difficult for me to understand what was so hard for her. I know that depression is not always a situational thing, but I still couldn't understand what she was so upset about.

She mentioned the men in and out of her life a lot, but for the first time I saw it a little differently than I had as a child. She seemed to be the one in control, the one who wanted it. It never seemed like she didn't want it, but it truly never seemed like she did either.

I turned page after page, looking for something with meaning. I wasn't sure what this big reveal or secret would be, but I kept on. It was late afternoon leaning into evening when I had reached my early teen years in her story and was still waiting for the plot to thicken. Up until this point, she had spent most of her time in her room or at the *Gazette*. She had told me many times that she wanted to be a better mother but was finding it hard enough to be Grace that she didn't know how to be a mom.

Dear Finn,

I see it in you. The beginnings of something I can't quite put my finger on. You are merely thirteen, but you seem to be battling the war of an adult inside. I remember puberty (I always hated that word), and I recall the turmoil and angst that came with it. When I look at you, I can almost swear that it is more than that . . . that there is something in you that you aren't letting out. I wish I would just walk over to you and ask, but here I stay, watching you from a distance. I hope someday you find inner peace. I hope you find more than I ever did. I see you and I love you.

Love,
G. E. H

There it was, the first time I saw her write the phrase that I had said so many times back and forth to my gramps in our letters. I wondered if she had read them or if it was something he used to say to her. Maybe it was pure coincidence, since it seemed like my gramps and mom weren't the closest of kin. Come to think of it, I don't know that I ever saw them hug or say I love you. I began to wonder how a man like that could be so affectionate with me and so cold to my mother, or maybe it was the other way around?

I breezed through a few more entries that seemed like small talk written on paper, and then I hit an entry that gave me chills. It was written in 2000 and was titled "Nick."

Dear Finn,

I never had the talk with you. Never sat you down and told you about the birds and the bees. I probably should have. That is what a good mother would do, I suppose. I am not sure what I would have said in that chat though, and that's one of the many reasons that I never bothered. Would I have told you that sex can be used a weapon? Would I have led with the fact that sex can be an escape? Would I have told you how many people I had sex with and that I only ever loved one of them? What kind of person gives that talk to a child? I suppose I was overqualified with all the experience under my belt (pun intended), but I was not going to wreck it for you.

I know that tonight was the night you experienced sex for the first time. You thought you were so crafty about it, I am sure, but a mother knows, and it wasn't just from the muffled noises I heard coming from the back porch. I could see it written on your face when you kissed Nick goodbye at the front door. From the crack in my door, I watched you smile, looking up at him with glowing post-coitus eyes, and whisper something in his ear and kiss him on the lips like a good girlfriend does. I watched you shut the door behind him, bend your head to the floor, and cry. I wanted to open the door and hold you, tell you it would get better, but I couldn't. I wanted to tell you that it would improve and you would learn to like it and control your emotions, but this would have been a lie. The best sex I ever had was in high school, and since then, I have used it as a tool to numb my mind and body from the pain I live with day in and out. I wish I could tell you that sex is amazing and wonderful, but I can't. To me, sex is a means to an end. The only man it felt any different with has been gone for fifteen years.

My wish for you is that everything I know about sex will be wrong. I hope sex is one of the best parts of your life, and I hope you find someone you will love and make it magical with. I hope you never again cry after, and I hope you have lots of it. Maybe not for a few more years (not that I am judging). I hope you don't follow in my footsteps. I want you to find your own way. I want sex to be part of a wonderful relationship you have with someone and not a means of escape from a shitty world.

I guess this is my birds and bees talk, a little late. If it helps, I did slip some condoms into your nightstand as a precaution.

Love,
G. E. H.


That explained how those condoms got into my drawer. I had assumed Nick snuck them in, hoping they would be put to good use. I felt my stomach turn a little at the revelation that my mother had heard me lose my virginity and then watched me cry about it. I wish she would have come out of her room and held me. I was such a mess in that moment. Sex had screwed me up, and I needed someone to talk with me about it. I surely wasn't going to tell Gramps, and Peyton would get all mushy about it, so my mom would have been a welcome ear back then. It infuriated me a little that she did nothing while knowing I was suffering.

My stomach flipped again, and I realized that it might not be the sex that bugged me but the fact that it was now past dinner and my only caloric consumption for the day had come from moonshine.

I set the journal back on top of the box and rose up off of the swing for the first time since that morning. I felt everything stiffen a little and my eyes take a minute to clear the moonshine fog from them and walked back into the house. The blanket on the couch called to me as the evening air had gotten a little nippy. I wrapped it around my shoulders and grabbed my phone. I plopped back down on the couch and deliberated on whether I should call James or Pey to bring me dinner since I knew the cupboards were bare.

Finally I slid the phone open and dialed.

"Hey," I said, "any chance you want to bring in some dinner provisions?" Being a city mouse, having access to a car wasn't something I was familiar with or even registered to me.

"I thought you'd never ask," he responded. "See you in an hour?"

"Perfect. Oh . . . and can you bring coffee? I'm out, and you don't want to know me without coffee."

"No problem." I could hear him smile.

Just like that, I hung up the phone and headed upstairs to

shower and make myself presentable for the man with who I was going to have the loving, sexual relationship my mother had always wanted me to have. I was going to make up for lost time and bad memories in this house. But tonight, in this house, he was going to help me right a bunch of wrongs. I was going to throw caution to the wind and let myself fall ever so slightly for a man I was sure I was going to leave.

"Didn't Finn used to date that Nick boy who died?"

"I heard she lost her virginity to him. I overheard her and Peyton talking about it one night on the phone."

"No way that was her first time. If she was anything like her mother, she was a pro by then."

"That's not fair, Tammy. Grace wasn't always that way. In high school she only had eyes for Beau. Remember?"

# grace

Grace felt like she was going to fall. Collapse straight through the chaise she lay on. It was one of the plastic chaise lounge chairs that she could never figure out how to close and never fully felt sturdy in when it was open. She had laid a towel over the plastic straw-like teal and green straps that were supposed to support a human, but she could still feel them press against the back of her legs.

Finn was in school at the same Hadleigh High School that Grace had once been homecoming queen of, and her father, Al, was in the next town over for a day or two for a pig auction. It was one of those rare moments when Grace was alone at Amgine Farm, and she didn't have to look over her shoulder. She wondered why they had decided to call this place "Amgine Farm." She knew it was her mother who had named it, and it wasn't really until Grace was in middle school that her mother started referring to it that way, but she had never bothered to ask why. It was a weird name, but it had come to roll off her tongue after years of saying it.

Under her sun hat, and behind those oversized glasses, she was hiding a black eye. She had gotten good at the lies by now and told Finn she fell down the stairs going to the basement. She only went to the basement to do the laundry, and usually to cry about her sad existence, but it had also become the place of her many "accidents."

She had "fallen" down those stairs, or "slipped" on water from the washer, too many times, and yet she was pretty sure Finn was still buying it. Paul, on the other hand, was getting suspicious. Every time she came into the *Gazette* with a fresh bruise, he would listen to her lie and shake his head. She didn't know how much longer she was going to be able to pull this off.

She sat up in the chaise, feeling the jelly straps give a little more as she turned and grabbed the sunscreen. She wasn't out in the sun much, in spite of loving the warmth it brought, though fleeting, but when she was, she was certainly not going to get skin cancer. Now lung cancer didn't faze her obviously, since a Winston was hanging from her mouth again, but skin cancer and wrinkles—now that was serious business.

Grace slathered the sunscreen on her legs and forearms, and was extra careful lathering the bruises on her biceps and back from that nasty "fall." She wiped her hand on the towel, took a long sip of her vodka lemonade (a summer tanning drink, she had decided), and picked up her journal and pen. Today was the day that she was going to let it all out. Someday Finn would read this, and it would devastate her, but she needed to know the truth. Grace reached down and took one more gulp from her cup of courage, took a deep breath, and began.

Dear Finn,

I told you when I started this story that I would tell you the whole story, the whole truth, every part of what makes me me, I guess. In order to do that, I have to go back to a time when I was just a little older than you are now. Back to one night back in 1983. . . .

Grace Harper was one of those kids who made puberty look beautiful. You know the ones, the kids who never had an awkward phase, just went from young to beautiful seemingly overnight. She rarely acted out and went from a slim, freckle-faced girl to a thin, stunning, full B cup in what seemed like an instant. She seemed to handle it all in stride, too. Where most girls would hide away and be ashamed of their new body, Grace seemed fine with just being who she was. No hiding, few issues.

The boys, of course, seemed to take notice right away. If they hadn't already noticed her (which was hard not to do), they definitely would now. She was the whole package—beautiful, smart, and sweet. She was destined to make her mark. She had Hadleigh in a twist. It had always baffled the town how a girl like that could have come from a woman like Elizabeth. The town talked and Elizabeth heard. Instead of being proud of her daughter, Elizabeth grew resentful and began drinking more heavily to drown the town's thoughts out of her own head. She became a raging bitch at her best and black-out drunk at her worst. Al, on the other hand, still seemed pleased with his only child. He wasn't thrilled with all the attention she was getting now though, but he tried to ignore it as best as he could. She had gone from fifteen to thirty overnight, and people were destined to notice.

It was the early winter of 1982, November to be exact. The Harper phone had been ringing off the hook for months with boys calling, all wanting to talk to Grace, begging for a minute of her time, hoping to bend her ear and eventually bend her over. Al had tried his best to fend off all these ill-fitted suitors, but if they didn't get a hold of her on the phone, they would show up at the front door. It seemed every high school boy in town wanted to date Grace, but she only had eyes for one— Beau Boyton.

Beau was a boy in Grace's grade who was easy on the eyes but a little slow on the uptake, which is why he didn't notice Grace's interest in him at first. Grace wasn't a brown leather pigskin knit together with white laces, and so he didn't notice her. Over Christmas break in '82 they had ended up at the same party, and after Grace had spent most of the night following him around like a puppy dog and hanging on his every word, he had finally gotten his head out of the game long enough to notice her beautiful smile and great rack. He drove her home from the party, and there in the front of his 1976 Ford F150, he leaned over and kissed her. She even let him cop a feel of her coveted breasts. After they had squarely rounded first base, she pulled away, kissed him on the cheek, and hopped out of the truck. She knew better than to give it all up like that. She wanted to leave him wanting more. Under that temptress body was a good girl trying to follow the rules. She had spent long enough chasing him, and now it was his turn to pine after her. She made sure to walk slowly, and deliberately arched her back a little more to flaunt her ass as she walked away from his truck. She didn't have to look back; she knew he was watching every step she took.

She had come into the house, grinning ear to ear, and quickly snuck into her room to journal the whole thing. She spent the rest of break ignoring Beau's calls and playing hard to get. She wanted to make him sweat it out, though it was killing her not to kiss him again.

Al had watched the whole thing transpire. He had heard the truck's tailpipes coming up the driveway and pushed back the curtains to see what the commotion was. He watched as his only daughter, his pride and joy, made out with some dumb jock and let him caress her untouched breasts. He fought back every inclination to storm out there and rip her out of the vehicle, and if they would have gone any farther, he would have. She was too beautiful for him. He watched out the window, breathing in and out so hard he sounded like a bull. Then he looked back at Elizabeth, already passed out on the bed, making sure his angered breathing wasn't going to wake the bitch he had married for her money. He turned back to the window and watched as Grace hopped out of the truck and sauntered towards the house. He let the curtains swing shut and vowed to never let anyone touch her like that again.

He watched as Grace spent the next few weeks leading the boy on. He carefully kept an eye on her, waiting to see what her next move would be. She did quite a job making the boy work for her affections well into January, until one night he heard she finally answered his call and agreed to go out with him again. The date would be Friday, January fourteenth. Al gritted his teeth together in the next room, knowing if he told her not to go that she would go anyway. He decided to let her go and deal with the repercussions of her actions when she got home.

"That's right. I totally forgot about the Grace-and-Beau era of high school. They were a sweet item. What ever happened there?"

"She got pregnant with someone else's kid."

"No way. I heard it was Beau's and he freaked out and bailed."

"Who is Finn's father anyway?"

# grace

Beau handled every detail of their first date, wanting it to be perfect. They spent their first real date together sitting under the stars in a field near Hadleigh Lake. Not another soul in sight, and in between kisses they had talked about their aspirations and their upbringings. Beau lived with his father and two sisters. His mother had died of liver cancer when he was eleven, and he had become his dad's main focus. It was a career in the NFL or bust. Beau seemed okay holding the weight of his father's hopes on his shoulders. He seemed unfazed, almost happy to carry the load for his dad. Grief will do that to a person—make them carry more than they can hold.

His sisters were both older and in college studying to be "God knows what," he had said and shook his head. Grace found his family life fascinating and alluring. What it would be like to have siblings to reference and act bewildered about was beyond her. She had always longed for a sibling but had been left with a simple father and a batshit crazy mother. She had let Beau get to first base again near the lake but told him she wanted to wait to go further. She wanted to ease into it, and though the bulge in his pants said otherwise, he agreed to take things slow.

He held the door open for her as she hopped in and buckled her seatbelt, staring at him the whole ride home. He turned and smiled at her between sentences, and she was sure no one's smile would ever make her melt like that again.

She almost hated the gently bumping of the dirt driveway of Amgine Farm bouncing her ever so slightly in her seat, bringing her back to reality and reminding her that the night was about to end.

He put the truck in park, leaned over to her, kissed her on the forehead, and said, "Grace Harper, you are something special, and I intend to make you feel that way for the rest of our lives."

She lurched forward and kissed him hard. She was in love, right then and there. In that moment on the saddle-bench, blanketed front seat of that Ford truck, her forever was beginning. She knew people wouldn't believe her, say she's too young to know what forever looked like, but she was sure of it. She kissed him again and hopped out of the truck. This time she looked back at him and smiled. She wanted to remember everything about this night for the rest of her life.

Grace walked in the front door and closed it behind her. She leaned back on the door, closed her eyes, and smiled. "Magical" was the only word that came to mind. She exhaled and opened her eyes to see her dad standing there at the bottom of the stairs. She smiled and was about to tell him about the best night of her life when he lunged toward her and grabbed her by both arms and squeezed really hard.

"Ow! You are hurting me! What the heck, Dad?" she cried.

"Dammit, Grace. Why do you have to do this? Why do you make *me* do this?"

"Ouch!" she hollered "What are you talking about? Let go of me!"

He pulled her off the door by her upper arms and pushed her backward into her bedroom door. Grace winced as the door hit the back of her head and her spine hard and flung open. Al squeezed tighter.

"Stop! What are you doing?" Grace called.

"Just shut up, Grace. Dammit!"

He threw her onto the bed, and when she tried to sit up, he shoved her shoulders back onto the bed and threw his forearm over her collarbone to keep her down. With his other hand, he reached under her shirt and under the wire of her bra and cupped her no-longer-untouched breast.

"What the hell are you doing? Stop!" she shrieked.

He lifted his arm off her collarbone for a second to slap her across the face.

She cried out and a tear fell on her now bright red cheek.

"Shut the fuck up, Grace. You asked for this," he roared.

With his arm back on her collarbone, he reached down and undid the snap of her jean skirt and slid his hand underneath her satin underwear she had worn just for Beau. He shoved his finger inside of her and she gasped.

"Please stop!" she muttered.

"No one deserves you but me," he countered and took his hand out and undid his pants.

"God dammit Grace," he said as he entered her. "Why do you make me do this?"

He forced himself in and out of her as she cried silently, her face looking as far away from him as possible. If she raised her voice, he would go harder.

After what seemed like forever, he was done. He took his arm off her collarbone and zipped up his pants. She kept her head facing away from him and tried to stifle her cries.

"If you ever tease me like that again, you will pay," he said. "You are too beautiful to waste your time on boys like him."

She didn't look at him, just kept trying to breathe in between silent sobs.

Once his pants were on, he leaned over her on the bed and grabbed her face with his hand and cranked her to face him.

"Don't you ever forget that no one will love you like I do." He looked her in the eye. "And if you ever tell anyone about this, I will make it my mission to make your life a living hell. I'll kill that little boyfriend of yours."

And just like that, he threw her face away from him, walked out her room, and slammed the door.

Grace lay in her bed, unable to move for a while. What in the hell just happened? How had her night gone so wrong? She finally sat up and saw the blood on the bed, and without even thinking, she ripped the sheets off the bed and threw them in the corner of the room. She wanted to call Beau, wanted him to come and pick her up and take her far away from here. But in the back of her head, she heard her father saying, "I will kill your little boyfriend if you tell," so she curled up in the fetal position and cried herself to sleep. All the while trying to figure out what she did to deserve this.

"Do you remember how Grace would always have all those bruises? Do you think Beau was hitting her?"

"He was always a bit of a muscle head."

"If he hit her, then why would she go back to him?"

"Back to him? What do you mean?"

"They have been together for the last like fifteen years. Didn't you know that?"

# finn

*I deserved this,* I thought to myself as I ran a comb through my still wet hair. Tonight will be amazing. I heard the doorbell ring and bounded down the stairs like a lovesick teenager and opened the door with a smile that damn near spelled out "I want to sleep with you."

He was standing there, looking handsome as always, smiling and raising his takeout bags. "Someone call for Chinese?" he said.

"I am not sure I would have called for Chinese in Hadleigh, but it will do." I smiled back.

He slid past me as I held the door open and turned back to give me a quick peck on the lips. I felt my body come alive and anxious all at once. I shut the door, and for the first time in its existence, turned the rusted knob that fought back against me and locked it. No one was interrupting this night.

He set the bags down on the counter and pulled a bottle of red wine out of one of them.

"I have seen you take down hard liquor like a champ, and even a beer or two, so I thought we would try out the only alcohol left." He smirked.

"Good idea. I am just not sure we have a—"

And just like that he pulled a wine opener out of his pocket. "One step ahead," he said. And I couldn't help but wonder what else he was one step ahead of me on tonight. What else were in those pockets?

I watched him head over to the cabinets and rummage through them, looking for glasses that I wasn't sure he would find. I enjoyed watching the way his jeans smoothly covered his every asset with perfection as he opened cabinet after cabinet. I could have cut to the chase and told him that the cupboards were bare, but I was enjoying the view from behind. Eventually he turned to me and said, "There are no glasses?"

"Oh." I tried to act surprised. "I guess not."

"Straight out of the bottle it is then." He smiled. "I am classy like that."

He began to twist the opener into the bottle when he looked up and our eyes met. He took his hands off the opener, walked towards me, and took my face in his hands and kissed me hard. His tongue and mine were exploring while my hands ventured down, reaching around and grabbing his ass, and then making their way to unbutton his jeans.

His hands stayed firmly on my face, grabbing me just hard enough. I got my hand inside his jeans just in time to spring him free and feel his longing for me in my hand. I stroked back and forth, and his hands traveled down to my pants, as well, and he began to kiss my neck, pulled my shirt off and kissed my clavicle. He unzipped my jeans and gently tugged my pants down to my knees.

My ribcage released as I realized he wasn't going to bother with my shirt. I had tested positive for the BRCA gene in high school and once away from this place had used it as an excuse to remove the large breasts that I had grown accustomed to hating, along with the back pain they had brought with them. Years of multiple sport bras still couldn't flatten them enough to make me feel better. So now, exposing my chest still gave me a sense of apprehension that I wasn't proud of.

As if feeling my body and mind relax, he then, all in one motion, spun me around and began kissing my shoulder blades, making his way down my spine as I moaned and braced myself against the kitchen counter.

He kissed his way up my neck again as his hands grazed down the sides of my hips, then traveled around front and pressed firmly against my inner thighs.

"Is this okay?" he whispered in my ear and then lightly bit my lobe, tugging down gently and making me arch my back.

"I want you now," I panted.

He released one hand from my inner thigh and used it grab a condom from his pocket. His other hand stayed on my inner thigh, rubbing up and down, making me crave him. He brought the condom to his mouth, and while holding it gently between his soft lips, ripped it open, letting the wrapper fall to the floor, and released his other hand to help ease it on.

He kissed my neck again, sending my body into overdrive. I would have done anything to have him inside me. I reached back and grabbed him, helping ease him in me, then placed my hand back on the counter to support myself. I let out a loud, quick exhale and bit my lower lip.

"You okay?" he whispered.

All I could do was moan and arch my back towards him, pressing my ass in his lower stomach. He kissed my neck and began moving in and out, slowly at first, and then more aggressively.

I gasped and closed my eyes. I wanted it to go on forever. He felt so good in me, something I had never felt before.

He was running his hands all over my spine and butt as he pulsed in and out. He was arousing something in me I didn't even know existed. I could feel him getting harder and harder. I could feel my body succumbing to his as his moans grew louder and louder.

Then he couldn't handle it anymore, and with one final thrust, I felt every nerve in my body convulse as I tried to dig my nails into the kitchen counter. Every gasp of air in my body exhaled as I lay on the counter and felt James's chest resting on my back. We stayed there a moment, both feeling exhausted and exhilarated.

He kissed the nape of my neck and then rose and playfully slapped my ass. I smiled as I lifted myself off the counter and went to pull my pants up.

I turned to face him as I finished buttoning, and he wrapped his arms around my waist and pulled me and kissed me again. A long, hard kiss . . . the kind that meant more than either of us wanted to admit. He pulled back, brushed my hair off my forehead, and kissed it. "I could get used to this, Finn Harper," he said and smiled down at me.

I had never been one of those people who fell in love fast or easily. In fact, I had spent most of my time since Nick actively avoiding feeling anything for a man whatsoever. They were simply a dick to me and nothing else. I played fast and loose with their feelings in high school and spent my years outside Hadleigh being nearly celibate. But this man had me revisiting things I hadn't felt since I was fifteen, things I had pushed so far out of the realm of possibility with my complicated past that I figured they would never be in the cards for me. He was looking at me the way I had always longed for someone to look at me.

Post coitus, we grabbed the wine and the Chinese food and

headed out to the back porch. The box still sat on the table with the journal lying facedown, half open, the pages touching the top of the box. We sat down on the swing, each grabbing a box of food and chopsticks, and leaned back, snuggling next to each other under the old blanket. It was strange how normal and easy this felt. It was almost like we had done it a hundred times before. He set his Chinese food box between his legs and reached forward and grabbed the wine. He put it to his lips and took a sip then passed it to me. I did the same, reminding me of Catholics drinking from the cup during communion like I had seen in movies, and I couldn't help but wonder if this God would ever forgive me of all my sins. I handed the bottle back to him, and he nestled it between his outer thigh and the arm of the swing. He leaned over and used his chopsticks to steal some of my food, winking at me as he leaned back to his side of the swing. We went on like this, eating, sharing bites, communing wine, and not speaking. There was so much to say, but in the moment it felt like nothing needed to be said. As the night sky went from gray to black and the stars began to do their twinkle dance, he finally broke the silence.

"So . . . are we going to talk about the elephant in the room?"

I could feel every hair on my arm stand up, not sure where he was going with this conversation and just which elephant he was referring to.

"Ummm . . ." I began.

He motioned his head towards the table. "The box," he said.

"Right," I said and tried to hide my exhale. "So far there hasn't been a lot to share. She seems to be struggling with something but hasn't come out and said it yet. Other than that, it turns out she knew the day I lost my virginity, right here on this swing, no less." I quickly looked away and started to blush, realizing I was oversharing.

"Right here, huh?" he patted the small space between us. "How old were you?"

"Wow. We are going there, huh?" I grinned. "I will answer as long as your next question isn't how many people I have slept with."

"Deal," he said. "And for the record, I am not as innocent as I look either."

"I never said you looked innocent," I started. "And with the moves I saw earlier, I can tell that wasn't your first time."

"It was one of the first times that ever mattered." He smiled and began to blush, as well.

"Dammit, James," I began. "This isn't supposed to be happening. This was supposed to be a quick thing for me. I was coming to bury my mom and throw out all her shit. Now here I am, knee deep in her life story, waiting for the big reveal, and my emotions are all tangled up with a guy I barely know."

He reached over and took my hand in his. "Finn, I didn't plan on any of this either. But one thing I know for sure is that this is something I haven't felt in a long time. I know it isn't orthodox, and it was a bit of a surprise, but I can't help myself. Every time I see you . . . I can't help it. I wish I could. I know this is far from simple, but I . . . I don't know."

I looked down at his hand enveloping mine and felt my stomach twist. This place was becoming one surprise after another. I didn't know what to say to him just yet. I wasn't ready to commit to this. I was still holding out hope that something would take a bad turn and I could make an easy exit. I looked up and we locked eyes. Fuck. I was screwed.

"Fifteen," I finally muttered.

"What?"

"You asked how old I was. I was fifteen."

"My turn for a question now. Why are you here? Why Hadleigh?"

He looked down into the white box with red Chinese letters across it and aimlessly dug around with his chopstick. I could tell this was something he wasn't proud of, but I didn't care. He knew all of me, and now it was time for reciprocity.

He finally looked up and swallowed before he said, "Honestly, I grew up in a simple house with an 'all too normal' family. No highs or lows, just in between. I know it sounds nuts, but I came here looking for something more. Something out of the ordinary. I am not sure why I thought I would find it in a small town, but I guess I was right," he finished and squeezed my thigh again.

"I found you," he reiterated, in case I didn't catch his drift.

"That you did." I smiled.

"So . . . fifteen . . . and he was one of your many conquests?" he joked.

"He was my high school boyfriend. My first love." I trailed off.

"What ever happened to you two?"

I scrunched my face a little, reliving the pain for a moment. "That's a story for another night and another bottle of wine," I said, hoping he would let it go.

"Finn Harper, you are going to be the death of me," he mocked.

If only he knew how close to home that statement hit.

"So, James, exactly how well do you know my Finny?"

"Not sure exactly. As deep as Finn lets one get, I guess."

"Deep, huh? Sounds awfully sexual, babe . . . ha ha ha."

"I don't kiss and tell. But I did finally read *A Light in the Darkness*, and I will say that Finn is one hell of a writer and quite a creative soul."

# grace

That night had been the death of Grace's innocence. She spent the next few years of high school putting on one hell of a show. She was fun, sweet, outgoing, bubbly, and more popular than any other girl in her class. She was now the longtime girlfriend of the quarterback, Beau Boyton, and she was his head cheerleader. People in the halls would whisper about her beauty and charm. Every guy wanted her, and every girl wanted to be her.

But every day when Grace walked in the front door at Amgine Farm, she would turn the act off and try her best to stay hidden and unnoticed. Her mother was usually too drunk or high to see her, but she knew that her mother was aware of what was happening behind the closed doors. Her mother would holler at her father from time to time to leave her alone, but she would end up meeting the same fate as Grace, minus the rape. He was too disgusted by her to even try to have sex with her. He would leave that act for Grace. He would sneak into her room in the middle of the night, hand over her mouth, and force himself on her, the whole time promising to end Beau's life if she told anyone. She would take it and she would like it, he would tell her. If she fought back, he would hit her hard, usually in places that she could easily hide, although the cheerleading outfit sometimes proved difficult.

When she and Beau would be intimate, she would lie her way through the bruises, saying they were from cheerleading practice and missed catches by the underclassmen. Beau seemed to believe her, so she kept up the lies, fearing if she told him that her father would kill him.

She still loved Beau with all her heart, and his touch still reeked of love to her. Perfecting her ability at separating her love for Beau from her abuse at home, she was able to have sex with Beau and enjoy it, all the while knowing that she would probably have to do it again when she got home. It seemed the more time she spent with Beau, the more aggressive and jealous her father got, and so the more the attacks happened.

She would look in the mirror and wish she wasn't so pretty, wish she was fat and ugly like her mother. Then maybe she wouldn't have brought this on herself. That is what he said, right? That this was all her fault; she made him do this. On the surface she knew this couldn't be true, but somewhere deep down, she believed it and blamed herself.

A few weeks before her eighteenth birthday, she began to get sick. It started with a bad headache and then turned into exhaustion and nausea. When things didn't let up after a few days and her period went missing, she drove her mother's old Celebrity to the five and dime and tried her best to secretly buy a pregnancy test in a small town. She didn't want to go home to do it, so she snuck into the bathroom at the Tin 'n' Grits, and there in the dark gray stall where Jill E. had written that she loved Tom P., Grace watched a light pink plus sign show up on her white stick. There with her pants still around her knees, she sat and cried.

She wasn't sure how long she was in there crying until she heard someone tap lightly on the door and mutter, "Are you okay, dear?"

"Fine," she lied between sobs. "Just fine."

She stood, pulled her pants up, wiped the tears off her cheeks, and threw the test in her purse. She and Beau tried to be safe, but most of the time they let passion get the best of them and just wanted to "really feel each other." She thought there was no way she would get pregnant. She was a teenager and that stuff just didn't happen. But here she was, knocked up by a boy/man who was about to leave on a full ride to Georgia Tech at the end of the year. It wasn't his wit that had gotten him that scholarship; it was his body and ability, the same thing that had gotten her into this mess, as well.

It wasn't until she was pulling back into the driveway of Amgine that it dawned on her that this baby might not be Beau's. While the attacks from her father were awful, they had become so routine that she almost totally blocked them from her mind altogether. He couldn't have gotten her pregnant. He was too old. He had to be shooting blanks, she was sure. He must have at least gotten a vasectomy. The way he looked at Elizabeth always made Grace assume the last thing he wanted was another kid with that woman. There was a don't ask don't tell policy at their house though, so she had no idea if he was still firing.

Elizabeth was a pro when it came to don't ask don't tell. Grace had watched her look at Al with suspicious eyes, and in her drunkest, most vulnerable moments, she would find the courage to holler at him about his disgusting ways, but usually she looked the other way. Grace knew if she pushed too hard that she would get a beating the likes of the ones Grace endured, and so Elizabeth took the easy route, in the process feeding her daughter to the wolf. It was in those moments Grace wasn't sure who she hated more, the wolf or the cowardly mouse.

She put the car in park and again began to cry. Resting her head on the steering wheel, she wondered what to do. How was she going to tell Beau? What would he do?

She collected herself to the best of her ability before heading into the house; she couldn't let on that anything was amiss or he would prey on her vulnerability. She opened the door, set her purse on the bench, and quickly, quietly snuck into her room and lay down. She quietly cried herself to sleep with one hand resting on her lower abdomen.

Grace woke up the next morning with her hand still on her stomach and the side of her cheek lightly stuck to her tear-crusted pillow. She wasn't sure the time or how long she had slept, but she was awoken by a light tapping on her window that at first she thought she was imagining. It came again. Tap . . . tap . . . tap. She sat up, walked over to the window, and lightly pulled back the paisley drapes.

Beau was standing there, smiling ear to ear, so proud of himself for successfully surprising her. He was holding a bunch of daisies he had picked from the side ditch on his way over, the black dirt still clinging to their rough-ended green stems, and motioned for her to come out and join him. She couldn't help but smile and think of what an amazing dad he would be. She held up one finger and shut the drapes. She quickly brushed her teeth in the small bathroom attached to her room and splashed a little water on her face. She threw on sunglasses to hide her red-streaked eyes. She knew she needed to tell him, but she didn't want him to read it on her face.

Grace tiptoed out of her room and gently opened the front door. The clock on the hallway read 5:05 a.m. as she shut the door quietly behind her. She turned and ran into Beau's waiting arms. He kissed her on the head and squeezed her tight. For a split second, she thought everything would be all right.

She hopped into his truck, never bothering to ask where they were going or why it needed to happen so early. She didn't care. As long as she was with him, she felt safe and happy. He pulled up to Lake Hadleigh, the same place they had their first date. He put the car in park and ran around to open her door before she could.

"Milady," he said and motioned for her to step out of the truck.

She smiled and looked at him a little quizzically. He shut the door and grabbed her hand. His hand felt rough, like the hand of a man who could protect her, a man who would provide for her.

They walked over to the lake, not saying a word as the sun began to find its place on the horizon. The closer they got to the lake, she thought she could begin to make out what looked like a boat on the shore. It wasn't as much of a boat as it was a canoe. Inside the canoe sat two fishing poles and a cooler. She looked over at him, smiled, and pulled on his arm to bring him closer to her.

"Is that boat for us?" she asked.

He just squeezed her hand tighter and kissed her head that was pressed against his bicep.

"Maybe, baby."

He smiled. She smiled, too, then looked down and winced as the word hit her.

"You okay?" he asked.

"Yeah. Of course," she said. "So what brings us to this boat at five in the morning?"

"Gracy! It's our anniversary. Don't you remember?"

Amidst feeling sick and the pregnancy revelation, she had lost track of the dates and hadn't looked at a calendar long enough to have the date ring a bell. Now she felt like an idiot.

"Oh, Beau! I am sorry! I haven't been myself. I didn't even look at the calendar. I am the worst!"

He stopped walking for a second, turned, and looked at her. "Grace Harper, you are the best thing that has ever been mine. You don't ever talk about the love of my life that way," he said and tucked one of her blond ringlets behind her ear.

She pressed up onto her tiptoes, allowing her toes to slip to the front of her flip-flops, just to kiss him. This man was her forever.

They got to the boat and he shoved it into the water, reaching back to help her in before hopping in without tipping the whole thing over.

He grabbed the oars and began to row them to the middle of the lake. Grace sat with a blanket he had put in the bottom of the canoe, now draped over her legs, and her hands grasped, anxiously rubbing together.

He watched her hands fidget and did his best to lighten the mood.

"We had to get up early because the best fishing happens at dawn," he said, hoping to distract her mind.

She smiled. "That makes sense, I suppose. Honestly I don't think I have been fishing since I was like eight."

"Well you are in for a treat, Gracy, because you are with the best fisherman in all of Hadleigh," he proudly announced and puffed his chest out a little.

She smirked. "Oh is that so?"

"Yes, ma'am."

She leaned forward and kissed him, trying ever so carefully not to rock the boat. She wanted them to be like this forever, happy, and carefree. She knew that she had to tell him, and she couldn't wait long.

They finally got to "the perfect spot," as Beau had called it. He set the oars down, and the boat came to a perfect stop. There was no breeze this early in the morning, and so it was them, the fish, and the stillness.

He baited a pole and gently stepped over to her, handing her the pole, and finding his way behind her, trying to keep his balance as the boat swayed. She grabbed the pole as he placed his arms over hers and his hands on top of hers.

"Okay, babe, let's get you fishing," he said, and she could feel his breath on her neck, slightly turning her on.

He helped guide her back and throw out a cast. She could feel his chest against her back and wanted to nuzzle into it and cry. Here they were fishing and smiling, but all that was about to change forever.

The bobber fell into the water with a plunk, and Beau helped her reel the line back a little to click it into place.

"Okay, babe, now you just wait for the bobber to go down and then reel like hell." He took his hands off hers and left her to man her pole alone. The absence of him behind her sparked the tears she had been holding back.

"Grace, you'll be fine. I am right here," he said, seemingly caught off guard that she was upset to be fishing alone.

She lowered the pole to her lap as the sobs came harder and faster. Beau moved out from behind her and took his spot on the bench across from her. He placed his hands on her knees and waited for her to ease up and talk.

"Grace, what is wrong?"

She finally looked up at him and saw so much concern in his eyes. He loved her so much. She hoped that wouldn't change after what she was about to say.

"Beau . . ." She choked down a few more sobs. "I'm . . . I'm . . . I'm pregnant."

His jaw fell a little but he kept his grip on her knees.

"Are you sure?" he said.

"Yeah. I took a test last night."

"Wow." He exhaled. "So . . . we are having a baby?" He looked at her half asking/half confused.

"Yeah," she muttered between tears, not able to make eye contact, afraid that she would see in his eyes that they were over.

He squeezed her knees. "Hey . . . look at me," he said.

She tilted her head up as her watery eyes met his.

"It is going to be okay, Grace. We are going to make this work. I love you, and you love me. This isn't how we planned it, but there are worse things, ya know?" he said and tried to eke out a smile.

She swallowed hard, realizing that somehow telling him about the baby had become the simple part, but what was about to come next would destroy him.

"Beau, that's not all . . ."

"You remember how everyone thought she would amount to big things, and instead she got herself knocked up by a random and amounted to nothing? What a sad turn of events."

"A child isn't sad. It is a gift. And I bet we don't know her whole story. I am sure there was a lot more to her than meets the eye."

"Oh, Wanda, you are such a damn optimist."

# finn

"And that's about all . . ." I finished telling James about all that had happened with Nick and my gramps. We lay among the dark, evening shadows out on the back porch swing for a while, playing footsie under the blanket and trying not to talk about the future or the box. It was after midnight when he turned to me and casually said, "Should we go to bed?" as if it was something we did together every night.

"Yeah," I responded to my own shock. And just like that, we collected the Chinese boxes, empty wine bottle, and blanket and headed back into the house. We threw everything away, and with the blanket still in hand, headed up the stairs to retire for the night. There was no sexual undertone, just two people going to simply sleep in the same bed.

Pausing at the top of the stairs, I wasn't sure which bedroom to head into. Naturally I wanted to head to my old room, but the queen bed suddenly seemed dauntingly small, and it seemed silly to let the master go unused, so we turned left and entered into the room that had now been passed on through three generations. I turned to him and casually said, "Sorry. It used to be my mom's room, and obviously I haven't had time to change anything, so please forgive the décor."

He smiled. "I wasn't even looking at anything but you."

"Smooth," I retorted.

"It wasn't a line," he responded.

"Mmmhmm." I winked.

I threw the blanket onto the bed, and headed into the bathroom to see if there was a spare toothbrush he could use. Never in my life had I looked for a toothbrush for a man to use. I never let anyone stay overnight, so there was no need for morning rituals.

Digging through the drawers, I came across several items that didn't seem like they would belong to my mother. A man's razor, a blue toothbrush, and some aftershave. I figured they were my gramps's left over from eons ago and went back to rummaging. The images of those items stayed in the back of my head, though. It didn't quite add up that she would have kept anything of my grandfather's, and my mother had cut back on the number of men in her life after Gramps died, so I wasn't sure who else's it could have been. That being said, I was aware that I wasn't super involved in my mother's life, and so she could have had a secret lover that I was unaware of.

I found a spare toothbrush under the sink and brought it out to James. He was fluffing the pillows and laying out the blankets.

"So this is your side?" I said jokingly. "What if I wanted that side?"

"I will take whatever side you deem worthy," he said.

I smiled and handed him the toothbrush. "I don't have a side. You pick."

He leaned forward and kissed me.

"I am going to take a quick shower," I said once our lips separated.

"Okay. I'll get comfy."

I turned and headed into the bathroom, and shut the door behind me. It wasn't that I didn't want him to come in the shower with me, it was just that no one had seen me fully naked in years, and I wasn't sure I was ready for that kind of exposure.

I turned the shower on hot, and as I waited for it to warm, I sat on the ledge of the tub, thinking about this night and smiling. I hated myself for my Hallmark emotions but also kind of loved the feeling.

I stripped down and hopped in. The warm water ran over my flat chest and instantly relaxed me. I couldn't remember a time when I had gotten in the shower after sex and didn't feel dirty or wrong. For the very first time, I felt nothing but joy and peace. This man liked me for me, not pretenses, no excuses, just me.

Suddenly I felt his hands running over my hips and towards my stomach. I felt my breath catch in my throat. I was about to turn around, but he pressed his body against mine and kissed my left shoulder blade.

"I—I thought the door was—"

"Locked?" he finished. "You must have forgot… or maybe you subconsciously meant to leave it unlocked for me." He kissed my neck and I could feel his smile.

"I just . . . I . . . um . . . " I stuttered, suddenly feeling the need to cover my body parts with my hands.

"Finn," he began, kissing my ear this time and pressing himself harder against me, "when I told you I wanted all of you, I meant it."

And just like that he spun me around and looked me up and down. I couldn't help but feel unmasked. I wanted to look away but waited patiently for his glance to meet mine. I knew that I cared about this man and that the new me should let him see me, all of me.

He ran his hand up from my waist, over my smooth, scarred chest, and up to my face, and I let him. His eyes followed. He took my head in his hand and kissed me. He leaned closer and pressed his chest against mine and whispered in my ear, "You are beautiful."

That was it, the moment I let my guard down. I wrapped my arms around him, grabbed his back, pulled him in, and began kissing his chest, making my way down his stomach, down to his sculpted abs that left a V pointing the way to his shaft. I put my mouth on him. James gripped my shoulder, torn between dragging me away and holding me in place.

Finally, he couldn't take it anymore, he pulled me up, kissed me hard, and spun me around. I could feel my body surround him. He leaned forward, going even deeper, and I gasped as I prepared for another amazing encounter.

Post intimacy and lots more kissing, we dried off and got into bed, still naked, yet oddly comfortable. I leaned over, snuggled into the crook of his shoulder, and let him kiss me on the forehead.

I looked up at him, and then I let myself close my eyes and fall into the deepest sleep I had experienced in a long time.

The warm sun beating on my face finally awoke me as I peered at the clock and realized I had slept until 10:07 a.m., something I hadn't done since my college days after stumbling home post–bar close.

I rolled over, excited to see James's face, but he wasn't there. On his pillow, on "his side," lay a note.

Finn,

Had to head into the office. Last night was incredible, to say the least. I put a pot of coffee on and left you a bagel from Blue Moon. Call me later.

Love,
James

I smiled, wishing he was here but appreciating his thoughtfulness and sincerity. I took the note and held it close to my heart, rolled back over to my side of the bed, pulled the blankets up to my chin, squeezed them tight, closed my eyes, and smiled. Dammit—this boy had me lying in my bed and smiling. I didn't come here for this, but I guess it found me anyway. I drifted back to sleep, hoping to dream about last night's events.

I finally got my ass out of bed for good at 12:16 p.m. I was well rested, and happy, a feeling I wasn't used to but which was growing on me. I threw on my sweats, ran a brush through my hair and another over my teeth, and headed down the stairs for some coffee and that bagel my lover had left. The thought of this made me smile again. The thought of last night kind of made me want a cigarette, too, but I was staying strong.

My phone still lay on the kitchen counter, and after I poured myself a cup of coffee, I grabbed it and the bagel and took a seat.

I ripped a piece off the bagel and threw it in my mouth as I unlocked my phone. I had thirteen new text messages, mainly from Pey and Letty wondering what I was doing and how it was going. One from James reiterating what his note said, in case I missed it, and two from my editor, checking in to see how the next book was coming. I cringed a little. The truth was that I had yet to start writing the next book. I had a few ideas, but nothing that motivated me to write quite yet. I knew he would want pages soon, but I was still trying to develop a character, a plot, really anything.

I did my due diligence responding to Pey and Letty, saying all was fine and I was still working on the house. I didn't mention more about the box or journal, since nothing of note had really come out of that yet. Pey responded, immediately offering to come help. I told her that I would text her later. Maybe she could bring dinner.

I texted James back, something corny that would have never come out of my mouth before, and told him I would call him later. I tried not to panic as I hit Send. Maybe I did need that cigarette.

Last, I responded to Hank, my editor, with some bullshit text along the lines of "It's coming along," and left it at that, hoping he would back off for a few weeks. I was sure he wouldn't.

I left the phone on the counter, grabbed my bagel and coffee, and headed back out to the back porch. I took my spot on the porch swing, smiled, thinking about last night out here, and leaned forward to grab the journal. I flipped it open, took a bite of bagel, and leaned back to read more of what I assumed would be the boring musings of my mother's simple life.

I immediately choked on my bagel when I saw the date at the top of the entry.

May 16, 2000

The date of the accident.

"I don't know. I think there may be something there."

"What! No way, babe! I have never seen Finny with some-one."

"I don't know. Maybe it is just in my head, but I like the idea in there."

"Might be a tough sell, babe. Finny wants out of here like yesterday. I don't know if you can change that."

# grace

Beau choked down his rage and could feel the fire burning behind his eyes when Grace got done telling him about what Al had been doing to her for the last three years. His fists were clenched, and she thought there a was chance that he would likely kill Al if given the chance. While no one would like Al dead more than Grace, she didn't want Beau's future, or their future, to be clouded by jail time, so she tried to talk him down.

In the end, they came up with a plan to run away together and get married at the end of the school year. If they were married, then she could live with him on campus in married housing and they could raise the baby together. She would go to school at night to become a journalist, and they would be far away from Al. They only downfall was that Grace would have to give up her job offer at the *Gazette*. She didn't love the idea, but she loved Beau more.

They had it all figured out as they pulled into the driveway at Amgine. Beau would do his best to protect her until the school year was over, and then they would get the hell out of dodge and never look back.

He put the truck in park and ran around to open her door

like the gentleman he was. He would have done it before, but now that she was carrying his baby, he was all the more loving, rubbing his hand over her stomach as she exited.

He walked her to the front door, fighting back against every instinct in his body to go hunt Al down and beat him to death. Beau was fairly sure it wouldn't be much of a fight—he was damn near twice the size of thin, old, farmer Al. Grace could see the rage brewing in his eyes and leaned forward to kiss him and remind him of the plan. Any interaction with Al would foil the plan, and they didn't want that.

She kissed him again and walked through the front door, dropped her purse on the table, and went into her room. She fell asleep again with her hand on her stomach and a mess on her mind.

Beau left the farm intent on getting her a ring. No woman he was going to marry wasn't going to have a beautiful ring. He headed into the next town over and spent a few hours in and out of antique stores and pawn shops looking for the perfect ring and a great deal.

Grace slept through most of the day, getting up a few times to try to choke down some bread or crackers. She lounged around, flipping through magazines or watching TV. She did her best to avoid Al and keep a low profile so he wouldn't notice anything was out of the ordinary with her.

Her day faded into night, and she crashed again early, trying to sleep off the nausea and worry.

The ear-shattering sound of the door being slammed awoke her from her slumber. The sun was barely on the horizon, and Al was yelling something at her from across the room, standing in her doorway. She sat up, sleep still lingering in the corners of her eyes, and tried to make sense of what was happening when he threw the pregnancy test at her. It landed on her lap on the bed. She looked up at him as he came closer to her and cold cocked her upside the head. She fell back onto the pillow, and closed her eyes as the tears began to flow and her eye began to throb.

"Sit up!" he yelled.

She lay there, unable to move, praying he would just leave, though she didn't have a religious bone in her body.

"Sit up, Grace. Dammit, girl. Look at me." He grabbed her by the shoulders and sat her up in the bed.

She tried to open her eyes to look at him, but between the tears and pain, she could only squint. She could smell the moonshine on his breath as he got right in her face.

"Pregnant?" he yelled. "You got yourself pregnant!"

She took a deep breath, trying to think of how to respond.

"Dammit, Grace. If only you didn't make me do it. If you weren't such a tease and a slut," he barked, his breath making her feel slightly drunk.

"What in the hell are we going to do now?" he yelled.

She exhaled and muttered, "It's not yours."

Al began to laugh. "Not mine . . . you think that dumb jock of yours has better swimmers than mine!"

"It is not yours," Grace said a little louder this time.

Al swung back and hit her again, this time on the other side of her face.

"You stupid girl!" he yelled.

She lay there, knowing better than to say anything at this point. Wondering if maybe he didn't actually have that vasectomy or whether he was just too drunk to remember.

"Now we have to deal with this," he said. "First things first. No more Beau."

She gasped and squinted at him. "You can't stop me from seeing him. I love him, and I am having his baby."

He grabbed her by the shoulders, sat her up, got an inch from her face and said, "If you see him ever again, or call this baby his ever again, I will kill him, you, and this baby! You understand?"

She turned her head away from him, trying to breathe in air that didn't make her feel tipsy. He took one hand off her shoulder and grabbed her face.

"You see him or mention him, he dies."

Then he threw her back onto the bed and slammed the door behind him.

Grace knew that Al was serious too. From the way he hit her and his extensive shotgun collection, the odds that he would follow through with killing Beau were good. He had nothing to lose. She, on the other hand, was about to lose everything.

Beau showed up later that afternoon with the ring he finally found two towns over at a vintage shop. It was from the 1920s, a half-carat diamond flanked with two smaller diamonds on each side. He loved how it represented their soon-to-be family of three. He spent everything he had on that ring and was incredibly eager to give it to Grace.

He knocked on the front door. Grace opened it, and immediately his jaw dropped. She looked like she had been in a bad bar fight. He lurched forward and enveloped her.

"Oh my God, Grace. Did he do this to you?"

She didn't say a word, just started crying.

"I will kill him, I swear," Beau snarled.

"No," she countered, quietly knowing what would happen if he did, but not fully able to convince herself that she didn't want him to do it anyway.

"Oh, Grace." Beau rubbed up and down her back.

Al appeared at the top of the stairs, watching them. Beau looked up over Grace's shoulder and they locked eyes. Beau squinted, giving him his best evil eye, when he realized that Al was holding a shotgun in his hands.

Beau flung Grace around behind him and blocked her with his body. Then he spread his arms out and yelled, "What the hell, Al?"

Al cocked the shotgun and pointed it in their direction.

Calmly he said, "Get out of here, Beau."

"No. Don't shoot. We are going to handle this. We are going to get married." Beau went to fish for the ring in his pocket.

"Grace!" Al shouted. "It's time to tell Beau what we discussed."

"Discussed?" Beau countered. "Looks to me that you did more hitting than talking, old man!"

Al yelled and shot his gun up into the ceiling. "Dammit, Grace, tell him or I'll kill him now!" Bits of drywall fell from the ceiling, spraying dust through the air.

Beau turned to Grace, who was sobbing behind him.

"Grace?" Beau said, the pain in his eyes digging a deeper canyon into Grace's broken heart.

"We can't do this anymore, Beau. We can't be together. I am sorry. I didn't want it to end like this. I love you, I just . . ." Grace mustered amidst sobs.

"That's enough. Get the hell out!" Al hollered, coming down the stairs still shaking his gun at Beau, so angry you could imagine the steam coming out of his ears like the cartoons Grace used to watch in her simple childhood that she was now longing for.

"Grace, what are you talking about? I love you. We have a plan." Beau reached out and put his hands on her stomach, his touch making Grace's breath catch in her throat.

Grace started crying even harder. "I know. I'm sorry. It's just that . . ."

And then Al shoved his gun against Beau's spine, begging for him to pull the trigger.

"You heard her, Beau. Time to go. And if you ever think about coming back here, it will be the last thing you ever do," Al yelled.

Grace removed his hands from her stomach and stepped out of the way for him to pass. Beau stood there for a moment, looking at her in utter confusion. Finally, he began to walk to the truck, opened the door, and turned the key in the ignition. Grace watched him look back at her one last time as he put the truck in reverse and faded into the distance. Every bone in her body wished he would rush back and save her, but she had begged him not to, and for everything Beau lacked, the one thing he did was listen, especially to Grace. She loved him for this, and hated herself.

Al ushered Grace back into the house with the tip of his gun and reiterated that she was never to see Beau again or he'd pay. He shoved her into her room, where she flopped on the bed and began to cry. For the first time in her life, she decided to pray. She didn't know how or where to begin, so she folded her hands and just started talking.

"Dear God, I know we haven't talked before. I am sorry. I am not even sure how to do this, so I hope it comes out right. I am in quite a mess and I don't know what to do. I can't be with the man I love and am being held captive by another who hurts me. I feel so helpless and hopeless. If you can find a way for Beau and me to be together again, I promise I will do right by you. I will attend church and be buried in a church. If you keep up your end of the bargain, I will keep up mine. Please, Lord, I am so lost."

She unfolded her hands and cried herself to sleep for many more nights to come.

· · · · · · · · · · · · ·

It turned out the only good thing about being pregnant was that Al laid off her. He seemed disinterested in beating or raping a pregnant woman, and so she spent her days with him dropping her off at school and him picking her up. She and Beau would exchange longing glances in the hallways, but she knew better than to let it go any further. Al was serious about his threats, and she wouldn't let that affect Beau.

Eventually school ended, Beau moved on, and she gave birth to a beautiful girl in October of 1985, naming her Finley, a hidden nod to the moment in the canoe with Beau, their last moment. The fins of the fish catching the early morning sun rays and throwing them around the water like glitter. That was the last day for a long time she saw glitter in anything around her.   Soon after Finley was born, the attacks from Al returned. They seemed less frequent and less intense once the baby arrived, but they still persisted. Grace resented that baby from the start because it had torn her away from Beau and had coincidently become the apple of Al's eye. She assumed this was because he thought it was his baby, but in her heart she always believed Finn belonged to Beau. As Finn grew, Grace would swear she could see Beau's eyes and jawline—even if it was just wishful thinking.

To combat her resentment and anger, Grace would sneak off and write for the *Gazette*, or she would bring home random men from the bar to try to screw away any pain she felt. She did it in part to feel something, anything, and also to piss off Al. She knew she was playing with fire, but she needed to feel at least a little in control of her life, so she tempted fate. A different man every week, a different reaction from Al. If Al ever found out that she was writing her thoughts and feelings for the world to see, though, he would have pulled the plug on the whole endeavor, so she kept it a secret from him and everyone else. That was the only way it would last. Writing was the only good thing about not running away.

She had no good reason to stay. The life she was leading was less about living and merely about staying alive. If she were truly honest with herself, the only reason she didn't run was Finn. A good mother she was not, but she surely was not going to let that old man do to Finn what he had done to her, and if sticking around and taking the brunt of it protected Finn, then she was going to make that sacrifice, the one her mother never did for her.

She missed Beau every single day. She would hear about him in town and write about him in the *Gazette*. He was the love of her life, and she knew she would never be that happy again.

Every time she looked at Finn, she was reminded of Beau and how much she missed him, so she decided it best to no longer look at her. She worried that by neglecting her she was feeding Finn to Al for a beating, but she truly believed that Al loved Finn in a way that would never cause him to hurt her. And he had Grace to beat on, so she hoped he would leave Finn alone.

For years she watched the two of them pal around and grow closer. After her mother died, Grace felt even more alone somehow. She hated her mother because she knew that her mom was aware of what Al did and didn't try to stop him, but somehow her being gone was worse than her being here.

Once Elizabeth was dead, the beatings came back in full force. Grace wasn't sure if it was out of anger or freedom, but Al had found a second wind, and Grace was suffering the repercussions. She sunk into a depression deeper than she had ever known. She became a shell of her former self, which wasn't that great to begin with. She wondered what there was to live for. Why should she go on?

Then one day she decided to end it all—not her, but him. She decided to kill Al. It wasn't without warning. He had finally crossed the line she told herself she would never let him cross.

It began one sunny afternoon at Amgine. Grace had returned from the *Gazette* and was indulging in a Winston on the back porch. Al, the man she had once called Father, and the child who looked like her Beau were out in the garden. Finn was a teenager now, with a boyfriend in tow, a mess of emotions. Even as a child, she had never wanted to wear dresses or play dolls; she'd always been rough and tumble, fight and dirt. She never concerned herself with makeup or clothes. As a former homecoming queen, social butterfly, and boy magnet, Grace knew what it was to be the girl everyone fawned over, and yet here she was watching her daughter try to go unnoticed.

Finn was picking weeds out of the garden, dressed in her usual baggy jeans and combat boots. The shirt was a light purple only because it was one of her "get dirty" shirts; otherwise, she would never be caught dead in purple. At times Grace wondered if Finn preferred women to men, but then she had come home with Nick, all starry-eyed and horny. *Her fashion choices obviously don't match her sexual choices,* she thought. But today she was in a typical girly color with her hair pulled back in a pony, as it always was. Had it not been for the garden gloves, one would have thought she was a regular teenage girl, one who could become prom queen, one who the boys would chase. Sure, she could use a stick of lipstick and an eyebrow plucking, but she was naturally pretty enough to hold her own.

Grace tilted her head, enjoying for a moment this beautiful child she had brought into this world. Born amidst chaos was such beauty. Then out of her peripheral vision, she spotted Al, the man who created the chaos, the monster behind it all. He opened the garden gate, said something to Finn that she couldn't hear, and approached her from behind. Grace took in another puff of cigarette and watched Al lean over Finn and pat her hair, starting at the scalp and stroking her ponytail, twisting the ends through his fingers.

Grace felt the smoke catch in her throat. What he was doing was something she knew all too well; she felt in her bones what he was gearing up for. He had seen the way Finn looked at Nick; it was the way she had once looked at Beau. His next move was one she wasn't going to allow. Like it or not, it was time to bring the pain.

She began researching at the paper ways to do it so no one would find out. She could poison him, drug him, or suffocate him while he slept. She knew this was a new low and extremely risky, but she didn't care. She had nothing to live for anymore, and so she decided he should die.

Grace finally found how she would do it. And as she snuck out to Al's truck and as she began cutting the brake line, she thought about Finn. Sure, this would affect her, but she was fifteen now, had a boyfriend, and was seemingly less interested in her "gramps," as she called him. Yes, it would hurt her. But in the long run, it would be better for both of them. Grace could finally be the mother she dreamed, free from fear and anger. And she would be protecting Finn from the possibility that Al might eventually attack her too. Grace decided the benefits outweighed the consequences as she shut the hood of the truck and went back into the house and smiled for the first time in sixteen years.

"I thought when she had the baby she would go back to the sweet Grace we knew in high school, but she went crazy instead. Man after man. Night after night."

"I know! I felt so bad for the baby. I wondered if I should go over there and help."

"Oh please, Pam. You weren't going to go help that tramp. Stop acting like you are such a martyr."

# finn

I wiped the smile off my face as I blinked my eyes again to make sure I was seeing the date correctly. *Holy shit,* I thought as I began to read.

Dear Finn,

I told you when I started this story that I would tell you the whole story, the whole truth, every part of what makes me me, I guess. In order to do that, I have to go back to a time when I was just a little older than you are now. Back to one night in 1983. A night that changed the trajectory of my life forever. You aren't going to like this, and I am sorry, but it is true. January 14, 1983, was the first night that your grandfather raped and beat me. I know that is a lot to take in, and again I am sorry, but you need to know that in order to understand what came after.

I sat up and reread the beginning of the entry again . . . "the first night that your grandfather raped and beat me." What?

This can't be happening. This cannot be true. The man who raised me was not a rapist or a man who beats women. This is wrong. This can't be happening. She must be lying.

Just like that I lurched forward, cupped my hands over my mouth, and ran over to the edge of the back porch and threw up on the lawn. I heaved over and over again. Every time I thought I was done, the text would play through my mind again and I would hurl. By the end, I was dry heaving. Nothing coming out, but I couldn't stop.

Oh my God!

OH MY GOD!

How did this happen? How didn't I know? There is no way he laid a hand on . . . and then I was dry heaving again, even though I wasn't sure if I fully believed her.

Once I finally gained my composure, I turned on the hose next to the porch and splashed some cold water on my face and took a gulp and swished it around and spit. I took a few more long swigs, swallowing and wishing this wasn't true. I could feel the iron minerals in the water tasting like blood in my mouth. I turned off the hose, wiped my face with my hand, and headed back to the swing to try to make sense of this. I needed to keep reading to decide if I really believed her or not.

I won't get into what happened or how often because it will just upset you further, but you need to know that it never fully stopped. It ceased for a while, only when I was pregnant with you, but otherwise was happening regularly. I wanted to run away or tell someone so many times, but he would threaten to kill Beau if I did, and he was the only thing in the word that mattered to me, so I kept quiet.

The night I found out I was pregnant with you led to me finally telling Beau everything. We made plans to finish out the school year and then run away together, get married, and start our family with you. I was never fully sure if you belonged to Beau or Al, but I swear I could see Beau in your eyes and jawline, so I liked to think you were his. Your grandfather thought otherwise and wanted me to end things with Beau. He told me if I ever saw Beau again, he would kill him, so I ended it, and it broke me.

The attacks resumed after I gave birth. I resented you because you made me think of Beau, and you were the apple of your grandfather's eye. He loved you in a way he never loved me. I wanted to be a good mother to you, but I was so depressed and abused that I could barely function. I used men to dull the pain, and alcohol to numb it away. I am sorry I was a shitty mom.

I used to watch the way you and Al interacted and wished I could be that way with you, but I didn't have it in me. I began writing to you after your grandma passed away and I felt more alone than ever.

As you grew, I grew too. I grew more depressed and more angry at your grandfather. Until one day I saw the way Al looked at you, his longing glance, one I knew all too well. That was when I decided I had had enough. I was going to end all the pain and hurt.

You need to know that what happened next I didn't plan on, I never could have planned for. You and Nick had been an item for some time now, and I knew you even gave up your virginity to him. I could see the puppy love in your eyes, even though something always seemed a little off. It reminded me of the way I felt with Beau, that new love, that exciting feeling, and I was so happy for you. You and Nick were seeing each other on a fairly regular basis, and I knew he was bound to make an appearance later that evening, as he usually did.

There was a knock on the door shortly before dusk, and I figured it was Nick so I ignored it, assuming you would get it. When the knock came again, and then once more, I finally got up out of my bed and went to open the front door. There he was. The first time I had seen him in fifteen years. Beau Boyton.

He looked the same, only slightly weathered by time. He was still strapping and handsome, and immediately I felt every nerve in my body come alive. I felt like I had been in hibernation for fifteen years, waiting for this exact moment. Without either of us saying a word, he leaned forward and kissed me. That kiss was more electric than any night I had spent with a man in the last fifteen years. We stood there, lips locked for several minutes. When he finally pulled away, he looked at me and said, "God, I have missed you, Grace Harper. I still love the hell out of you." I smiled and we kissed again. Finally I stepped back and told him how much I missed him and never stopped loving him. In between falling back in love, we would kiss and kiss again. It wasn't until we heard a shotgun cock behind us that we even noticed the world existed outside of us.

I turned around and saw your grandfather standing there with his shotgun at the ready. We all three got into a yelling match, which you must not have heard through your headphones you usually had on. Finally, Beau grabbed my hand and we ran out to his truck, your grandfather in pursuit. I hopped into the passenger side, and we took off down the driveway, your grandpa banging on the hood before turning and running off to the garage and getting in his truck to follow. We raced off down the road and headed to wherever we could that would get us far from here. I looked back a few times and saw your grandpa gaining on us. It was around the bend near the high school that I looked back and saw your grandpa try to brake and lose control of his truck, swaying back and forth before crossing the center line and hitting a Toyota Corolla head on.

Obviously you know that inside that Corolla was Nick, on his way to see you at Amgine. I hollered for Beau to stop, and we got out and tried our best to tend to Nick while we waited for the ambulance to come. I would like to tell you that I tried to help your grandpa, too, but that would be a lie. Not only did I not help him, I was the one who caused the accident, and not just because of the "getaway" with Beau. I had cut his brake line earlier in the day, hoping that he would lose control, as he did, and meet his fate. What I never meant to happen was for him to hurt someone else in the process. He had spent too much time hurting other people for him to have one final act on his way out. I never meant for Nick to get tangled up in this. Never meant for anyone to die but your grandfather. I know that doesn't help.

I know it must hurt you to find out that I am the one who killed your "gramps," and coincidently your Nick, but I need you to know that I had my reasons. Not for Nick, of course—that was a tragic, terrible accident—but for wanting your grandfather gone. He made my existence a living hell, and I wanted it to stop. I know you may not understand, and I have to live with that, but I did what I did, and I never looked back. I am so sorry about Nick. I wish I could have saved him.

Love,
G. E. H.

Tears had fallen all over the journal. I hadn't even realized I was crying until I looked up, placed my hand on my damp cheek, and felt my face was sopping wet. I thought for a minute about going to the police, but she was dead now so what did it matter? I thought about how devastated I was to lose my gramps and Nick in the same night, but now to know what my gramps was doing to my mother and what my mother did to him? How in the hell was I supposed to process all of this? I needed a cigarette and a drink. The house had neither, and so I called Pey.

"Hey you," she answered. "How's it—"

"I need a stiff drink and a pack of cigarettes now!"

"Oh my, Finn. Are you okay?"

"No. Cigarettes and booze. Now."

"I thought you weren't smoking any—"

"Dammit, Pey. You said you would do anything for me. What I need is liquor and Winstons—like yesterday."

She stammered a little. "Okay," she said, "I'll be right there. I'll bring you something for dinner, too, okay?"

I hung up. I was too upset to speak anymore. We had gone from my mother's mundane musings to several of the biggest bombshells of my life. My gramps used to beat and molest my mom. I could be his child, or the love of her life's. My mother is the reason that Nick and Gramps are dead. What the fuck!

And then there I was again, running with my hands cupping my mouth, ready to vomit over the edge. Nothing came up. I sat there, leaning over the edge, crying and dry heaving until I felt myself become faint. It was one of those moments in life when, as you get older, people start telling you who the characters in your life truly are, not the kid-friendly versions of them. I used to think he was my hero. I used to think he was the good guy. I used to be so naïve. Adults aren't simple; they are complicated. The hero can morph into the villain with just a simple scene change. You want them to stay the way you saw them in your child eyes, but once the rose-colored glasses are off and the darkness is able to seep in, you see for the first time they are flawed, just like everyone else in the world. They will hurt you. Disappoint you. And above all, they will break you. But there are those few who do their best to only bend you, handle you with kid gloves you didn't know they were wearing because you never got close enough to even see their hands. Those hands under the gloves belonged to a woman I thought was hiding behind a mask instead.

The sky started to spin as I went crashing down onto the grass below me.

"I didn't know that she and Beau were back together."

"Duh! They have been all over town together for years, and he brings in the crops from Amgine every week. You must have known."

"Such a shame, I suppose. He was always such a catch."

"You never had a chance. He was Grace's from the get-go."

# grace

The weight of what transpired came crashing down over Grace. The incident with Beau, Al, and Nick left her pretty shaken. But while she knew she should feel remorse, what she mainly felt was freedom. Tears of joy ran down her face as she moved the paint roller up and down over the blue walls, painting them a fresh shade of peach to match her new outlook. She knew she would have to help Finn through these tough times, but for the first time in her career as a mother, she felt like she was going to be able to do just that.

Grace saw Finn watching her out of the corner of her eye and decided this was her moment. She went out in to the hallway, engulfed her in a hug, and reassured her. Grace could feel Finn's pain and knew it all too well, but she was going to help her get over it, just like a good mother would do. She was her savior, a martyr whose story might never be told.

·  ·  ·  ·  ·  ·  ·  ·  ·  ·  ·  ·

The next few months and years with Finn were anything but the bonding experience Grace had planned. It seemed like every time Grace extended a hand, Finn pushed her farther away. Grace began to feel that all those years absent from her daughter's life were taking their toll as their relationship never seemed to find firm ground. Grace watched Finn follow in her footsteps, looking to men and sex to numb the pain. She felt awful having set that kind of example for her daughter, especially now that Beau was back in her life. They had been together since that tragic night. She knew she should introduce Finn to him, but she was hesitant since her relationship with Finn was already on shaky ground, and so they kept it a secret.

Grace knew that Beau was a simple man who would put her needs first, even when he may not like or agree with them. So, Beau watched Finn from a distance, watched her rebel and struggle. Respecting Grace's wishes, though she guessed it was breaking him inside. His love for her was something she knew was one of the few things in her life she would never understand what she did to deserve.

Grace could see that the men weren't fixing what was off for Finn. She was struggling with something much more profound than skin deep. She knew she only had a limited amount of time with her before she would head to college and likely out of her life forever. She couldn't get through to Finn, so she attempted to bond with her best friend, Peyton, instead, hoping the effect would trickle down to Finn.

Grace would steal Peyton away for a quick chat when she would show up at the house. It seemed like Peyton grew to like Grace, or at the very least respect her attempts to get to know Finn. Grace could tell that Peyton wanted to help, wanted to provide deep insight into Finn, but it was beginning to seem that Finn kept everyone on the outside, even Peyton. Peyton would try to relay Grace's messages about men and drinking not being the way to fix things, but they went right through

Finn. She wouldn't listen to anyone or anything since Gramps and Nick had died. She lost everything she loved in an instance, and if vodka and dick helped her escape for a while, then she was going to indulge.

Finn finally graduated in June of 2004. She had many rough qualities, but school wasn't one of them. She had graduated near the top of her class, but she refused to be acknowledged at graduation. All those people watching her be the center of attention just wasn't her thing . . . it was Peyton's. She spent the summer after graduation the same way she had spent every other day in Hadleigh: drinking, writing, and counting down the days until she would get out of there. She even convinced Grace to let her head to Austin a couple weeks early to get situated. Finn hadn't liked the idea of a forced friendship, so she opted out of the dorms situation and rented a studio apartment near campus. It was going to be her and her studies, just the way she wanted it.

Grace felt lonely at Amgine once Finn left. They hadn't been close, but simply being the only person in this big house made her feel isolated. And since Finn was now gone and would likely never return, regardless of how much Grace begged, she decided it was time for Beau to move in.

So that October after Finn had left, right around the time nineteen years ago that Grace had given birth to what she always thought was "their child," Beau moved into Amgine Farm, and they began their "happily ever after."

·  ·  ·  ·  ·  ·  ·  ·  ·  ·  ·

Peyton was the type of kid who would come home for holidays, and when she did, Grace made sure to invite her over and get the scoop on Finn. Finn had been talking with Grace once a month, if Grace was lucky, but the conversations mainly centered around school and niceties. Grace wanted to know more but didn't want to pry. She weirdly felt like something was different about Finn, something in her voice. She seemed happier, more at ease out there in Texas. Grace began to worry that it was her all along who had made Finn so miserable, so she allowed the distance to remain, not feeling the ability to push right now.

Peyton was of little to no help on the Finn front. Finn had pretty much cut her out of her life after they left Hadleigh. All she knew of Finn was what she posted on Facebook, which wasn't much, not even a profile pic, just a long-standing gray question mark in a circle. There were no drunken, frat-party pics. Finn didn't even drunk dial her. Peyton had tried time and again to reach out to Finn, but she was left in the dark. She still went to Grace's when she was home more to hear what Grace knew about Finn than to dish on what she knew.

Time passed, and Grace and Beau were entwined in the blissful existence they had hoped for twenty-some years ago. Beau had taken to farming the land at Amgine, and Grace continued her writing and home duties. At times when she was cleaning the stove or vacuuming the stairs, she would wonder if she had been this person when Finn was little, if things would have turned out differently. She would try to shake that thought away and focus on their present, deciding that she couldn't blame herself for the situations that were beyond her control. She knew that Finn hated her for her happy demeanor since Al was dead, but she couldn't help herself. She wanted to help Finn mourn, but every time she saw her cry, all Grace wanted to do was confess everything, hoping it would make Finn realize that him being dead made them better off. She knew it would only make things worse for Finn, so instead she kept her mouth shut, something she had spent her life perfecting.

After Al's death, Grace came into a ridiculous sum of money that had been willed to her along with the house. She was dumbfounded when she heard the news, thinking that with the way her father treated her, he would never leave her a nest egg. In her heart, she knew it had nothing to do with her and everything to do with Finn, so after she went on a little shopping spree, she made another big purchase, one she hoped would secure Finn's future.

She sat down with Paul at the *Gazette* and pitched him on the idea of her becoming 51 percent owner of the newspaper. She wasn't sure he would go for it, but she pushed hard. The *Gazette* was quite the moneymaker in this small town, and she had invested the best parts of herself into it for the last several years. Her only happy times outside of Beau had been inside that old flour mill, writing and freeing her mind, if only for a moment. She wanted to stake a claim in it now. She had given her blood and tears, and now she wanted to put her money where her mouth was. Paul, on the other hand, had been there way longer than he ever expected and was looking to get out a little of what he put in before he retired. He wasn't sure when that would be, but he would like it to be sooner than later. He loved the idea, and just like that, Grace had become majority owner in a newspaper.

She went on writing her column as usual, never bothering to change the fake name to the real one. Even though she didn't have to hide anymore, she decided if it ain't broke, don't fix it. She kind of liked writing as someone else, too. She felt less restrained. Only her, Paul, and Beau knew about the pseudonym, and that was how it would stay. She didn't even tell Finn, not wanting to steal thunder. Grace preferred to fly under the radar after years of being the talk of the town. It wasn't until about 2015 that she even let them put her name in the paper as a contributor; it felt too revealing. She had come a long way in the last fifteen years, but something about having her name in print still made her cringe a little.

During Finn's time in undergrad, their conversations grew less and less frequent. Once a month her freshman year, every other month her sophomore year, quarterly her junior year, and only on special occasions her senior year. Grace hated this, but when they did speak, Finn sounded so happy and settled that she let it be.

Finn's graduation was one of those calls in late April of 2008. Grace's newfangled iPhone (a gift from Beau) lit up as she was shucking the corn Beau had harvested to go with the chicken he was out back grilling for dinner.

She looked down at the screen and saw Finn's senior picture flashing, and immediately it brought a smile to her face.

She swiped and put the phone between her ear and shoulder, just as she did when they still had a landline.

"Hello," Grace said.

"Hi, mama," Finn responded.

*Mama.* The word alone made Grace smile and drop her phone on the counter. She quickly realized these new fancy phones weren't going to stay between her ear and shoulder like the old, cordless ones did.

"Hello?" she could hear Finn saying as she wiped her hands on her pants and picked the phone back up to her ear.

"Oh, Finn, I dropped you. This fancy new phone has me in a twist," Grace said.

"Got the iPhone, huh?" Finn asked.

Grace thought twice before responding. For some reason she still felt strange telling Finn about Beau. She worried that if she told her, then she would have to tell her the whole story, and she wasn't ready for that. She felt wrong about lying, but it had become one of the only characteristics about herself that seemed to come without thinking twice, something she didn't love but had come to grips with.

"Yeah. I finally caved." Grace laughed once.

"You doing okay?" Finn asked.

"Oh fine. Same old, you know. What about you? What is new in the big world outside Hadleigh?"

"Well . . . I am calling because I got the date for my graduation ceremony. I don't expect you to come; I know you have never left Hadleigh. But I didn't want it to be a thing that I didn't tell you. So . . . it is May 10 at noon. I will send you pictures on your new fancy phone." Finn chuckled.

"You can send pictures to my iPhone? Well, I'll be," Grace began, then swallowed hard, knowing this moment would come. "Finn. If it is all right with you, I could like to come. I would like to be there."

Finn was a little caught off guard, not expecting Grace to want to come and watch. They hadn't seen each other in almost four years now. Finn was humbled by the effort but wasn't sure it was time. A gentle pause, a moment of thought, and then Finn thought better and said, "Of course you can come. I would love for you to see me here."

Grace was over the moon. Never mind the fact that she was about to get on a plane for the first time in her life, she was going to get to see her only child walk across the stage and get a degree, something she had always wanted for herself but was happy to watch Finn accomplish instead.

The silence lasted too long, so Finn cut in on her thoughts. "I will book you a flight and hotel, if that's all right."

"Oh, of course. Thanks, honey!" Grace exclaimed. "I will see you soon!"

"Yep. Bye, Mom."

"Love you, Finn."

And the line went dead. Just like that, Grace went back to shucking corn with the biggest smile on her face. She was going to see Finn graduate, she was getting out of this town for a little while, and she was hoping they could reconnect while she was out there.

•  •  •  •  •  •  •  •  •  •  •

Luckily for Grace, the days flew by quickly, and before she knew it, she was on her very first airplane, off to Austin. Outside the airport, she put out the last cigarette she would have for the next few hours and headed inside to navigate the airport. People were moving all over the place, and it instantly raised her blood pressure, leaving her wishing she could sneak in one more Winston.

By the time she made it through the security process, she felt slightly violated, leaving her flashing back to the bad memories of old, if only for a moment. She boarded the plane, took her seat, and immediately began twirling her necklace between her pointer and thumb, a habit she did unknowingly whenever she was tense.

The flight attendant walked by and noticed Grace looking a bit nervous, so she crouched down next to her as if approaching a child and said, "Don't worry. Everything will be just fine. I promise."

Grace looked at her and cracked a fake smile. "It is my first time flying."

The redheaded flight attendant extended her hand and placed it on Grace's arm. "You are in good hands. I've got you." She smiled, winked, stood back up, and went about shutting all the overhead bins.

Right before takeoff, the flight attendant came back and slyly handed Grace a tiny bottle of vodka, the ones Grace had seen at the liquor store checkout. Again she winked and walked away.

Grace gently untwisted the cap and chugged her mini bottle of courage. She took a deep breath, leaned back in her seat, and closed her eyes as the plane began to speed up.

• • • • • • • • • • •

The captain came over the intercom and announced they would be landing in twenty minutes, forcing Grace to realize she had fallen asleep. She blinked her eyes a few times and tried to peer out the tiny window a few seats away from her. She took another deep breath and braced herself for the landing as she began to twist her necklace again.

A few bumps and a forceful stop and they were in Austin. Grace had survived her first plane ride unscathed. As she grabbed her purse and headed to exit the plane, the flight attendant stopped her, asked her to reach out her hand, and placed a plastic wing pin in her hands.

"We give these to all the first-time flyers. They are usually on the younger end, but I thought you still deserved it." She smiled and put her hand on Grace's shoulder. "You did great! Enjoy Austin."

"Oh I will." Grace smiled as she exited the plane and went to find Finn, who was meeting her at baggage claim.

Grace followed the signs and got on the escalator down to the baggage-claim level. She was still half-confused and not sure she was going the right way and in desperate need of a cigarette when she first saw Finn at the bottom of the escalator. She had to catch herself from gasping as she stared at this person who didn't even look like the same girl.

"I remember hearing that Grace flew out to see Finn in Austin and that she looked quite different."

"Has anyone seen her yet?"

"I heard she is going to speak, but I haven't seen her yet."

"Maybe she thought better and skipped town. I am sure she doesn't have anything great to say about Grace anyhow."

"Come on. Cut the woman some slack. She's dead, for God's sake!"

# finn

"Finn! Is that you?"

"Oh my gosh! Finn! Are you okay?" Peyton was yelling at me as I squinted my eyes open and realized I was lying on the grass.

"Finny! Say something! What the heck happened?" Peyton kept on.

I tried to sit up and immediately realized my head was killing me and my eyes and throat hurt. I was so confused and not sure what the hell had actually happened. I took a deep breath in and out and could smell the stench of old food, acid, and shit mixed together. It smelled like I had been eating cow poop drenched in gasoline, or dog vomit. Then it hit me. I had been throwing up . . . and then it hit me as to why. I felt myself start to convulse all over again, knowing full well there was nothing left to spew. I tried to calm down, tried to catch my breath.

"Finn! Are you sick? What is wrong?" Peyton said as she reached down and placed her hand on my back and began to rub.

I looked up and locked eyes with her, distracting my mind long enough to stop the convulsing. I took in a few short breaths, willing them to be longer, and tried to rise off the lawn.

I stood up, a little shaky at first, and took a seat on the edge of the porch, opposite of the side where I had spent the afternoon vomiting. A couple more deep breaths with my eyes closed and I finally spoke.

"Hey," I said.

"Hi," she replied in her sweet voice, now holding the bags of booze and cigarettes she had been asked to fetch but had been embarrassed to pay for as the store clerk eyed her ever growing belly.

I reached out to take the bags from her, but she pulled them back. "I've got them. You are in no shape. I'll go make you a plate before you dive into these other bags. And then you are going to tell me what the hell is going on with you," she said sternly but with a smile as she walked past me and into the house.

I sat there, looking out over the acres of field, wondering how this place could have been full of this many secrets, this many mysteries. How could one person act a certain way and then be something totally different. That thought made me pause, realizing I knew that feeling all too well, but I wasn't going around hurting people, at least not physically, I suppose.

Peyton came back out carrying a box of pizza and a six-pack of beer. I had somehow missed the pizza box when she had come in but was incredibly glad to see it now, despite my churning stomach.

She set the box down next to me on the steps and then slowly made her way to sit, leaning and using her arms to brace herself so her stomach didn't make her topple forward. Once her butt was firmly planted on the wooden stoop, she opened the box and looked over at me. I had my head rested against the porch's newel post and looked paler than the clouds in the sky. The day was on the edge of evening, and I was in desperate need of food and a cigarette.

She quietly tore a piece of pizza from the pie and motioned it in my direction.

"Come on. You have to eat something. You look awful."

I couldn't even find the strength to muster up a sarcastic response. I reached for the pizza and put it to my lips. Slowly I took my first bite, chewed it, and swallowed, waiting to see how it would sit. I sat for a few minutes, staring out at the fields, letting my stomach churn, deciding if the pizza would stay down. I could feel Peyton's eyes on me as she quietly chewed her piece. She was waiting patiently as a good dog should, but I knew I had to give her something. She had gone to all this trouble for me, and I needed to return the favor.

I have never been one for sharing or divulging too much about myself. It always came more natural to keep it in and let others think what they wanted. I learned a long time ago that people have their own agendas, so I kept mine to myself.

This was one of those things I should definitely keep to myself. There was too much here for people to feed on and misconstrue. I wasn't even sure how I felt about the whole damn thing, so how was I going to tell someone, anyone, else? I took another bite of pizza and swallowed hard. I turned to her and began, knowing if I didn't get it out, I was likely going to continue in my quest to get everything else out of my body and onto the grass.

"So . . . my mom kept this journal for me all these years." I took a breath and another bite.

"Oh yeah," Peyton responded quietly, looking away rather sheepishly.

I stopped mid-chew, "Oh yeah?" I asked her, irritation starting to boil to the surface.

"Well, after you left, I kind of kept an eye on your mother and Beau. I didn't want them to feel alone. She always wanted to know about you, and I felt bad that I never really had much for her since we didn't keep in touch. I felt like I let you and her down, so I kept coming by when I could. She mentioned the journal once or twice, something about it explaining things, I guess."

I didn't know which part of this new information to digest first, so I decided to start with the visits. "You visited her? How often? Why didn't you tell me?"

"It wasn't that often, maybe once a month max. And I did mention it at dinner the other night. But you and I weren't really in touch, Finn, so when was I supposed to tell you? I reached out to you a couple times in college, but I heard nothing, so I let you be."

"You should have told me when you showed up on my back porch when I first got here, Pey," I said, feeling slightly upset but mainly guilty that it was her who visited and not me.

"I'm sorry," she began. "I didn't think it was important. I figured whatever she truly wanted you to know she would tell you, and the rest was simple small talk. Really all that ever happened was she would talk about you and I would listen. She was so proud of you."

"Okay, fine. But what do you mean you would visit her and Beau? How did you know him and where he lived?"

She looked at me quizzically. "Finn, Beau lived here with your mom."

"What? No he didn't."

"Yeah, actually he did. He moved in shortly after you left for college. They had been back together since the night of the accident, but I don't think she wanted to upset or complicate things for you, so she kept him away until you left."

I set my pizza on my lap and ran my hands up through my hair, landing them in a praying motion, one on each side of my mouth. I was dumbfounded. The hits just kept coming. I wasn't sure if I was angry with her for never telling me or happy that she had someone with her, the seeming love of her life.

Peyton set her pizza crust back in the box. She never ate the crust, even in high school. There are two kinds of people in the world: the ones who eat pizza crust and those who don't. I didn't know what it said about either, but I knew there was not a middle group.

She reached her hand over the box and onto my shoulder. "You okay? What are you thinking? I didn't mean to upset you. I thought you knew."

Anger caught in my throat, thinking about all these things Peyton "thought I knew."

I didn't know what to say. Why didn't she feel like she could share this with me? I was an adult, for God's sake. I could have handled this. I know our relationship was complicated to say the least, but I thought we were at least honest with each other, or at least she was. Now here was this journal full of secrets *and* a secret lover. I was done with the secrets, done with the hiding.

I looked at Peyton, picked up my pizza, and said, "It's fine. I am glad for her, I guess." I took a bite. "Where is that beer?"

Peyton reached behind her and grabbed a beer, turned back to me, and said, "I wish you would eat more first. You still don't look great."

I took the beer from her hand and twisted it open with my teeth, spit out the cap, and chugged it down. I didn't much care if it came up. I needed to feel it go down.

She watched me in utter amazement with a hint of disappointment. I swallowed the last drop and set the bottle on the porch. I looked over at her and motioned for another. This time she didn't turn around, though. She kept her stare fixed on me and waited.

"I am not getting another one until you tell me what is going on with you!" she blurted.

I took a few more bites of pizza, ignoring her motherly death stare for as long as I could. Finally I turned to her.

"Pey, that journal is full of some really fucked-up stuff," I said and the looked away.

"What kind of stuff?" she asked, bristling at my vulgarity, always the good girl.

"I am not sure you want to know. Or maybe you already know, being as though my mother and you were so tight and all." I guess my sarcasm had returned.

"Finn, it wasn't like that. We only talked about you. She never told me anything about her or anyone beside you."

"Right." I looked at the grass again.

"Finn . . ." she pestered.

"You remember the night of the accident?" I asked.

"Of course I do. How could I forget?"

"You remember how my mother wasn't home initially, and when she did get back, she seemed oddly calm, almost happy?"

"I don't know that I would say she was happy . . ."

"Oh she was happy," I snapped.

Peyton was starting to get pissed at me at this point. "Why on earth would she be happy? Two people close to both of you died."

"Yeah, you are right. . . . She wasn't happy. She had only meant for one to die. Nick was a casualty of war."

Peyton looked at me and tilted her head slightly. "Finn, what do you mean she only meant for one to die?"

I went on for the next hour or so between explaining every detail of the story and sipping the beer she had handed me once I began to talk about murder. Murder felt like it warranted a beverage stronger than beer, but that was all we had left, and so it would be a murder "light" kind of chat. I had never been so honest with someone in my life, and though my instinct was to be guarded, I suddenly felt the need to purge, and this time not onto the bright green grass.

I looked down for most of the conversation, somehow ashamed of something I had no part in. Peyton watched me the whole time. I could feel her eyes burning with anger and pain. She reached out to touch me, comfort me, a few times. I just kept barreling through the story. Every time she opened her mouth to ask a question, I refused to halt, and she sat there with her mouth twisted in the "w" waiting to ask. If I was going to get it out, I needed to do it as quickly as possible.

At the end, I finally took one long exhale and looked up to meet her eyes, which were red and wet. She wiped them with the back of her pizza-greased hand and scooted her huge belly toward me and enveloped me in a hug. I could feel her chest rise and fall as her tears dripped on my shoulder. I stayed stoic, not sure whether I was emotioned out or just trying to play tough.

Finally, she released her arms and looked at me.

"Finn. Oh my gawd. I had no idea. I am so incredibly sorry. You must be feeling a million things right now. I don't even know what to say."

"Yeah, me either."

"It is such a torrid tale. I have so many emotions about it. I don't even know who was wrong in the story."

"You are telling me," I said.

"I mean. Gramps. I just can't. And then your mom. And on top of all of that there is Nick and Beau. And you. I just . . ."

I took another gulp, wishing the answers were at the bottom of that bottle. I looked out over the farm, and in that moment I knew it. I knew how this story ended. I knew how to make peace with the madness. I needed to write it down. I needed to tell it from my perspective. I needed something good to come out of this mess.

The feeling engulfed every part of me, and I immediately felt the need to start. I needed her story to meld into mine and become better. I needed a Hallmark ending to the shitshow that had become of my life. I needed to figure out what I was thinking, and the only way I knew how was to let my fingers do the talking. Most of the time, I didn't say the right thing or do the right things, but I always wrote the right thing. This was the one thing I was still sure of after these last few days in Hadleigh. I needed to write. I needed to release. I needed Peyton gone.

As if reading my mind, she stood up. A glimmer of hope flickered in my eyes that she was leaving without the awkward "me asking her to go" thing, but instead she headed over to the coffee table where the journal lay facedown, still full of secrets I was sure I wasn't ready for.

She picked it up and looked at me.

"Don't you want to know what happened next?" she asked.

Part of me never wanted to read another page in that damn book again, but the rest wanted to know how her story ends. The victim finally kills her attacker and then what? Does she ever lose sleep over it? Does she get a taste for murder? Revenge? Does she get her Hallmark happily ever after?

As I sat silently contemplating my next move, Peyton flipped the journal over, turned the page, looked over at me, and began reading.

"Dear Finn . . ." she started.

I shot her a look, still unable to speak, still unable to decide if I wanted to hear this. I couldn't find my voice to protest, and so she continued.

Dear Finn,

I am sitting in my room at The Westin in Austin with the biggest bed I have ever slept in in my life. I wish I would have brought Beau with me, now that I am here. He would have loved to watch you graduate. He would love to see the person you have become. I watched you struggle for years after the accident. You used sex and smoking as a crutch, and I let you. I should have fought for you. I should have stood up to your vices. I should have been a real mother. I will forever be sorry for that.

I am here now, though, and I am so proud of you. Seeing you in this place, the new you, the new life, the new outlook. You look happier than I have ever seen you, and for the first time ever, I see why you had to leave Hadleigh. I understand now why that place held you back. I know I did a lot wrong, but the one thing I did right was let you go. You are thriving here, and I see it. I can't wait to see what this world has in store for you. Part of me wants you to move home and write for the *Gazette* with me, but I know that is not realistic. I know you need to find your own way. I just hope you will take me along for the journey.

I am so proud of you, Finn.

Love,
G. E. H.

Peyton looked up from the soft book bent gently over her hands and sniffled, trying to choke back the tears.

"Finn," she started, "she loved you more than you knew. This is the kind of stuff she would say to me all the time. I know it is complicated, but you must see this. You must see her in this, right?"

I tried to inconspicuously wipe a tear that was forming in the corner of my eye. I raised my hand, wiped it away, and placed my hand on my cheek resting my elbow on my knee, hoping it looked like one fluid motion, just needed to rest my head on my hand.

The look in Pey's eyes let me know it wasn't as discreet as I had hoped.

I looked away from her and out at the farm. I did understand. In that moment, something shifted in me. I wasn't sure if I was going to toss my cookies again or pass out. I hoped neither. I took a deep breath, closed my eyes, and for the first time, I let myself step into my mother's head. The things she had endured, the life she had led, the hopes that shattered, and the pain she buried. I felt the weight of all of it fall upon me and immediately understood why she needed him gone. He wasn't the man I knew. He never would be again. He was a monster disguising himself as a loving grandpa. He would never again be my gramps, he was now just a man . . . another man who broke my heart. First Nick, now him. James flashed into my mind, and I was worried he would break me too. I tried to flush the thought out as the rage started to cloud my mind.

I felt my teeth start to grind together and my temples start to pound. I used to think she was the reason I was fucked up, but it was him—all along it was him. I would play with him, write to him, and love him, and all the while he was slowly killing her inside, leaving behind a corpse of a mother that I deserved more of. He was the reason she couldn't be there for me. He was the reason I didn't have a mother.

It wasn't until I heard Peyton off in the distance that I realized every muscle in my body was clenched.

"Finn?" she called. "Are you okay? Talk to me."

I rolled my shoulders back, felt the V neck of my shirt rise a little, and turned to her.

"I am fine. I think I just need to be alone. I need to process," I responded.

"Really? Are you sure?"

"Yeah. Thank you so much for the pizza and beer. I needed to purge and nourish."

"Well . . . isn't the writer in you just throwing out big words now?" She laughed.

"I guess it comes with the territory," I said, trying to keep it short, willing her silently to leave.

"Okay, if you insist. But just know that I am a call away if you need," she chirped, setting down the journal and turning to clean up the pizza box and beer bottles.

"Leave them," I said half-politely/half-pushy.

"Okay . . ." She set the box down and turned to grab her purse.

Before walking off the back porch, she stopped and kissed me on the top of my head.

"Everything will be okay, Finn," she said, and then she left, waddling as gracefully as one could as pregnant as she was.

As soon as she was out of sight, I stood up and headed inside. I picked up my phone and glanced as the screen. I had a few texts from James and a missed FaceTime from Letty. I wanted to talk to both, but inspiration had hit, and there was no time to chat.

I quickly texted them, saying I would call later and that I was all right, even adding a smiley emoji for effect. After hitting Send, I realized the emoji was probably overkill and would make them wonder if I had gone off the deep end. *Too late now,* I thought and set the phone down on the counter.

I retrieved my computer from that Frye bag I used to resent. I found myself running my fingers over the soft leather, now looking at it in a different light. She wasn't trying to buy my love; she was simply trying to do something she thought a proud mother should do. I felt like an ass thinking back to my reaction that day. If only I had known instead of relying on my assumptions like we tend to do.

On my way back outside, I walked by the office and saw the desk that my grandfather . . . no . . . that Al had made. Suddenly it looked different, dirty, made by hands that caused so much pain. I went into the office, set my computer down on the chair in the corner, covered in faded paisley fabric of course, and took my seat in the leather chair behind the desk.

Opening the side drawer, I found his old letter opener, took it out of the drawer, and set it on the top of the desk. I then ripped the half-open drawer out of the jambs and threw it across the room. The few items that remained in there all these years later sailed around the space. I took a breath, grabbed the next drawer, and did the same. I continued until no drawers remained in the desk and the room was littered with papers, staples, pens, and old receipts.

Exhaling out hard, I picked up the letter opener, turning it from side to side in my hand and watching the light catch the etching on the edges. I had watched him use this so gracefully to open letter after letter and longed to have such an item. The opener had always seemed like the quintessential adult item, something you had to earn. I had longed for the day I would wield one in my hand and gracefully rip something open.

I flipped the blade around, and using all my strength, jammed it into the top of the desk I used to revere. I dragged it across the top, leaving a gouge deep in the wood. I repeated it over and again, each time ripping apart all the memories and affection. I hadn't realized I was screaming until I finally came to a stop and felt sweat dripping down my neck, my cheeks wet with tears, and my throat burning.

I jammed the opener into the desk one last time, the final blow, the archetypal nail in the coffin, and slumped back into the leather chair. Using the back of my arm, I wiped my tear-stained cheeks and wrapped my hand around the back of my neck to wipe the sweat. I was done crying over this man. Everything he was to me had died right here on this shredded skeleton of desk. Made by his hands and destroyed by mine.

I blew the remaining hot air out of my lungs and stood up, grabbed my computer, and headed to the porch. On the chair next to the office door sat the pack of Winstons that Peyton had grabbed for me against her better judgment. I smiled and pulled out a few of them. If I was going to write my truth, it was going to take more than a run and my "better self." I needed to allow the old me to peek through, just a little bit. And that was going to require a cigarette . . . or two.

"You remember that accident, right? The one that killed Al and Nick? I heard that Grace and Beau were there that night."

"No way. It was simply an old man who should not have been behind the wheel. My grandma still thinks she can drive, even though she is half blind. Those old birds can't give it up."

"I felt so awful for Nick's parents. A young life lost too soon. It was so sad."

**33**

# grace

Grace lit her cigarette and sat on the back porch swing, watching Beau pick weeds in the small garden next to the wheat field. In between clouds of smoke, she watched the way his hands moved so smoothly, as though he had been born with the hands of a gardener and not a football player. She smiled, remembering him in his football pads, and those tight white pants that turned her on. It had been almost thirty years since she had seen him in those pants, but he still had the same effect on her. He looked over and smiled at her, almost as though he could read her thoughts. She felt goose bumps rise on her skin at the warmth of his smile. Then he motioned for her to put the cigarette out, and she remembered that he was still just a man, one who could drive her mad, as well. *Damn him and his healthy habits,* she thought as she took one last puff and stubbed it out in the ashtray that Finn had made her in elementary school.

She hadn't kept much from Finn's childhood, but somehow she had managed never to lose this ashtray, and every time she used it, she thought of her only child and smiled. The thought of Finn hadn't always made her smile, and the thought of that now made her shiver. She pulled the old blanket lying on the swing up over her as if it could block the thoughts.

She looked back over at Beau and watched him work, wiping beads of sweat off his brow every once in a while, and she could swear that Finn had looked so much like him when she was out in Austin. She had loved every minute of her time there. Watching Finn walk across the stage and move the tassel from one side of the cap to the other. Such a small gesture with such huge meaning. She had always wanted to move a tassel like that. To feel the silky threads in between your fingers and gracefully swing them over the corner of your cap to signify that you were closing a chapter and moving forward. That tassel meant the world was at your feet, and yet her feet had never left Hadleigh soil, not until Austin, that is.

Austin had renewed her, invigorated her. She came home happier than she had ever felt and excited to dive back into her writing at the *Gazette*. She may never swing a tassel, but she could try to leave her mark on this small town.

She had spent the months and years since leaving Austin with a new outlook. She was going to try to be the best partner, the best writer, and the best mother she could be. She would call Finn every week, and they would talk, but she knew it would never be more than surface deep unless she could really reveal all her secrets, and she never felt ready. She was making an effort, though, and that felt better than the nothing of before.

Finn enrolled in a master's program and had since completed it, an MFA in creative writing. Then Finn had been quickly offered a job at the *Boston Herald*, writing puff pieces. Grace had been internet savvy enough to figure out how to subscribe to the *Herald* online and was diligently reading Finn's work.

Piece after piece, she was blown away. All her life she thought she was a good writer, but it turned out that her child's writing chops put her to shame, and she weirdly felt okay with that.

As much as Grace had loved reading Finn's articles online and their casual conversations on the iPhone, she always felt Finn was hiding something from her. Not a lover, or a scandal, but something more personal. She never had the nerve to ask, she assumed she had given up the right a long time ago, but she could sense it was there. Call it mother's intuition or just a hunch, but either way, she knew something was off.

Finn seemed happy in Boston with Letty, the roommate who was fun and liked women, which was something new for Grace. She had never been a judgmental person, and if her life and Finn's life hadn't braced her to accept everyone as they were, then she wasn't sure what would. Letty and Grace had spoken on the phone a few times, and she seemed like the kind of person Finn needed.

Austin had been a good stepping stone for Finn, but Boston seemed a better fit. More diversity, more accepting, more obscurity . . . and as far from Hadleigh as one could get (lifestyle-wise).

Grace tried to tell herself over and again that it was fine, Finn was fine; whatever she thought Finn was hiding was just nothing.

That nothing became a something in September of 2013.

The air in Hadleigh was just starting to crisp with the fall chill. The leaves were still holding onto their green pigment as long as they could, though the tips were turning the lightest shade of yellow. Grace and Beau had decided to get out of town for the day, maybe stay a night in the bed and breakfast the next town over. They wanted a romantic getaway, and that town had some new restaurants and a few unique shops.

Favorite among the shops for Grace was a bookstore/coffee shop, called "Hot and Read-y," where she would spend hours searching the shelves, flipping through books, and sipping her favorite cold press coffee. The shop was a bit of a haven for Grace, a place where she wished her name belonged, but knew it never would. She would flip through book after book and get lost in the story or wonder about the author's story. She had always wanted to write a book but could never actually bring herself to do it. She had started a novel here and there, but they never amounted to much more than a couple thousand words before she quit. She knew the book she should write, the one people would be in awe of, but she was never brave enough to write it. It still cut too deep.

Grace threw her overnight bag into the back of Beau's truck and climbed in the passenger side, where she had once leaned over and kissed him as a teenager. The truck was long overdue to be put down, but she wouldn't let him get rid of it. They kept it in the garage, in the way back, and only brought it out for special occasions. Each time they climbed in and started the engine, they both said a silent prayer that it would start when they climbed back in after their adventure.

The tires gently bumped over the gravel driveway on their way out of town. They needed a night off. Things weren't bad per se, but sometimes being in that house was too much for Grace. She looked out the window at the few leaves beginning to fall from the trees and began to roll down the window. As she cranked, the warm breeze filled the truck, and the sweet smell relaxed her. Fall was always a favorite for her. It was the calm before the storm. Spring would bring the farm chores back in full effect, but for now she had Beau to herself. She looked over at him, slid her body across the bench seat right up next to him, leaned her head on his shoulder, and closed her eyes, letting the warm air and his sweet smell bring her full tranquility. She felt his lips touch the top of her head and leave a sweet kiss on her starting-to-gray hair. They truly were going to grow old together, just as she had always planned.

She hadn't realized that the gentle bumps and warm air had lulled her to sleep until she felt the truck come to a stop and Beau reach between her legs to put it in park. She tilted her head up and looked at him, sleepy eyed and a mess. He kissed her on the nose and hopped out of the truck, turning around to reach his hand out for hers. She took his hand and hopped out the driver's side, excited for what the next day or two might bring. She felt like the teenagers they once were, out for an adventure. No responsibility and no worries.

They checked in to The Marmalade B&B, where they were able to put them in the honeymoon suite. Beau and Grace had looked at each other and smiled before she nestled into his bicep. There had never been a wedding, so therefore no honeymoon. They had talked aimlessly about it, but she always pooh-poohed it. She had no rhyme or reason for saying no. She loved him, so she wasn't sure what the reservation was about, but every time he asked, she said, "someday." When she finally pulled her face out of his arm, he was looking down at her with those eyes, the same eyes she had fallen for so many years ago.

"Well, Mrs. Boyton, shall we?"

She smiled.

"It's Mrs. Harper. I am not about to go changing my name now." She giggled.

"That's up for debate." He smiled, threw their bags over his shoulder, and grabbed her hand to lead her up to the honeymoon suite. Once in the room, with the door shut behind them, Grace came into his arms and then into the bed. They lay there in the bed together, Grace burrowed into the curve of Beau's shoulder, feeling his chest rise and lower. Beau was running his fingers up and down her arm that extended over his still-taut stomach, holding him as close as she could.

"Grace," he said, low and anxiously.

Grace tilted her head up at him and could feel the stubble on his chin brush her forehead as she waited for him to go on.

"Grace Harper," he started again, a little more seriously this time, "I have loved you all my life, and I won't ever stop loving you. You are my miracle."

She knew where this was going. He had never said it like this before, but she could tell where this would end. She braced herself for the fallout as his fingers stopped running up and down her arm and his voice lowered.

"You and me make sense, Grace. We always have. I don't want to go through life without you. And I know it seems silly to you, but I want to call you my wife. I want us to wear a ring. I want to make this right. I want you forever. And if you'll have me, I'd like to be your husband."

He stopped for a second and looked down and met her eyes. "So I guess what I am asking is: Will you marry me, please?"

Something about his sincerity or his manners at the end made her smile, and without thinking, she whispered, "Yes. I would marry you tomorrow, Beau Boyton." Then she climbed up to kiss him, and her body rose up to meet his. Afterward, Beau fell asleep with Grace still on top of him, and when he woke up, he brushed her hair away from her face and watched her sleep, trying not to disturb her, but trying to take all of her in. He arched his head up and kissed her hair. She fluttered her eyes open and met his. They smiled.

"Well, let's go get some coffee," he said with the biggest smile she had ever seen, instantly reaffirming her decision.

It was only late afternoon and already so much had happened for Grace. She made love with her beloved . . . twice . . . got some much-needed sleep, and became a future Mrs., all before stepping into Hot and Read-y for some coffee and words for the soul.

Grace and Beau walked hand in hand over to the barista and ordered two large cold press coffees. They noted the barista waited, cup in hand, for them to somehow tweak the order. Everyone did that nowadays. No one just ordered a latte. Now it was a half-caf, skinny vanilla latte with two pumps, light foam, and nutmeg on top. So when the barista realized they were as simple as "large cold press," she smiled and silently thanked God people like these two still existed.

Beau and Grace, meanwhile, were so wrapped up in one another that they didn't even notice the barista's response to them. They couldn't stop smiling and cooing with one another. They would have made any normal, fancy coffee-ordering person sick, and also incredibly envious.

Once their coffees were ready, they continued on, hand in hand, over to the magazine section where a small table, barely equipped for two, sat, and Beau set down his coffee. Here was where they would usually say goodbye. Beau would flip through car, football, and farming magazines, while Grace would spend hours perusing all the book sections in the store one by one, pulling books off the shelf and flipping through them. The next few hours would be the only ones they would spend apart this whole trip. As Beau set his coffee down and Grace went in to kiss him and release his hand, he held it tight and looked at her before fishing in his jacket pocket and pulling out a green velvet box. Green had long been his favorite color. It was the main color on his football jersey, his glory days, so it stuck. He dropped down on one knee, and there in one of her favorite places on earth, by their too-small-for-two table, he opened the box he had been keeping in his jacket pocket for almost thirty years, waiting to put it on the love of his life's finger.

She hesitated for the slightest of a second. Her natural inclination to put up a wall tried to rise, but she shoved it down, smiled, and shook her head yes. Beau slid the beautiful ring on her finger and stood up as best as his old football knees would let him. Once off the ground, they kissed, and then she looked down at the ring. It was perfect, exactly what she would have wanted, and she marveled at how well this man knew her. Little did she know he had picked that ring out so long ago and had kept it, hoping one day it would grace her finger.

They kissed again and finally released each other's hands. Beau headed toward the magazine rack, and Grace picked up her coffee with her right hand so she could still marvel at the rock on her left. She headed off into the store to spend time being in awe of those who could do the one thing she had never been able to: write a book.

She began in the history section. She always loved to see what was new there. She liked the irony of looking for something new in history. She flipped through a few books about new theories on assassinations and attacks but eventually grew tired of the speculations and blood. Today was a day of happiness, and so she needed light books about love and hope.

She picked her coffee up off the floor, shoved the books back in their place on the wooden shelf, and made her way over to fiction. Usually her route would have been history, art, biography, home and garden, true crime, and lastly fiction, but today felt different, was different, so she skipped ahead to her favorite section—the place where people's imaginations ran free. She walked right past the "new releases" in fiction because, being a purist of literature, she believed those were just the books that the publishers were trying to force feed you, and she was no one's sucker, so she kept her eyes akimbo.

The sunlight of that warm fall afternoon made its way through the foggy front windows, hitting her new ring just right and bouncing the light over to the "new fiction books," almost as if someone was forcing her hand. Grace turned, admittedly slightly interested in what new books were out, even if she was trying to be better than that, and that's when it caught her eye.

In the middle of the books, right where the sun had forced her eye, was a book, a book from an author she had never seen before but immediately felt connected to.

*A Light in the Dark* by Finnegan Hadleigh. Grace set her coffee on top of the shelf and picked up the book with both hands. She mouthed "Finnegan Hadleigh" as she ran her fingers over the name on the front cover. She didn't even flip the book around to read what it was about. She didn't have to; she knew it was going to be worth it. She spun around, letting her back lightly hit the bookshelf and slide down onto the ground, folded her legs crisscross applesauce, licked her right thumb and pointer finger, and flipped open the cover of the book.

The book's dedication gave her goose bumps. "To anyone who has ever felt like someone else." She couldn't explain it, but she felt her suspicions confirmed. She knew in her gut that Finn had written this book. She flipped to the start and began. Her gut might have been fully confident, but her head still needed confirmation.

She wasn't sure how much time had passed, nor had she noticed the that the sun was now setting outside those same foggy front windows, when she felt a shadow hovering over her. She looked up from her book, binding now bent, and met Beau's eyes.

"Grace, are you okay? Are you crying?"

She hadn't realized that she was until she raised her fingers to her cheek and felt the tacky, gloss layer over them. She quickly used her sleeve as a towel and wiped both cheeks, still leaving the blackened mascara smudges under her eyes.

"What is going on?" Beau asked.

She wasn't sure if she should tell him yet. Part of her wanted to shout it from the rooftops that her child was an author, but part of her wanted it to stay her secret, one between her and Finn, even though Finn wasn't in on it. The latter won out for now, and while she hated lying to him, she told herself that she didn't want to wreck this day for them. He was so proud of his ring and proposal that breaking the news about Finn being an author would overshadow that.

So Grace smiled, put her hand on the ground, pushed to stand, leaned in, and kissed him before pulling back. "It's just such a great story. I think I am going to buy it so I can finish it at home," she said through her secretive, smiling teeth.

They paid for the book and left the store, hand in hand walking back to the B&B for a night of celebration and lovemaking. Grace loved the warmth of her hand in Beau's, and her other hand wrapped around Finn's book, which she was clutching to her chest, wanting to feel as close to Finn as she could in that moment. At the store she had declined a bag, claiming to help the environment, but really she just wanted to never let the book go. She didn't know if she would even let Finn know that she knew, but she relished in the accomplishment the same.

That night as they drank champagne and toasted their future, she said a silent celebratory toast to Finn becoming the author Grace never could, and that made her smile even more than the man clinking glasses with her.

"I actually heard that Grace and Beau were married."

"No, they weren't. You are full of it, Poppy."

"No, I swear. Didn't you see the ring on her hand and his? Jim and I saw them out on a walk before she got sick, and they both had rings on."

# finn

The thing about being an author is that you have to write, and lately I had nothing of significance to put down on paper. But now. Now I did. I snubbed out my sixth cigarette on the edge of the back porch swing that I had once so adored. It had fallen from high esteem to my ashtray. The tops of my thighs were warm from the heat of the laptop that I had been pounding on for hours. The only thing reminding me that I was still part of the outside world was the cord I had gone to get at some point in the night when my battery began to flash. The porch light flickered overhead from time to time, almost as though it was also trying to get me to step outside of my head, but I couldn't. This was the first time in my life that the words were coming easy. *Easy* might not be the right word. They were definitely hard, but they were flowing. Flowing out of a place I never knew existed until a few days ago when a little green notebook changed everything. Ironically, just like it had in *The Notebook*. Man, I am a sucker.

I thought I had had enough of change when I left Hadleigh the first time. I was leaving behind a part of me and moving towards a new and better me. Now I was back in the place that had scarred me before and was ripping those scars open, letting them bleed out to the point of passing out, and then rubbing salt in them just to really let the pain sink in deep. I knew I wasn't going to get out of here unscathed, but I could have never imagined this.

My night was fueled by beer, cigarettes, anger, and toxicity—a lethal combo for some, but a creative outlet for me. Page after page I typed, never stopping to reread, check spelling, or even think twice about grammar. I just wrote, let the words fall where they may. Most of the time it was through writing that I found my true feelings, and as the night dragged on, I felt myself go through the stages.

There was the anger, the reason I was still beating the keys as though I could rub the letters right off if I hit hard enough. Then there was the realization, the profound, earth-shattering moment when I realized that I might be a child of incest, and worse yet, that my mother was abused most of her life. And for what? So a man could be in control, so he could show her who's boss? During this stage, the cigarettes were back to back and the bile crept up in my throat. I managed to shove it back down with swigs of warm beer and sheer will. Telling myself I was done letting him upset me.

But then I wasn't. Then I was crying over a man who pretended to love me, cherish me, know me, when really he was a monster in disguise. He was a wolf in sheep's clothing, and I bought it hook, line, and sinker. I blamed her for my issues. I held her responsible for my failures and my lack of intimacy. I hated her.

There it was, staring at me on the page. It seemed to grow bolder without me ever editing it. I hated her. It might have been the only time I paused all night and reread it. Over and again. I hated her. But the fact of the matter was that I didn't even know her. And now that I did, it was too late. She was gone, he was a monster, and I was a mess. The mother I thought I knew, the one I resented, wasn't the woman she was; neither of us were.

Once he was gone, she was different, but I was too angry and confused to see it. She was trying, she had spent years trying, but I was ignorant. I never gave her a chance. The beginning of our relationship might have been her fault, but the end was mine.

I had always been a mess. That's what the people in town had said.

"Something is wrong with that Finn girl. Why doesn't she behave like the other girls? Why doesn't she take a page out of that Peyton girl's book? I guess the apple doesn't fall far from the tree," they would whisper.

I used to hate them for it too. I was nothing like her. I wanted to be anything but her, but the truth was . . . is . . . now that I know her, I am just like her.

The secrets, lies, walls, regrets. Both of us hiding our true selves for reasons we weren't even sure mattered. Eventually we both became who we really were, except she had gotten a glimpse into the real me and accepted me for it. In turn, I didn't bother to see, and I held it against her.

Maybe that was part of the problem all along. I hated her because I hated me. She was just an easy target for the anger. The self-realization hit hard and made the bile rise again, which just brought me back to him. He deserved to die. That I was sure of. I just wish I could have known, could have been in on the truth back then. Maybe I wouldn't have believed her; maybe I would have helped her do it. There is no way to know. I don't blame her for what she did, nor am I upset about it.

Alisha Perkins

I felt like I would be when I first read it, like she took something away from me for her own selfish reasons. But the truth was that he was never mine to begin with.

Anger, upset, realization, and then pain. The pain of reliving what happened to Nick. At the time I had assumed if anyone were to blame, it was Nick. It seemed easier to blame him than try to rationalize an accident. So every boy I ever screwed, every beer I ever drank, and every cigarette I smoked was to spite him. He would have opposed all of it. He never liked when girls acted like boys, and so I did it to show him I blamed him. *I would show him,* I thought. But now, the blame had shifted. He wasn't to blame. She was.

I felt a catch in my throat. I wanted to cry again, but I didn't know who for. For Nick, the puppy love I lost too early, or for me, the person he left wrecked. Most of all, I think I was crying for my mother, who only intended for a good outcome from that accident, not a bad one. She would have never done anything to intentionally hurt me, but she had.

"Everyone you love will hurt you eventually," my grandmother had said to me in one of her drunken states, and she was so right. If you let someone get close enough to love you, then they are close enough to knife you.

Nick was a casualty of war. The good ones always are. I didn't have to like it or be okay with it, but I had to understand it, and I did. He left me so long ago that the fresh pain had long subsided, and I was slowly coming to grips with this new information. It stung, but not in the way I expected. All's fair in love and war, right?

It wasn't until the evening had turned dark and then light again that I realized this whole time I had been writing, I was writing to her and for her. It was my own little green book of secrets from Amgine Farm. All the things I wanted to say

264

but never did. All the things I wanted to say now that I would never be able to. She had left me a window into her soul, the window she wanted to jump out of, the window where Beau used to throw rocks. She left me the best piece of her, the only piece she knew how.

I was still lost in thought when the aroma of coffee came seeping out the screen porch door and I began to hear the dripping of fresh-brewed coffee hitting the glass pot. My mother had never sprung for one of those fancy coffee machines with the timer. She insisted that making coffee was meant to be part of your morning ritual. Only lazy people or those wasting their time with outside worries didn't have time to grind up beans, measure out the right amount, put in a fresh paper filter, and breath in the aroma of the miracle that was coffee. If you didn't have time for that, then she didn't have time for you.

I, of course, had bought a Keurig with my first paycheck from the *Herald*. It felt good to know I could make fancy coffee at home and a little good to spite my mother at the time. But now the smell of coffee percolating was soothing and odd, bringing a smile to my weary face.

I was too busy still ruminating in the smell of time passed by when the porch door swung open and there stood James, holding two cups of steaming coffee. It hadn't dawned on me that someone had to have been making the coffee, of course.

He smiled at me. I smiled back but kept my lips pressed together. A night of smoking, drinking, and angered breathing surely hadn't done me any favors in the breath department. I reached for the cup as he moved closer, hoping to take a swig and somewhat mask last night's debacle on my breath.

He leaned in and kissed me on the cheek as I pressed the cup to my lips and swallowed. The warm liquid rushed down into my empty stomach and brought forth the realization that I hadn't eaten for a while. I took another gulp to make sure the coffee was strong enough to cover my breath and then looked over at him.

He had taken a seat in one of the rocking chairs that flanked the swing. Using the balls of his stocking feet to gently push himself back and forth, he was looking out over the fields and sipping his coffee as though this was his regular routine, and for a moment I felt a pang of wanting this to be our standard practice.

He must have felt me staring and turned to meet my eyes.

"Hi," he said slowly, as though he was approaching a wild animal and didn't know how it would react.

"Hi," I repeated and brought the mug to my lips again.

"The front door was unlocked, and Peyton told me what happened yesterday, and so I just . . . I mean, I hope it's okay I came over."

"Oh. Yeah. I guess old habits die hard in this town. We can't keep the secrets in or the people out." I smiled.

"I don't think she was trying to gossip. She was just—"

"No. I know. I was kidding. It's fine."

"Fine?" He looked at me quizzically.

"Yeah. Weirdly, I feel fine."

He motioned his head towards the computer I had set next to me when he walked through the door.

"That have anything to do with why it's suddenly fine?"

I glanced over at the computer. The screen was still lit up on the white pages of my word document and littered with thousands of words that had poured out over the course of the last twenty hours. The cursor was still blinking at me, taunting me to finish.

"Yeah. It might be," I said and raised the cup again, hoping he would let that be enough.

He waited.

*Give him more,* I thought. *The new you is done keeping secrets.*

"I haven't slept," I finally said.

"At all?"

"No. Once Pey left and I let out a little anger, I turned my rage to the keyboard, and that's where I have been since."

"Yeah. I saw the office on my way out here. Is that the scene of the crime?" He smiled a little.

I wasn't sure if I was ready to laugh about it quite yet, but I did know that what happened in there felt good.

"Um . . . things got a little crazy for a little bit," I said.

"That seems like one way to put it," he said and sipped from his mug. "I don't blame you. That's some messed up shit you found out."

I was a little struck by this. I don't think I had ever heard Mr. prim and proper lawyer swear up until now. But he was right—it was some messed up shit indeed.

"That's one way to put it." I winked at him.

He smiled, sipped his coffee, and looked out over the fields.

We sat in silence for a few minutes. A moment that should have felt strange, but instead felt oddly tranquil.

"You have a lot of people worried about you, Finn," he finally said.

"A lot of people, huh?"

"Well, Peyton, Will, and myself, of course. And on my way out here, I noticed your phone as it lit up with another text from Letty. Seems she is looking for you. It was her eighth text."

"Shit," I muttered

"Yeah. You have us all in a twist worrying about you."

I looked over to him and we locked eyes again.

"I am sorry. I am not used to having people worry about me. This has all been a lot to process, and it seems like every time I have a grip, something else pops up."

"That's precisely what I am talking about. You have to let us be there for you."

"I am fine. I'll be better at getting back to people. Last night was just a bit of a catharsis for me, and I didn't want to stop the process," I said.

In truth, I was so transfixed with what was flowing out that I had forgotten a world outside of my computer existed. People who weren't writers couldn't understand that. To them the real world is first and foremost, but to a writer, the outside world can drift away, and you can get lost in the words on the page. And I was.

"I get it. We just want to help. Let us help." He looked at me earnestly, and I could feel his generosity cut through my exterior like a knife.

"I'll try" was all I could get out.

"That's enough for me," he said. "For now." And he smiled.

I smiled back and looked out at the fields, trying to find whatever peace that James was finding out there. I closed my eyes and tried to breathe in the country air. The air of my youth, the air of simpler times.

"You should probably get a nap in before this afternoon," James said, obviously seeing me sitting there with my eyes closed.

I slowly opened them and exhaled out the hay-ladened air.

"This afternoon?" I said and looked at him quizzically like he had something up his sleeve.

He furrowed his brow and tipped his head back the slightest bit as though I had rendered him bewildered.

"Your . . . um . . . mother's funeral," he said and cleared his throat, either for effect or because I had made him uncomfortable in mentioning it, I couldn't tell.

"Shit!" I exclaimed and stood up off the swing. I had been so busy word vomiting my feelings that I had forgotten about the funeral. I was supposed to give the eulogy, but now more than ever I had no idea what to say about my mother.

Should I tell the truth? Should I reveal our family secrets to the town? Should I act as though she and I were still estranged?

I had no idea what to say, but I knew I needed more coffee and a shower.

And I needed a fucking cigarette.

"Finn must be here because I saw the lights on at Amgine all night."

"What, are you spying on the place now?"

"No, of course not, but I can see the lights from the road where I jog, and the other night they were on after ten p.m., so something is going on over there."

# grace

Beau had never liked when Grace smoked. He had begged her time and again to quit, and while she would give it the old college try, it never stuck. She hid it for a while, but eventually she gave in and just lit up when she felt like it. He always told her that it was going to kill her. He was wrong.

Here they were now, sitting in the Tinsley Hospital, with Grace hooked up to a bunch of machines, dying. Not from smoking but from breast cancer.

He knew what people in town were saying about her. He knew the rumor mill was running overtime, but he didn't care. The only thing he ever cared about in this world was lying on the silk peach sheets he had brought from home and replaced on her hospital bed, breathing in and out under an oxygen mask, making her sound like Darth Vader.

This was the beginning of the end. Well, truthfully, the beginning was five months ago when she was diagnosed with inflammatory breast cancer. It had all started so simply, with what she thought was a rash.

"Probably some seasonal allergy," she had told him.

But as time passed and the seasons shifted, the rash didn't go away. Instead it got worse, so he had finally talked her into going to the doctor, a trip he knew she would fight. She hated the doctors because they would wag their finger at her smoking. She had begun to leave it off the forms she would fill out, but she knew deep down they could smell it on her.

Dr. Simen's initial reaction to the rash was all they needed to see. The jolly doctor's bedside manner left his face as he closed her gown and began to mention running more tests. The lump he swallowed in his throat told her everything she needed to know. She was dying. Cancer, she was sure, and she was correct, just like her mother.

IBC stage 4. No cure and no treatment. They could make her comfortable, was all they could say. Grace stayed stoic, not sure whether she was in shock or just being strong, but Beau was a wreck. He didn't know how to live without her. She was the strongest woman he knew, and he couldn't do anything without her. This wasn't their plan; this wasn't the way it was supposed to go. He was going to die before her so he would never have to know a life without her. She wasn't supposed to get sick, and not from breast cancer especially.

They sat there in the doctor's office, holding hands and not speaking until Grace stood up, shook off her gown, and began to put her clothes back on. He walked up behind her, ran his hands around the smooth skin of her waist, and slowly ventured up and took her breast in his hands. He rested his chin on her shoulder and just held her in his arms as she began to cry.

It had all gone so fast from there. They had gone home and tried to go back to normalcy, but everything felt so different, so forced, so painful. Every morning felt like a gift, but as the night fell, he would worry he would wake to her no longer breathing. Beau lost his sleep as she lost her will.

After three months, it was too much at home for her. She didn't want to die in this house, the place she had called her home her entire life, so they had gone to Tinsley Hospital, where Dr. Simen had referred them to a Dr. Gavin, who could make Grace comfortable.

Beau had begun to hate that word, "comfortable," as he watched her labor through breathing, looking so small and helpless in the bed. He spent his days holding her hand and talking to her and his nights with his head lying on the bed next to her. Grace would wake up in the middle of the night and see him there, her loyal husband and soul mate. She would beg him to go home and get some real rest, but he always refused. He wasn't going to go until she did.

When she had the strength, she would run her hand through his hair as he lay there on the side of her bed. She did it gently enough not to wake him, but deep enough to remember how every lock of his still-lush hair felt running through her now-bony fingers.

Usually after meals she would have enough energy to converse with him for a little while. Her contribution to the conversation was minimal, but monumental to Beau. He would hang on her every word, just like he did in high school. Which is why on one of her last days when she asked him to find the green journal he had given her in her bag and finish her final story to Finn, he obliged.

Beau had always been more brawn than brains, and the idea of writing the final chapter of his soul mate's life scared the shit out of him. He found the journal and kept it next to him while he sat with her. When she dozed off, he would open to the dog-eared page where she had left off and stare at it blankly. He had no idea what to write, what to say, how to encapsulate everything this woman was on these pages. He would stare at it for hours as she slept and lift the pen a few times to begin, but he never had the courage to start. After he felt he could no longer look at the blank page, he would lift the journal to his face, gently breathe in the smell of her, close his eyes and forget it all for a moment. Breathe her in, breathe the words out. But they never came. He would shut the book and promise her he was working on it when she would wake and ask.

Beau had wanted to phone Finn so many times in those last few days, but Grace had forbid it. She didn't want her only child to remember her in this way. Their relationship was far from perfect, but at least she could keep the few good moments intact. Finn had fought so hard to become this amazing writer and person, and Grace didn't want to burden Finn with her own issues. Beau had won the fight on whether to tell Finn about the cancer to begin with, but he wasn't going to win this one. She made him promise not to contact Finn until she was gone.

Beau, for his part, had let Grace dictate everything when it came to Finn. He felt he had no right to lay claim to anything when it came to the child that may or not be his. He was a simple man, and though he felt in his heart that Finn was his, he was not going to risk losing Grace to explore that further, so he let it be. Finn was the only thing Grace ever felt good about outside of him, and he wanted her to have that just for herself.

The decline happened much faster once they were in the hospital. Grace's will was gone, and Beau's smile was all that was keeping her there. She would watch through the slits of her eyes as he spun his wedding ring around his finger and stared at those blank journal pages while he thought she was asleep. They had never actually gotten married in the traditional sense. That wasn't their way. They had simply bought him a ring and exchanged vows while holding hands under the old willow tree where the back lawn met the hay fields.

The sun had been setting on another perfect fall evening, and as the sky faded from blue to pink, with a final blaze of yellow as it set, Grace dawned a flowy, nude chiffon dress with a deep V neckline that met the chiffon ruched belt below her chest. The V separated her breasts perfectly, leaving her silky peach skin between them exposed and skirting a fine line between sexy and graceful. The hem of the dress dragged a little behind her as she walked barefoot with Beau to their spot under the tree. They shared side smiles before turning and facing one another. Beau took her hands in his as the see-through, billowy sleeves of the dress floated in the light breeze, and he began his vows. She smiled and tried to allow her hands to stay interlaced with his as tears started falling from her bare eyelashes. Beau had requested no makeup at their wedding. He wanted her in her natural beauty, the way he had fallen in love with her.

Once he finished, it was her turn. She swallowed hard after every few words as she tried to profess her love to this man. The only man she had ever truly trusted and loved. The one who knew her truths and flaws and loved her in spite of them. The man who would stand by her as they grew old together. Only they wouldn't grow old together.

As Grace thought about their wedding day and all the love they had shared in their short lifetime together, she tried to smile but was too weak. She mustered up every ounce of love and strength in her body to move her hand onto Beau's and squeeze it so slightly he wasn't sure if he had imagined it or if it was real.

He looked up at her from his blank stare at the green journal, and as a teardrop fell from her cheek, she kept her hand in his, just as she did that evening under the willow tree when they had become man and wife. He knew this was the end, and as she took her last breath, he whispered, "You will forever be my saving Grace." When her hand relaxed, the teardrop fell, and he knew what he needed to do: write to Finn. And so with the tears falling down harder than he expected, and his one hand still holding his wife's hand, he picked up the pen and began.

Dear Finn,

I know we have never met. I have wanted to meet you more than you will ever know. By this point in the diary (or whatever your mother is calling this), I am sure you know the whole story of my Grace, but you don't know the full effect of our love. Before I tell you, I want you to know that it was your mother's wishes that I didn't meet you. Don't be upset with her for that. She was scared. But know this—you have always been in my heart and on my mind. I have cherished every bit of information your mother shared with me about you and relished in your accomplishments as a father would. In my heart you are my child, always have been. I can't explain it, but something tells me you are mine. I don't need a test to prove it, I know it. I have seen pictures of you over the years, and I swear you have my eyes and jawline. I would love to take credit for your intelligence, perseverance, and bravery, but we both know that is all Grace.

Your mother was my everything. She was my light and my truth. Being apart from her for all those years was the darkest part of my life. She was, and always will be, my saving Grace.

I don't know if you know this, but a few years ago, your headstrong mother finally agreed to make an honest man out of me. Interestingly, I asked her the same day she discovered your book at our favorite book store, and while I like to think that the proposal was the best part of her day, I know it was finding your book. She never knew that I knew, but it was written all over her face. And with the way she carried that damn book around like a security blanket, I knew it was the one thing that might have been more important than the ring on her finger.

But that ring on her finger meant the world to me. It was a symbol of our lifetime together. A symbol of a love that was the greatest I will ever know. I think the very best way for you to understand it is to read our vows. I know you are a word wizard like your mother, so try not to hold my lack of creativity against me.

"My saving Grace, I choose you. Again and again. Every minute of every day. From now until forever. Before you, I didn't know what love was. After you, I feel complete. All these years you've surprised me, captivated me, pushed me, distracted me, and loved me with reckless abandon. I promise to spend every second of every day loving you with that same recklessness. I will love you when our love is easy and when it is hard. Without you, I can't breathe. I swear I couldn't love you more than I do right now, and yet I know tomorrow I will."

And after I mumbled through the truest words I had ever said, your mother looked up at me with tears streaming down her face, and with her hands still in mine she began:

"My Beau, I sometimes wonder how you fell in love with a girl like me. I feel like I am scattered in a million pieces like a puzzle. It seems overwhelming, but you take every piece and try to put it together, not knowing if you even have all the right pieces. You are steadfast and persistent. You love all my broken pieces. You have shown me that love can exist for even the most broken and imperfect people. You have seen my worst and loved me through. I have fallen in love with you over and over again without reservation, which scared the hell out of me at times. You have been the only man to break down my walls and still be on the other side for me to run into your arms. I see these vows not as promises, but as privileges, and so if you will allow me the honor, I would love to spend the rest of my life loving you as deeply as I do in this moment. Today might seem like the start of a new journey, but I already belong to you. Today, it feels like we are finally going home."

Your mother's and my love story wasn't always a fairytale, but it was real, fought for, true love. She was my everything, and as I write this, she is gone. The woman I spent a lifetime loving has left me. I don't know where to go from here, but I do know three things . . .

1. I will spend the rest of my days loving your mother and working hard to live a life she would approve of.
2. The only good thing that can come now is that fact that after thirty-something years, I will get to meet you, Finn.
3. I hope you can find a love like ours, and if you do—never let it go.

Love,
Beau
P.S. I am not sure that anyone else told you but right before Grace passed, your mother found a letter addressed to your Grandmother from before you were born rambling about all the things going on at that "damned farmhouse of hers" (her words, not mine). She ended the letter by referring to

Elizabeth as a backwards drunk living at Enigma Farm. Apparently, that is how the farm got its name…. Enigma backwards is Amgine. How 'bout that huh? Thought that was a fun fact you might like to know if you are anything like me.

"It is kind of sad that she is gone. I think she had finally found peace in her life."

"Yeah, I am super sad. Sad we won't be able to gossip about her anymore."

"Seriously, you are a terrible person!"

"I just call it like it is."

"Let's be honest. We haven't had much to tell about her for a long time. She kept to herself, happy as a clam with Beau at Amgine."

"I heard Beau moved out of Amgine after she died, was just too sad for him to be in the house. Poor fella."

# finn

I shut the journal gently and set it on top of the manuscript I had spent the night writing. Beau. He was the man who had stood by my mother her whole life and loved her despite everything. He was the kind of man any person would dream of having as a father. His blind love and tenacious need to protect and provide for my mother impressed the hell out of me. And for a split second, my mind wandered over to James. Was he that kind of man?

I shook my head slightly and grabbed my suit coat off the hanger and slid each arm into the sleeves. The black-on-black combo with a paisley shirt seemed appropriate for the occasion. I looked in the mirror and stared for a minute too long. *Am I ready for this? What in the hell am I going to say?* I wondered.

I took a deep breath, noticing I was now twirling my chain again. I let it fall to my collarbone and flattened the front of my jacket with my palms. *I can totally do this,* I reminded myself and turned to head down the stairs.

I felt the familiar gentle bumping of the gravel under the car as I headed down the driveway towards church, driving in my mothers old car, yet another first since I got here. It had only been a week since I had landed in Hadleigh, and yet it felt like I had been here for years. I realized it had seemed like my own Lifetime story, complete with the new love, murder, and death. There was no theme music coming to end the scene, fade to black, and go back to real life. This was my real life, and I had no idea what was next for me. All I knew in this moment was that I was going to my mother's funeral and I was going to speak. That was it. Period. What came after was still unwritten.

It wasn't until I was putting the car in park that I realized I was in front of the church. It was one of those moments in life when you are driving, and your mind is focused on something else, and yet you still end up at your destination. It had happened to me before, but never when I was going to a place I hadn't been in so long. I would be driving home from work in Boston, thinking about the novel, and somehow pull into my driveway without remembering how I got there. That occurrence made sense. How I ended up at the church without direction or sound mind didn't, and yet here I was, shutting the driver door behind me, again smoothing my jacket and walking toward the church.

The church looked a little like the outside of Amgine Farm, weather-worn white paint flaking off the siding boards. The windows were stained glass images of biblical figures and scenes, none of which I knew besides the Virgin Mary hanging above the large arched-front double doors. I watched as a few people filtered through the doors; some I recognized and others I didn't. I was slightly caught off guard at the fact that there were people here at all. My mother spent most of her life keeping to herself, apparently hunkered down with Beau at Amgine. She was not the type of woman who needed girlfriends or a book club—those things led to people asking questions, and she wasn't ready to handle that. So she held on tight to Beau and her secrets.

People in town did love to hit up the funerals and celebrations to make sure they didn't miss out on any of the gossip, though. Just a bunch of morbid gossips faking their condolences while bursting with eagerness.

I looked down and walked through the thin patches of grass to the back door of the church. I knew it was there because we had broken in a few times as kids to play in the confessionals at night. I pulled the large, heavy, wooden door towards me and stepped inside. As the door slammed shut behind me, the room became so dark I had to wait a moment for my eyes to adjust. Suddenly, to my right, the pastor, or priest, or whatever the hell he was appeared.

"Hello, my child. Can I help you?" he said softly behind his cream robe adorned with colorful tassels wrapped around his neck and hanging over his shoulders. His bald head reflected the only light coming in from a small window beside him.

"Hi. I am Finn," I stammered, for the first time in my life nervous as to whether I was speaking correctly in front of a man of God.

He looked at me but remained quiet.

"Grace was my mother," I said and rolled my shoulders back a little, trying to fake confidence.

"Right," he said, still a little suspicious. "Of course." He could see the sin in me already, front and center like a robe I was draped in.

"This way, my child," he said and reached out his right arm and motioned me to a chair behind a large, red, velvet curtain.

"You can have a seat here if you want. I will begin and call upon you when I am ready." He smiled.

"Or, if you are more comfortable out in the congregation, you may do that, as well."

"Thanks. I am good here," I said and took a seat in the large oak chair with intricate carvings adorning it.

"Okay. We will begin shortly," he said and suddenly disappeared.

I exhaled, hoping I had been polite and correct in my actions towards him. Though as I sat there, I wasn't sure why I cared.

I stood up after a minute or two and gently pulled the red velvet curtain to the left, leaving a sliver just large enough for my eyes to peek out if I tilted my head.

I scanned the crowd, looking for anyone I would recognize.

First I saw Sandy talking behind the back of her hand to Tammy about something not flattering, I was sure. There was Harold, Frank, and Johnnie in a circle near the back, trying to hold back their laughter as Frank chewed on his thumbnail.

Tom was quietly seated near the front, waiting for the service to begin, and in front of him sat Peyton, Will, and James, all quietly whispering.

One of the large arch doors swung open and flooded the room with light for a second, and once it had faded, I could see Letty walking up the aisle, looking around for a seat. She slid casually next to James, turned to him, and smiled. I smiled behind the curtain, knowing she knew me well enough to ignore what I had said and come anyway.

In the back corner, I could see a bit of a scuffle and heard a few louder voices before I saw a man rise up off the floor as another man was being restrained by others. *What in the hell is going on,* I wondered.

Both front doors flew open this time, and I squinted as the light flooded in again. I waited for it to fade as I watched a man with sandy blond hair sprinkled with gray with broad shoulders and a simple black suit come into focus. I felt my breath catch in my throat a little because, even though he was still a little blurry, I knew instantly it was him. That jawline, those arms, and the way he walked right to the front without hesitation. Beau Boyton.

He took a seat alone in the front row, and for a brief second I felt an overwhelming need to rush out and sit next to him. To take his hand in mine and remind each other we were going to be okay.

Instead I let the curtain go, watched it droop shut, and took a few steps back into my large oak waiting chair. The reverend or father or whatever would be starting any second, and I needed to collect my thoughts.

"Hello," I heard the once soft-spoken minister bellow over the crowd.

Then I felt my mind go blank. All I could hear was my breath going in and out. I wished with every bone in my body that I could have just written something for someone else to read. I could say so many things on paper, but when they had to come out of my mouth, they became word salad.

"Now, we have someone here who wants to speak in Grace's memory."

I heard the footsteps coming toward me and felt the heavy, old hand rest upon my shoulder.

"Child?" he asked. "Are you okay?"

I blinked a few times and then looked up at him, his bald head still reflecting the light and his smile radiating warmth. *Maybe this is why people come to church,* I thought. Maybe the judgment we associated with it was simply a byproduct of our own insecurities.

"Yes, sir," I croaked.

His smiled widened as his hand squeezed my shoulder.

"Do your mother proud."

I felt myself crack a smile in his general direction as I willed my legs to stand. I tried to focus on breathing in and out as I reminded myself to put one foot in front of the other. I could feel the red velvet curtain escaping my peripheral vision as I walked towards the podium.

I stepped up, adjusted the microphone, and looked out over the rows of people staring back at me. They were waiting for me to say something, anything. *Give them more,* I thought.

I cleared my throat and gripped the sides of the lectern, feeling my fingers pressing in hard enough to make them tingle. I could feel the color draining from my face as I exhaled and opened my mouth.

"Thank you for coming," I began. Then I stopped, taking another breath and trying to release the tension in my fingers. I looked over, and for a split second, I locked eyes with Beau, and he nodded his head ever so slightly, acknowledging that he, too, knew who I was, even though it was still blurry.

"I . . . I am Finn Harper . . . Grace's son."

The audible gasp throughout the church sucked all the air out of the room as I gripped the lectern tighter than before, bracing myself for blowback.

The lack of oxygen made it hard to breathe as I tried to continue my inhale/exhale routine. My eyes were staring at the wood grains on the podium, afraid to look up and meet the curious eyes that would be staring back at me.

This was too much for this small town, stuck in their small ways with their small minds. They now had to come to grips with the fact that James might be gay. That I could come out as trans in a place like this and life would simply press on under a normal guise was nothing more than wishful thinking.

Another throat clear, I closed my eyes, lifted my chin, took a deep breath, and opened them again.

"I recognize this may shock and confuse some of you, but I don't care. I have realized that things are not always what they seem, and that's not always a bad thing. The old me wouldn't have had very many great things to say about my mother. But I am not that girl anymore . . ."

# EPILOGUE

The rest of the service was a blur. I escaped the same way that I came in. I knew the right thing to do was to stay and thank people for coming, but I had had enough face-to-face time for one day. Those who mattered to me would find me, and those who didn't would find me a gossip-worthy topic for some time to come.

The car ride back to Amgine felt freeing. Coming clean to the people who held you back can do that to a person. I felt like someone had taken off the lead vest I had been carrying around over my baggy tees to hide my breasts as a teen, and for the first time in years, I could breathe . . . really truly breathe.

I was no longer gasping for pockets of air in the shadows where I was safe and unnoticed. I was out in the sun, gulping in endless amounts of oxygen that were laced with freedom and peace. I felt a little high, though I hadn't held a joint between my fingers since college.

Maybe this is what that damn runner's high felt like. Like you didn't have a care in the world and your mind was no longer drowning.

I cracked the window a little to let even more air consume the vehicle. The warm, fall air filled the car as I followed the familiar route back to Amgine.

The bumping of the gravel driveway felt less jarring for the first time, and as I looked at the beautiful farmhouse approaching, I began to wonder what was next for me. What was I to do with this place?

As the house grew closer, I suddenly felt its vastness overtaking my elated mood. I had come to grips with just about everything in my life, but I couldn't discern how I felt about this place. What once had been a haven where I shared sweet notes with my gramps had become the hellhole I shared with my mother after his death. I had left Hadleigh not caring if I ever saw Amgine again. But when I had first stepped out of that taxi, the proverbial pang of familiarity warmed my heart, and it almost felt like home. I couldn't explain it, but it was there. I was coming to terms with the fact that some things didn't need explaining.

Stepping out of the car and shutting the door behind me, I wasn't sure how I felt about this place. The pang was no longer there, but neither was the rage. I was somewhere in the middle. The emotions had ebbed and flowed. Sometimes I was nostalgic, and other times I was hateful. I reached for the front door handle, thinking about my mother and Beau spending all their happy time here. This house should have been his, not mine. His memories here couldn't be confused; he knew how he felt about this place.

I tried to turn the doorknob and immediately realized it was locked. Never in Boston would I just reach for the knob without the key ready to unlock it first, and yet here I was, baffled that the door wasn't unlocked. I reached into my pants pocket to fish out the key and realized that all my changes had followed me back to Hadleigh. The door that had never been locked was now bolted. I had just left my mother's funeral, where I had let my long-kept secret out from behind lock and key, and yet here I was, facing another catch. As I slid the key into the hole, turned it, and walked in, it dawned on me that I would probably always be facing locks here. I would never live a simple life. But, then again, my mother had. She had found the love of her life, holed up at Amgine Farm, and lived happily ever after. Was it possible for another town outcast to find happiness in the midst of small town USA, among small minds and big gossip? I thought of James and happily ever after. I thought about Beau and a future with my dad. But mostly I thought about my mom. I wondered what she would want me to do with this place. It had been her haven and her hell. How does one come to grips with that?

I slipped my shoes off and threw my coat on the back of the couch. I grabbed the bottle of moonshine still sitting on the kitchen island and headed to the office to find my one last Winston among the rubble of a life I thought I knew. I walked lightly over the splintered pieces of desk and the mounds of paper and office supplies lying about. It looked as though a tornado had gone through here, and maybe, in fact, it had. My eyes darted all over the room, trying to see through the rubble if my last cigarette lay waiting for me. If I ever needed a smoke, this was it. Fuck all those other times I thought I was jonesing for a hit. Coming out as trans in a town still stuck in the fifties—now that was cause for a smoke.

Just as I turned to leave, convincing myself that I must have taken the pack outside, I spotted it. Lying there on the chair in the corner, the only thing among the mess that seemed untouched, almost as if it was fate. I grabbed the pack and headed to the hallway to fish a lighter from the hall table. I dug through the first two drawers only to be left empty handed. Then in the last drawer, I found a pack of matches from The Marmalade B&B. I flicked open the top and was relieved to find two matches still intact. The table wiggled slightly as I shut the drawer.

I grabbed my maunscript. I had spent hours writing my truth and hadn't had the time to reread it or edit it. Seemed like no better time than the present.

I headed out the back screen door and stopped momentarily at the porch swing to grab the green journal, my mother's story to me. I had strangely begun carrying it around like a security blanket, much like Beau had described by mother doing with *A Light in the Dark*. I smiled and clutched the journal to my heart as I walked out to the lone teal-and-green plastic chaise lounge chair in the lawn. I was glad it was already open because I could never figure out how to effectively open them and tilt each end to the right angle.

I plopped down in the chair, praying the thin plastic straps could hold my weight. I began to carefully unload my armful of goodies, setting the glass jar of moonshine in the grass and watching the liquid catch the light, reminding me of the kind minister and my lack of religious knowledge. Maybe I should join a church?

I set the journal on the ground next to the moonshine, watching as it blended into the spare grass around it, almost as if it belonged to the earth. Setting the manuscript on my lap and putting my cigarette in between my lips, I looked at the house I once called home. So much had happened here in my thirty-four years, much more than anyone would ever believe. Part of me wanted to stay here, grow old with James, write many books, and live the life my mother led in the end.

I fished in my poket for the matchbook, quickly tore a stick out, and swiped it onto my maunscript, from left to right directly under the title: *Enigma Farm* by Finn Harper & Grace Boyton.

I watched the matchstick ignite as I raised it to my lips. I looked back at the house and saw a manly figure walking along side the weathered wood exterior. He got close enough for our eyes to meet.

"Dad?" I said out loud before realizing the word had left my lips.

The match still flickered, burning while my eyes remained locked on Beau, my mind couldn't help but wonder if I should just burn the whole damn thing to the ground.

## ALISHA PERKINS

Writer. Speaker. Mental Health Advocate.
TEDX Speaker. Mother. Wife.
Not necessarily in that order.

Find Alisha at www.alishaperkins.com

Other books by Alisha Perkins

## MARTYRED

## RUNNING HOME

Made in the USA
Coppell, TX
08 June 2022

78617564R00173